BE THE CHANGE

BE THE CHANGE

MENOPAUSAL SUPERHEROES - BOOK 4

SAMANTHA BRYANT

For O'Neill, who always knew when it was time to get up and take a walk and when it was time to sit on the blanket so I couldn't get out of my writing chair. I miss you, boy-o.

THURSDAY

PATRICIA'S NOT A LIGHTNING ROD

D o we have to talk about this now?" Patricia O'Neill flung herself behind a park bench as a streak of lighting flashed across the lawn, blackening the patch of grass where she'd been standing moments before. Reflexively, her scales thickened, strengthening her armored skin to something akin to rhinoceros flesh.

Luckily, the new communications earpiece stayed in place through her transformations. Leonel could still hear her. "I'm kind of busy," Patricia managed to say.

Standing near the center of the field, a slender Black woman stretched her arms toward the sky. Wind swirled her hair despite the stillness of the day and crackles of white light popped around her like small fireworks. It would have been beautiful if she weren't lashing out with deadly force at anyone who approached her. Two agents had already been carted off the field. Patricia didn't want to be next.

While being bulletproof had its advantages, it also meant the Unusual Cases Unit or UCU tended to send Patricia in first. "Bulletproof Lizard Woman" played well in the press, even if the work could have been done by anyone in tactical gear.

She was damned tired of being used as the biological equivalent of a tank. Bullet impacts still stung; and if the weapon was powerful

SAMANTHA BRYANT

enough, sometimes she bruised. She didn't even know for sure how much her armored flesh would protect her if she took a hit from this lightning-flinging woman.

So far, she'd managed not to get burned, but a nearby park bench hadn't made it through in one piece. Patricia considered her next move as the woman's hands began to glow with a bluish light again.

"You coming?" she growled into the headset.

The plan had been simple enough. She would draw the lightning-wielding woman's attention while Leonel and the rest of the agents took up positions behind her, someone would tranq her, and then they'd get her back to the UCU for containment. Not much different from relocating an angry bear that wandered into the picnic grounds…if bears shot lightning at you.

But Patricia had been dodging the woman's attacks too long, and she was tiring.

Ducking her head, she bent into a crouch. Running away hadn't proven effective. The woman was burning the grass and destroying the furniture and statuary. Time to go on the offensive.

Patricia leapt from her hiding place, screaming a wordless battle cry, and ran toward the woman at full speed, the earth trembling beneath the heft of her fully transformed body, her vision reduced to blobs of color and movement. She'd tackle the woman and hope her scales would protect her from the worst of the electricity.

The woman, apparently stunned by the sudden attack from the person she'd been flinging electricity at for several minutes, gaped, glowing hands held at the ready. Patricia picked up speed and bent so she would strike her shoulder against the woman's middle.

She was nearly there when her target slumped to the ground, collapsing in a heap. Patricia threw herself to the side, unable to stop her forward momentum and not wanting to trample the now-unconscious woman. As she careened toward the tree line, Patricia hoped she wouldn't make the op-ed page again for destruction of public property during crime fighting. The gazebo had not been her fault.

Then she collided with something—not a tree, but nearly as solid.

2

Something that exclaimed in Spanish when she barreled into it. Something that smelled suspiciously of spicy aftershave.

After they skidded to a stop, Leonel's arm wrapped around Patricia's body like a tango dancer's, Leonel "Fuerte" Alvarez spun away from her with a dancing flourish and took a bow. "And you said you couldn't dance."

Patricia grunted, bending at the waist to catch her breath. The man infuriated her, and she was damned glad he'd been there to catch her —but she'd never tell him that. "What took you so long?"

"*Ten un poco de paciencia*, Patricia," he said. "We had to get the civilians out of the way first."

"You sure took your time about it. I was the one having to outrun lightning, you know."

Dusting bits of dirt off his hands, Fuerte cocked his head at Patricia, concern pressing his mouth in a flat line, his ridiculous red shirt and gold mask shining in the sunlight.

Sometimes his history showed. Looking at him, you'd never guess he'd spent the first forty-eight years of his life as a woman, until Dr. Liu's soap had transformed him into a super-strong man. But when angry or disappointed, the shadow of his former self loomed large.

Though his eyebrows were hidden by the half-sun mask, Patricia could still tell one was raised. The raised eyebrow always went with the all-too-familiar arms crossed over the chest and the tapping, booted foot. The complete set of Latina-mother disapproval, Leonel-style.

Not in the mood for a lecture, she held up a hand. "Come on. We'd better get back to the scene and see how we can help."

The lightning woman lay on the grass. Someone had rolled her onto her back. Leonel turned her head gently to examine her face. "Does she look familiar to you?"

Patricia knelt, a little awkwardly since her feet were still fully taloned—she guessed she must still be too full of adrenaline to pull her transformation back in.

The woman looked to be somewhere between forty and fifty years old, if one could judge by the small lines around her eyes and mouth.

Maybe a little young for the bits of silver streaking through her bush of black curls. Dressed in ordinary clothing—blue jeans and a pink hoodie—nothing about her suggested the dangerous woman Patricia had engaged a few minutes before. She looked like someone's auntie who had fallen asleep watching clouds.

It was hard to tell with the woman's eyes closed, but Patricia did think she might have seen her somewhere before.

She stopped one of the blue-jumpsuited agents moving around the scene. "Do we have an ID?"

He pulled out his phone and knelt between the two heroes to show the profile of one Marietta Cooper, age 64, longtime resident of Springfield. Damn. She looked good for 64. There was hope for Patricia yet!

The blue star in the corner of the screen marked the woman as someone the UCU had been monitoring for power manifestations, or as they called it amongst themselves, "potential freakiness." The agent clicked the star for more information, and they read that Ms. Cooper had low-level electrical powers, sometimes resulting in surges that blew out her apartment lights or destroyed her electronics.

"Low-level, huh?" Patricia huffed out a frustrated breath. "Her electricity didn't feel low-level when it singed my hair and stung my nose with ozone."

The agent nodded. "I guess something changed."

A strange feeling roiled in Patricia's guts. "Yeah. I guess something did."

She got to her taloned feet, turning to make her way back to the transport. She'd gotten a few yards away before Leonel called after her. "Wait!"

Patricia's shoulders slumped, spikes waggling. She really wasn't in the mood to talk about her lack of patience and the importance of being a team player. She wanted to get a shower and maybe pop in to see Suzie, since she'd missed their lunch date to handle this situation.

Leonel stopped by her side. "Well?"

"Well, what?" Patricia blinked at him, twice, once with each set of eyelids.

"What about the bachelorette party?"

Ah, yes. Tonight, after work. For Jessica "Flygirl" Roark, about to marry Walter Peeples, the head of research.

She'd been teasing Leonel all morning, threatening not to attend. He'd been shocked at the idea that a bridesmaid would skip the celebration. They were arguing about it over comms when the fight kicked up a notch and they'd had to quit talking.

Patricia sighed, feigning reluctance. "All right. Yes, I'll come to Jessica's bachelorette party."

She'd always intended to go anyway. Her girlfriend Suzie would hardly have allowed her to skip the girl's night celebration of their friend and colleague. Plus, Suzie dancing? She wouldn't miss an opportunity to watch Suzie when the music took her. Too sexy.

But it had been fun to let Fuerte think she would refuse.

A wide grin spread across Fuerte's face, but before he could say anything, Patricia raised a green, scaly hand. "But I'm not wearing matching t-shirts, or a stupid hat, or a lei."

Fuerte smacked a hand down on her shoulder, avoiding the yellow spikes sprouting from her armored flesh. "That's all right. We're getting tiaras!" He turned and started jogging toward the UCU van, leaving her to follow.

She called after him, "A tiara is still a hat!"

DARRIN WORKS AN ANGLE

Darrin Berger, reporter for *Springfield City News*, stood obediently behind the yellow tape with a small crowd of onlookers. He hoped the drone camera had captured something of the fight in the park—he'd bought it himself when the station refused the expense because he knew it would be worth it if he got some footage of the actual fight. Even from this distance, there had been quite a light show and a loud crack that had frightened everyone waiting and watching.

Ever since the UCU had stepped out of the shadows and into direct partnership with the city, covering the crime beat had been a lot more interesting. Now Darrin was angling to be the voice of the superhero beat in their city.

A small child, maybe four or five years old, let out a whoop, and Darrin snapped his head up. The boy yelled, jumping up and down on tiny blue sneakers that lit up with red flashing lights each time they impacted with the pavement.

"Fuerte! Fuerte! *Habla conmigo!*"

Across the street, a plain white van stood, and after squatting down to a kid's line of sight, Darrin finally spotted what the child had: Fuerte. The photogenic Hispanic strongman, dressed in his trademark red shirt and golden sun mask, was visible through the open doors of the vehicle.

Darrin's heart sped with excitement. This could be the break he had hoped for. A crowd favorite, known for his graciousness with fans and generosity with his charity work as well as for his feats of strength and courage, Fuerte might provide a clip for the news if he could get his attention. Even a few words would for sure make the nightly newscast and raise Darrin's cachet with his supervisor.

After a quick consultation with the young woman watching the child—an older sister, he guessed—to make sure she approved, he knelt and whispered to the child conspiratorially, "Hey kid, let's get you up a little higher so Fuerte can see you."

Taking advantage of his tall, lanky frame, he lifted the kid into the air where he could see over the top of the van. He encouraged the boy. "Call for him again. Maybe he'll see you now!"

The child squealed out again, his voice high and piercing in the vacant street, traffic having been rerouted to avoid the park while the fight raged on. The boy threw his arms in the air and waved them madly, making Darrin work to keep him held securely.

"Fuerte! Fuerte!"

It worked. Fuerte ducked out around the side of the van and waved at the crowd, eliciting a cheer and some applause from everyone watching. Seeing the boy, Fuerte held up a finger, then disappeared behind the van. Darrin saw him lean into the vehicle for a moment and talk to someone back inside, then come to the curb. After ostentatiously looking both ways, long wavy locks catching the breeze to blow behind him dramatically, Fuerte jogged across the street. He had to hand it to Fuerte—more than any of the other powered heroes of their city, he understood and embraced the whole "role model" thing.

Darrin released the child and gestured at the cameraman, but the man was already on it, following Fuerte's path toward the little boy, who practically vibrated with excitement.

The hero knelt to talk to the tiny fan, camera rolling and the crowd spreading to give them a little space to talk. Phones and cameras came out of pockets as everyone tried to watch and record it to show their friends later.

Holding out a hand for the boy to shake, Fuerte spoke, "*¿Cómo te llamas, niño?*"

The boy went adorably shy, and Darrin did an internal fist-pump knowing the kid would make a great impression on the news tonight. "M-m-mateo!" he finally managed to squeak out, face gone beet red.

"*Hola Mateo. Es un placer conocerte.*" He shook the boy's hand, and the child lit up, his smile revealing a missing front tooth that ought to be worth a few more ratings points on its own.

Twisting at the waist, Fuerte gestured behind him to a silent blue-jumpsuited woman with a UCU patch on the shoulder of her uniform. Darrin had been so focused on Fuerte and the boy that he hadn't noticed her arrival, but he recognized her. He'd seen her at more than one scene involving the powered UCU agents.

Reaching into a bag at her side, the short Black woman pulled out a comic book and a marker. She tossed the marker to Fuerte and when he caught it in his hand, he shattered the plastic, sending ink dripping down his palm. For a fleeting moment, her face registered surprise before she schooled her expression into something more professionally detached.

"Oops!" Fuerte said. After accepting a towel from the same silent agent with the satchel, he wiped off the ink. "Let's try again."

This time, the agent handed him the comic book and another marker directly. Fuerte held it delicately between his fingers and signed the book, his flowing signature sprawling across the brightly colored cover. "Here you go," he said. "Remember, *leer es poder!* Reading is power."

The boy grasped his prize to his chest and melted against the knees of his caretaker. Fuerte turned to the crowd, waving. Darrin stepped forward. "Fuerte! Darrin Berger, *Springfield City News.* Can you tell us a little about what happened over there?"

Fuerte flipped the marker in his fingers. "The credit for today belongs to Patricia. I was merely her back up." Putting his hands around his mouth, he yelled across the street, "Patricia."

A gasp went out from the crowd, and Darrin spun to watch Patricia, the infamous Lizard Woman of Springfield, making her way across the street. She didn't smile at the crowd, but that was probably for the best—Darrin had seen her attempts to smile. It was disconcerting at best, bringing to mind the toothy maw of a predator. He could hardly believe his luck. Two of the powered agents of the UCU. If he succeeded with fight footage, they'd lead with his work tonight.

Patricia stopped beside Fuerte, and the crowd noticeably shrank back, though the cameras and phones were still in hand. Darrin didn't blame them—Patricia was amazing in her own right, but also more than a little frightening. Those yellow eyes and shining green scales made his inner caveman want to run and hide, despite all the evidence that she fought on the side of right.

Fuerte put a friendly arm around the Lizard Woman's back, seeming oblivious to the tall yellow spikes protruding from her shoulders and upper arms. "Señora Patricia kept the Lightning Woman's attention while our team cleared the park to keep you safe."

Patricia looked uncomfortable and a little annoyed, at least that's the impression Darrin got. It could be difficult to read a reptilian face for emotion. But she shrugged and spoke to the crowd, a rare moment Darrin was thrilled to have captured for the news. "All in a day's work. I managed not to get too singed, though I'm afraid the park bench wasn't as lucky."

Fuerte laughed and a few members of the crowd joined in with nervous titters. The little boy who had jumped up and down for Fuerte now clutched his sister's leg, thumb in his mouth and saucer-like eyes staring at the Lizard Woman.

Darrin tried again for information. "Can you tell us anything about the Lightning Woman?"

Spreading his hands, Fuerte sighed. "The UCU will release a fuller statement later, but I suspect the poor woman did not intend to hurt anyone. She just needs help getting her electricity under control. We will make sure she gets the care she needs."

"Do you know if this woman has any connections to the other strange happenings across Springfield?"

Fuerte opened his mouth to respond, but the woman in the blue jumpsuit who had handed him the comic book stepped forward, tugging the hero by his red-shirted elbow. She bowed to the crowd and shot Darrin a warning look that silenced him. "I'm sorry, but Fuerte and Patricia will have to go now. They're needed back at head-quarters."

Shrugging an apology, Fuerte turned his brilliant smile on the crowd and blew a kiss as he turned to leave. Darrin didn't miss the poke he gave Patricia to remind her to wave. He also didn't miss the way the blue jumpsuit failed to hide the taut muscularity of the unnamed UCU agent with the fierce eyes. Maybe she wasn't powered like Fuerte and Patricia, but she exuded strength. He'd have to look into her.

Darrin could hardly contain the giddy feeling bubbling within his chest. The only way that could have gone better would have been to get Flygirl, too. He'd own the newscast tonight.

PATRICIA'S TIARA

By the third bar of the evening, Patricia had a pleasant buzz going. She twirled a frothy pink concoction around a large martini glass, watching the light catch in the ice cubes. The happy chatter of the other women washed over her. It had been too long since she'd had a night like this, longer than she had realized.

Even before her Lizard Woman alter ego had become a factor, she'd never been very good at relaxing—nights like this felt like a waste of time. Her once-best-friend turned enemy, Cindy Liu, used to say Patricia needed to learn to live as hard as she worked. Throughout their forty-year friendship, she'd encouraged Patricia to get out more, to enjoy the fruits of her labor in the form of travel, tickets, and trouble. Even though Cindy had been wrong about so many other things, she'd probably been right about that.

Suzie reached across the table and squeezed Patricia's wrist, a private couple's signal to let Patricia know her scalier self had surfaced. Refocusing her vision, she saw the sparkly fake fingernails she'd allowed Suzie to affix now lingered on the ends of very long nails more akin to talons.

That was always a mistake, wandering the hallways of memory

that led to Cindy. She pulled in a deep cleansing breath, pushed away all memories of her former friend Cindy Liu, and focused on bringing her hands back to normal before anyone else noticed.

Patricia tended to get scaly in public if she let herself dwell on her betrayal at the hands of Dr. Liu, the woman she had believed she knew best in all the world. It turned out Cindy had some pretty big secrets in her laboratory, including the one that made Patricia into the Lizard Woman of Springfield.

Patricia hadn't been the only woman to experience startling side effects from Cindy's products; there were three others at the UCU—two of them at this party. New cases kept popping up around the city despite their best efforts to get all Cindy's products off the market. None quite as dramatic as Patricia's transformation, there were still some definitely far-left-of-normal reactions to skin creams, soap, and tea.

"Excuse me, ladies," Patricia said as she made her way to the restroom, hoping to clear her head of regrets and recriminations and enjoy the night.

The door clattered shut behind her, and Patricia shook her head to clear away the residual ache from the thumping music. When she'd been younger, she never got headaches like this. Partying until dawn and putting in a full workday the next day had been par for her course. She pulled out her phone to check the time. Still only ten o'clock. They'd be hours yet. She felt older than her sixty years.

A second or two later, the door bounced open again and Suzie came in, her high heels clattering on the tile floor. "Everything okay?"

The younger woman pulled out a glossy pink lipstick and reapplied it, filling Patricia with a desire to kiss the sparkle off those perfect lips. Suzie must have felt the heat of her gaze because she winked at Patricia in the mirror as she slipped the tube back into her tiny yellow purse.

Patricia ran the water and dipped her fingers in the flow, then patted the cool liquid on the back of her neck. "I'm fine. It's a little loud for me."

Suzie squeezed her arm. "I know it's not your scene, but Jessica is so happy."

"Don't worry. I'll be fine. I needed a break is all."

Suzie linked her elbow with Patricia's and pulled her toward the door. "Well, break's over, Sweetcheeks. Time to dance."

Patricia grinned, hearing the opening notes to "Dancing Queen" by ABBA as the two stepped back into the hall. Suzie must have requested it. The bouncy fluff of a song never failed to bring out Patricia's dormant inner party girl, and she spun Suzie out onto the dance floor dramatically, making her girlfriend's white gauzy skirt flare out around her slender legs. The two women made a circuit of the dance floor, weaving in and out of the crowd. Patricia let the music buoy her out of her fit of melancholy and soon didn't have to fake the smile.

The rest of the party rushed the dance floor with the next song, something Patricia didn't recognize, but it had a catchy beat. Jessica Roark and their team leader, Sally Ann Rogers, took the spotlight in the middle of the dance floor, and a crowd encircled them to watch the women do their version of breakdancing.

The two athletic women showed off their flexibility with backbends, flips, and convoluted gyrations, and Patricia found herself clapping along with the crowd. If not for the differences in their complexions—blond and fair-skinned Jessica, and russet-brown-skinned Sally Ann—they might have been sisters. Both short, but solid and well-muscled, each was fiercely determined to outdo the other on the dance floor.

Jessica didn't even cheat gravity much. The past year working with the UCU had her so fit, she didn't need to use her power of flight to wow the other dancers with her moves. She just had to keep up with her former trainer.

Sally Ann claimed she didn't have any powers beyond her ability to read psychic imprints and emotions off paper. But watching the positions she effortlessly held, Patricia wondered if Sally Ann had some secret enhancements of her own. Or maybe it was youth. Sally Ann's years still numbered nearer twenty-nine than thirty-nine: by Patricia's estimation, a mere babe.

Patricia had never been that flexible, even when she'd been the terror of the field hockey team back in Indiana. Her athletic nature came across in strength and intimidating ferocity, traits that also served her well in the corporate boardroom before her retirement.

Hanging out with Jessica's soon-to-be sisters-in-law and old college friends had been easier than Patricia had expected. Old or not, she found herself enjoying the night out being mundane with regular people. Even Leonel had relaxed—after a third margarita—to the point that he was giggling with the twenty-something lab tech Jessica had invited at the last minute when they'd all been leaving work together, a shy Black girl who hid her teeth behind her fingers when she smiled.

Somebody should have let the girl know Leonel wouldn't be interested in her—she already appeared a little moony-eyed over the muscle-bound hero. Leonel still forgot sometimes that his interactions were perceived differently than they had when he'd been a woman. She probably thought he was flirting with her, while he thought they were having a good "girls" moment. Maybe Sally Ann could drop a hint about Leonel's husband and save the girl a bit of heartache.

It was good to see Leonel laugh. He could be so serious, and the stress of negotiating with his husband took its toll, making him downright dogged. David had finally moved back in full time a week or two ago, but things were far from settled between them.

After Leonel took a bullet in Indiana, David had demanded Leonel give up his new and dangerous line of work. Leonel had refused.

The two had already been through so much upheaval, with Leonel's unexpected gender change—a transformation from a short and curvy Latina grandmother into the Hispanic Adonis on the cover of the city magazine. Watching the drama at *la casa* Alvarez made Patricia feel lucky not to have family around her. At least no one would try to tell her what she could or couldn't do with her newfound abilities. Suzie would certainly not try to hold her back.

Whenever Jessica or Sally Ann pulled an especially impressive move, Leonel clapped his hands and threw them into the air calling out with an impressive mariachi *grito*. While Patricia had escaped wearing a glittery, decorated t-shirt like the other bridesmaids, Leonel opted for a printed tuxedo t-shirt with a sticker announcing his role as *"Hombre de Honor"* and the promised tiara. His was more of a crown, but it did have pink jewels on the plastic golden spikes, leaving him looking like some kind of merman beauty queen.

Nestled in Suzie's blond curls sat Patricia's refused tiara. It flattered Suzie's widow's peak, though it also emphasized her youth, and Patricia twinged at the difference between their ages.

Patricia donned a blue pantsuit, sharp and sophisticated. In concession to the party atmosphere, she'd worn a blouse with a bit of silver thread running through the stripes that caught the lights. At least Jessica had chosen dignified gowns for her bridesmaids, something for adults instead of Barbie dolls. No pink taffeta or slick, teal satin.

Patricia found it strange enough to be a bridesmaid at nearly sixty years old, alongside the far younger women. Suzie said the dress had classic Hollywood charm and made Patricia look like a taller, more dangerous Katherine Hepburn. Patricia had been surprised Suzie even knew who that was, given her youth.

In her back pocket, Patricia's phone buzzed. A quick glance revealed a phone number she hadn't seen in a few months, with an Indiana area code. She tapped Suzie on the shoulder and wiggled the phone to show she needed to step outside and take a call. Suzie waved and spun back in to join the wedding party, now trying to learn some kind of group dance involving bumping hips and jumping apart. Patricia shook her head as she stepped out into the night.

She pressed the phone against her ear as she elbowed through the door onto the sidewalk. "Hello?"

"Patty?"

The voice on the other end warbled. Though she hadn't heard it in months, she recognized Annie, her youngest half-sister, the one young enough to be her daughter. Patricia didn't correct the nickname—

Annie had picked it up from their mother who never respected Patricia's desire to give up her childhood moniker. "What's the matter, Annie?"

"It's Mom."

Patricia waited. Her mother might be seventy-six years old, but Patricia would put little past her. She only ever heard from any of her half-siblings when disaster struck; and disaster tended to strike every three to five years. Did they need bail money again? Patricia tried to remember if Annie had been in trouble. She didn't think so. Barely eighteen herself, the girl's father, her mother's seventh husband, was so overprotective he hadn't even wanted her to get a driver's license. How much trouble could she have gotten into?

On the other end of the line, Annie snuffled noisily, honking her nose as she tried to calm herself enough to talk. Patricia stifled her annoyance.

Annie had been a later-life surprise, born when their mother was in her fifties. There had been plenty of family jokes about how Mom's eggs had been past their use-by date when Annie arrived. Kind-hearted, if not necessarily quick-witted, Annie tested Patricia's patience on a good day, and it seemed today wouldn't be a good day.

"What's going on, Annie? Is she in trouble?"

Annie's snuffling broke into a loud wail, and Patricia moved the phone away from her ear, turning to walk further down the street, away from the party music and smokers huddled at the edge of the allowed distance from the door for indulgence. A light rain misted the air and Patricia raised her head to watch the streetlights prism against the night sky.

"Annie." Patricia took on an authoritative air. "I can't help until you tell me what's wrong. Did she have a fight with George?"

A long pause stretched out. Patricia might have thought she'd lost the call, but she could still hear her youngest sibling breathing.

"No. It's not that."

A snarl crept into Patricia's voice. "Then what is it, Annie?"

"Mama's missing."

Patricia's phone slipped from her grasp, and she had to scramble to keep it from hitting the pavement. "What?"

Annie yelled it. "She's missing, Patty!"

Patricia's mind raced. Mom had been sober for a long time now. Annie's father, George, had been a good husband, a calming influence on her incorrigible adventuress of a mother, and Patricia thought they had a good life together. Babs had made her way through the ranks of AA and earned a ten-year coin the year before. Patricia had dared to hope her mother might be done bringing extra drama into the lives of her children.

"Can I talk to your dad, Annie?"

"He's not here." More sobs broke in the girl's voice. "He didn't want me to tell you."

"Why not?" Her heart clenched. She'd never been close to her family, but she liked George better than she'd liked any of her other stepdads, except maybe Wayne. She'd been nicer to George than she'd been to any of the others, too.

"He said he'd find her himself, that we didn't need to bother you."

That hurt. Did he think her so cold that she wouldn't care that her mother was missing? "How long has she been gone, Annie?"

"A week," she said.

Twenty questions streamed through Patricia's mind at the same time. Where had she last been seen? What did the police say? Why the hell had they waited an entire week to call her?

"I have to go," Annie whispered into the phone. "Daddy's home."

And she hung up, leaving all of Patricia's questions unasked and unanswered.

PATRICIA STOOD on the sidewalk staring at the lightly falling rain for a few minutes. She might have lingered there longer, but her phone buzzed. It was Suzie, looking for her. She ran her hands over her head, pushing the now-damp red locks into spikes atop her head, and hurried back down the block.

She found the wedding party gathered around a table asking Jessica details about the wedding and her romance with Walter Peeples. Most everyone there already knew how the couple had met, but she recounted the story for the new lab tech, glossing over the "he helped me learn to manage my powers of flight" part, since only some of the guests knew her secret, and focused on the "meeting at work and tripping and landing in his arms" part. It did make a romantic tale; it was all the more charming for being mostly true.

Suzie slid in next to her as Patricia rejoined the group and wrapped an arm around Patricia's hips, sneaking a thumb beneath the waistband of her slacks. "Everything okay?"

It wasn't, but Patricia couldn't talk about it here, so she shrugged.

A worried furrow sprouted between Suzie's brows, and Patricia leaned over and kissed it. "I don't want to spoil the party. I'll tell you on the way home."

Suzie nodded, but her mood had already shifted, and a few of the other party guests shot them curious looks. Patricia waved an arm, calling the waitress back over. "Another round for everyone," she said. "It's time to toast the bride."

Jessica spun in a circle, shaking her glass to encourage the ice to rattle, and everyone clapped. Jessica and Walter really were made for one another, Patricia decided. He deserved some of the credit for the new assurance in her every movement. Her hero work as Flygirl accounted for the rest. If anyone deserved success in love, it was Jessica.

Sally Ann climbed up into her stool and stretched out across the table so everyone could hear her. "Tell us, Jessica. How does Walter rate a woman so far out of his league?"

Jessica's face reddened, but she held Sally Ann's gaze and retorted, "Walter has hidden talents."

Patricia laughed, but one of the other bridesmaids covered her ears —Francine, Walter's sister. "Shut up! That's my baby brother you're talking about!"

Laughter overtook the table again, and the timely barmaid arrived with a fresh tray of drinks. Suzie grabbed her whiskey sour and passed Patricia her cosmopolitan. "To second chance romance!"

Jessica raised her stout and added, "To getting it right this time!"

By the time everyone had toasted, Suzie had tucked her arm through Patricia's and started making their excuses. Patricia might fool her friends and colleagues, but there would be no getting anything past Suzie. She could smell trouble a mile and a half away.

WALTER BURNS THE MIDNIGHT OIL

Walter Peeples sat in his office, reviewing lab notes. With his fiancé Jessica out celebrating with the bridal party, he seized the opportunity to put in some extra hours at work. Life had never been dull, working with the Director, but the new crop of recruits fascinated him. He could study cases like Leonel's, Patricia's, and Jessica's for the rest of his career and barely make a dent in what there was to learn.

And the woman who started it all paced her cell three floors below. Cindy Liu. Turning to a console at his left, Walter brought up the latest reports from Lab F, the one designated for her use in her incarceration with the Unusual Cases Unit.

He kept a closer eye on her work these days, after the invisibility incident a couple of months earlier. He still hadn't forgiven himself for underestimating Dr. Liu. Looking at her youthful visage, one could easily forget that teenaged body housed a nearly seventy-year-old woman with several advanced degrees and an overwhelming lack of respect for boundaries and personal decency.

If not for Patricia's quick thinking, and what she termed her "lizard vision" they might well have lost Dr. Liu and any chance of understanding the nature of the changes she had wrought in the women who used her products. The loss for science and for the peace of mind of his bride-to-be would have been immense.

Thinking of Jessica made Walter's stomach flip gently. He still couldn't believe she had agreed to marry him. Better yet, she seemed to think earning his love qualified as a stroke of luck on her part. What could be luckier than loving someone who feels lucky to have you? Even better—there would be no need to live a double life, pretending to produce boring drugs for Big Pharma or some equally dull cover story. Jessica, as Flygirl, served the same agency as Walter. No need for secrets between them.

Turning back to his tablet, Walter read that Liu had again requested access to Jessica. Reluctantly, he refused it.

Since her arrival in their custody, Dr. Liu had insisted Jessica held the key to understanding the strange effects her products had on some of their users. Liu's formula, a basis for most of her work in treatments for the ailments and complaints of aging and menopause, was borrowed from a strain of cancer, retrained and repurposed.

As the only known cancer survivor among the affected women, Jessica was of considerable interest. Dr. Liu believed if she could fully study Jessica's case, she could further their understanding.

The scientist in Walter found that theory sound, but as Jessica's fiancé, he would not force her cooperation with the woman who had kidnapped her and held her captive. Jessica herself mattered more than anything they might learn from such research.

Clicking over to the security monitoring system, Walter checked in on each of the special cases in turn, always the last thing he did before he signed off for the night—most were sleeping peacefully, though Helen's fire suppression systems were working overtime to keep up with the increased number of night-fires she produced in her sleep. He made a note to check the system functions with the tech crew in the morning.

He saved Cindy Liu for last and found the petite figure pacing the darkened cell, a pathetic vision of lonely adolescence. It was convincing if you didn't keep reminding yourself the truth of her age. He watched her stalk the small room and was reminded of a tiger at the zoo trying to fit a wanderlust designed for ten miles into ten square feet. No rest for the wicked, he guessed, and signed out of the system for the night.

Checking the time, Walter was startled to realize it was nearly midnight. He hadn't intended to stay quite so late. Standing, he patted himself down to verify the presence of his glasses, wallet, keys, and phone, humming the children's song "Head, shoulders, knees, and toes" as he did so, a habit he'd picked up from Jessica's boys. As he closed the door behind him, his phone buzzed in his pocket.

A text. "Stop by my office before you leave." From the Director.

Did the man never sleep?

Walter spun on his heel to make his way to the elevators.

THE DIRECTOR STOOD with his back to the office, gazing out the windows at Springfield. The city lights distorted his reflection in the glass, making the normally imposing man appear slope-shouldered and weaselly. Walter cleared his throat. "You wanted to see me?"

The man nodded but didn't speak, and Walter flopped down on the sofa. The Director liked his drama and wouldn't be rushed. Sometimes Walter wished he would speak to the point.

"It's peaceful out there tonight."

Walter shrugged. "That's probably good. Some of our best agents are unavailable tonight."

The Director turned around. "Oh yes. The bachelorette party was tonight, wasn't it?"

Walter didn't miss the arch tone in The Director's voice. He had wanted to make a media event out of Flygirl's marriage, but she had refused, opting instead for a quiet affair. The man had even concocted a plan to disguise Walter as some kind of mystery bridegroom.

Sally Ann, head of street operations and Jessica's trainer, had helped talk him down, reminding him not everything should be about public relations, and making Walter and Jessica's wedding into a media circus would not help keep her children and family safe. That promise of protection was a condition of her cooperation with the UCU, no matter if the Director thought her over cautious.

The Director listened to Sally Ann when he wouldn't listen to anyone else, but that didn't mean he wouldn't stoop to sardonic comments when he didn't get his way.

"What did you want to talk about?" Walter yawned. "It's late."

"It's about the Liu-vians."

Walter stopped mid-yawn. Liu-vians were the in-Department name for the women affected by Dr. Liu's products. "I'm listening."

The Director swished his drink in his hand. "You heard about the case this afternoon?"

Walter shrugged. He'd heard only cursory details—he'd been too immersed in his own work to follow the chatter. "Patricia and Fuerte handled it, right? Something involving lightning?"

Nodding, the Director crossed the room and perched on the edge of his desk. For a moment, Walter thought the man's feet didn't fully reach the floor—odd for such a tall man. He rubbed his eyes.

"She was on our watch list."

"Was she?" Walter pulled out his phone, intending to search for the details, but the Director cleared his throat, indicating he wasn't finished, so he set the device aside.

"Marietta Cooper. She'd been using a TENS system in coordination with a deep tissue cream produced by Dr. Liu to help with her arthritis."

Walter thought back to his last debriefing on the watch list. "I remember. We found her because of the continued brownouts in her neighborhood." He bit his lip, puzzled. "I thought her condition had lessened, once she stopped using the cream."

"Given the burnt grass in Springfield City Park this morning, I'd say we were mistaken."

A spike of worry jabbed into Walter's heart. Liu-vian cases had become a lot more personal after he'd fallen in love with one of the doctor's victims. "Do we know if she kept using the cream despite our warnings?"

"They've got her in medical right now. As soon as she's stable, we'll know more. But that's not everything."

Walter stood. A spike in a previously stable Liu-vian worried him enough. If there was more, he needed a drink. The Director kept an old-fashioned drink cart behind his desk and Walter poured himself two fingers of whiskey. He made himself sip it, though part of him wanted to shoot it in a single swallow.

"All right," he said. "Let's have it."

"It's a pattern. Not just Ms. Cooper, but several other cases, all in the past month."

The Director spun his tablet computer around and clicked a few things, then passed the device to Walter. Going back to the window, the Director gave Walter time to peruse the files.

Walter thumbed through the case files, noting the dates and the sudden surge in severity of symptoms or manifestations of power. This wasn't good. Eight cases. Almost half the people on the watch list had experienced anomalies of some sort in the previous month. The lightning incident had just been the most public.

After a few moments of scanning the files, Walter dropped the tablet back on the desk. "We're going to need to bring them all in for testing. It's the only way to know."

The Director sighed. "I thought you might say that. But we're going to need to handle this quietly. We've finally begun to make headway with the press and popular opinion. The last thing we need is to give the public a reason to be afraid of our beloved 'freaks' again. We wouldn't want to undo all of Jessica and Leonel's good work."

"Understood." Walter checked his watch. "I better get a little rest. Can you have Suzie set a meeting for Monday first thing? All the medical and scientific leads? We'll review the data and make a plan."

Anxiety radiated from the Director as he stood staring out at the city view through his window. Walter was surprised. Usually imperturbable, he had seldom admitted stress or concern in all their years of working together.

Walter took a step closer to the windows, tilting his head. Was there still more? Something the Director hadn't yet shared? He cleared his throat. "Is there something else?"

Turning around, the Director smiled and shook his head, and Walter felt instantly soothed, sure in his core it would all work out fine. A wave of calm assurance spread from his chest out to his extremities, and he felt his shoulders relax and the tension leave his jaw. After all, they'd solved tougher problems than this, hadn't they? The UCU had the resources and brains to solve this one, too. There was no reason to worry.

"No," the Director said, low and calm, a lullaby of a voice, a voice to be trusted. "Nothing more."

"Okay then, good night. We'll get to the bottom of this on Monday."

"Of course."

Walter set the glass on a side table and made for the door. He didn't know if he'd be able to sleep with the whirlwinds spinning through his mind, but he should at least try and get some rest. Monday would be a whole new kind of stressful.

"Don't worry," the Director called after him. "We won't let anything happen to them."

Walter left without answering. He couldn't say he wouldn't worry, and lying to the Director was a waste of time. He always knew.

LEONEL ON OVERDRIVE

L eonel over-tipped the taxi driver and the young woman grinned as she pulled the door open for him, bowing in a flirtatious flourish. A wave of dizziness overtook him as he moved to get up; he shouldn't have ordered that last margarita. It had been a long time since he'd had more than a beer or two, and the drinks had seemed to grow stronger as the night went on.

"You got this, Mr. Alvarez?" The smile slid off her face, and the girl squinted at him doubtfully. He understood her concern. She shouldn't have to pull a drunk out of her backseat and, in this case, she actually couldn't. He doubled her size at least.

Leonel shifted his bulk, then paused, waiting for his head to stop spinning. "I've got this. I need a second." With one quick movement, he pushed himself to his feet. He teetered there for a moment, then managed to get both feet up onto the curb. He bowed to the driver, covering his clumsiness. "Thanks again."

The girl smiled, her gaze flicking across his biceps and then back up to his face, admiration keen in her face. She patted his shoulder. "You have a good night."

Behind them, the porch light came on. The girl closed the door and crossed to the driver's side. "Looks like someone waited up for you." She sounded as if she might be sorry about that, and Leonel worried he'd overdone the charm. If Jessica were there, she'd tease him about collecting more young women for his fan club. His alter ego, Fuerte, had quite a following among the young women of Springfield, and it appeared that Leonel might as well.

Leonel waved as the car drove out of sight, then weaved his way to the garden gate. The Alvarez house was pretty at night, with fairy lights strung into the shrubberies and small solar lamps resembling colorful mushrooms lining the path. Unfortunately, all the colors blurred before Leonel's eyes, and he had to work hard to bring the walkway into focus.

He made it to the porch with minimal stumbling and laid a hand flat against the house for balance as he climbed the four stairs. His fingers pushed into the wood, leaving a handprint, and he snatched his hand back before he could do more accidental damage to the house. A hapless moth circled the porch light while Leonel fumbled in his pockets for his keys. He dropped them on the welcome mat and was kneeling to pick them up when David opened the door.

David loomed above him, arms crossed over his slightly paunchy belly. As he looked down at Leonel, a smile lifted his cheeks, and he offered Leonel a hand to get back to his feet. "Come on, *borracho*, we'd better get you some water or you're going to wake up with a headache."

Leonel decided not to argue about being called a drunk, but waved away the hand, choosing to pull himself up using the doorframe. He glared when it creaked under his grip, then turned a wide grin on his husband. "It was a great night, *cariño*. You should have been there."

David laughed. "No men allowed, I thought. Except, of course, you. But you're a special case."

Dropping heavily into a kitchen chair, Leonel groaned. The room spun.

A glass of water appeared in front of him, and David urged him to drink it. "You have always been a lightweight, *querida*. I guess that's one thing that hasn't changed."

Having David back at home should have made everything better.

Sitting here at their kitchen table together certainly felt right. His teasing brought back memories of many nights over the years, when the two of them had sat up late into the night figuring out what they would do.

But the recent tension between them still lingered, and even through his fuzzy head, Leonel could hear the false note in his husband's voice—the pretense that everything was okay. It didn't seem fair that when the rest of his life had firmed up, their marriage had wobbled.

So much had changed. David still hoped some things would change back. Leonel liked the changes.

Sighing, Leonel stood to fetch another glass of water. Hydration really would save him some suffering in the morning. Luckily, morning meant it was Friday, and he had the day off. No meetings. No training. He might sleep as late as ten o'clock, if his body allowed it.

He gripped the chair back for balance. To his astonishment, the wood crumbled beneath his hand, leaving him holding only wood dust. The spindles, now without a top bar to hold them in place, dropped to the tile, echoing hollowly.

David whirled around, his mouth agape. They both stared at the dust falling from Leonel's hand. The glass in his other hand trembled, and Leonel dropped it onto the table like it might bite him. It teetered on its bottom before settling.

Wiping his hands on his jeans, Leonel took a step backward into the marble countertop. His gentle bump cracked the stone and dropped a chunk onto the floor.

David moved toward him, but Leonel held up a hand. "I don't know what's happening."

In his first days after his transformation, it had been like this. Leonel—Linda, then—had not known how to manage her incredible new strength and had done considerable damage to their house and belongings while figuring it out. But he'd not had trouble like this in years. He knew his strength and navigated ordinary life. It couldn't be the alcohol, could it?

Afraid to touch anything, Leonel sat down on the floor and pulled his hands into his lap so he wouldn't accidentally break anything else. Across the room, David watched, his eyes wide and his face rigid with tension. He reached out a hand. "What can I do?"

"Don't come any closer." Leonel sobbed. "I don't want to hurt you."

David blanched, and withdrew the hand he had offered. Keeping an eye on Leonel, he backed out of the room. Standing in the corner of their kitchen, he picked up the handset of the old-fashioned, wall-mounted telephone they had installed when they first moved in. They cut off the service years ago but left the green plastic relic of their past hanging there, a sentimental keepsake.

Without dialing anything, David spoke into the handset, utilizing the Department's emergency system. "Emergency," he said. He waited, listening. Leonel quelled his rising panic with long, deep breaths, thanking God David had been there to make the call. Help would come.

FRIDAY

MARY'S MOM IS TOO HOT TO HANDLE

M om!"

Mary Braeburn touched a hand to the fire-protective glass in the UCU observation room, disbelieving. She yanked it back, her palm scalded red from the momentary contact. On the other side, her mother was in flames. The room billowed with white clouds of steam and the observation window had blackened at the edges. Mary could see the mist of fire-retardant projecting from the ceiling-mounted system, but Helen Braeburn's body burnt it off as fast as it could fall. Boiling rivulets streamed down the glass, evaporating only to reform.

The temperature readout blinked an error message, which meant the air in her mother's room now topped 400 degrees. Even on the other side of the glass, Mary sweated through her thin sweater. Helen's former hospital bed had become a puddle of melted plastic, glowing metal fragments, and the smoking remains of the mattress. Gray ash and sparks swirled in the air.

Helen herself sat on the floor, unconscious and unmoving except for an occasional twitch of her hands, which kept raising cones of fire, seemingly against her volition. Each new eruption of flame added to the conflagration of the room.

"Mom!" Mary screamed into the microphone again, wondering if the system could even still function in the face of the heat, if her mother could hear her over the roar of flames encircling her. Behind Mary in the observation room, the attendant who had brought her in shifted from foot to foot.

Mary licked her dry lips. When the Director sent for her, Mary had expected to be asked to handle some kind of psychic crime situation. That had been the deal after all. The Department kept her mother locked up, safe, and she used her resistance to psychic manipulation to assist in the work of the UCU. No one was equipped to deal with the special kind of hazard known as Helen Braeburn, not even Mary.

Pulling down the sleeves of her sweater to afford her pale, tattooed skin some protection, Mary pounded on the glass with both fists. The guy who had brought her in gasped and pressed himself against the far wall. *Idiot. How did he even get hired if he freaked out this easily?* This glass had been built to withstand her mother's heat. It wouldn't break or melt from the ordinary force of a panicking daughter's fists. She wasn't the one with super strength around here.

Mary pounded the hazy gray glass with five thuds, as loud as she could manage. She had just drawn back to try a sixth when her mother started, as if awakening, drawing in a huge gasping breath.

Mary lunged for the call button. The system squealed before her voice came through. "Mom! Can you hear me?"

Helen looked down at her fire-engulfed hands and brought them together in her lap, extinguishing their flames with a gesture resembling prayer. Pressing a hand against the wall, she used it to help her get to her feet. She crossed the room, gesturing at the fires as she did like she might at a dog she wanted to sit. It worked. The fires shrank and went out one by one. The temperature gauge came back online, dropped fifty degrees, then another thirty. It kept falling.

Mary's heart slowed, her panic calming into something more like the ordinary fear she felt these days whenever she had to face her mother.

Helen had refused to talk to her daughter for the first two months of her captivity, spending visit days making snarky, passive-aggressive comments to the impassive guards. When she finally spoke to her again, it had been a single word, dripping in venom. "Traitor." Helen hadn't forgiven her daughter for her part in the events that led to her incarceration at the UCU.

But Mary had kept visiting, kept telling her mother her side of the story—the one where she accepted what help she could find because her mother had tried to kill Cindy Liu and didn't seem to care if everyone else burned to ash beside her. Not even her daughter. Mary tried to make her understand she'd been a danger to herself as well as to everyone else, and she hadn't known any other way to help. She'd gone to the only people capable of helping—the very same people she had helped her mother escape from months before: the UCU.

They'd made progress. While Helen still scowled when she saw her daughter, she no longer covered her ears and sang when Mary spoke. A thoughtful look crossed her face from time to time, giving Mary hope her mother might understand and forgive her someday. Or maybe she was desperate for any kind of company after months alone in a fireproof room. Mary would take it either way. Progress was progress.

Recently, Helen had become more cooperative with her caretakers and even seemed to look forward to Mary's visits—at least the staff told her Helen asked when she'd be coming. Mary didn't know if her mother would ever get to a place where she could be trusted and set free again, but maybe she could get to a place where they could talk.

Helen stood on the other side of the observation glass, her face unreadable. Mary had already set the opacity to let her mother see her in turn. She pulled up the shoulder of her sweater and used it to wipe tears off her cheeks, leaving a black streak of makeup on the sleeve. They stood looking at each other on the two sides of the glass for a long moment.

Finally, Helen spoke. "What the hell happened?"

"We were hoping you could tell us."

Helen looked around the room, then walked back over and kicked the wreckage of what had been her bed on the floor. "Did I do this?"

"You did."

She looked up at the ceiling where a faint mist continued to fall. Somewhere, a fan kicked on, drawing some of the smoke and fumes out of the room. Helen's voice warbled. "I thought this place was supposed to be fireproof."

"We thought so, too."

Helen glared at the ceiling again, presumably angry at the observation cameras. "What did they do to me?" Two of her fingers lit, a candle flicker tickling the air.

Mary forced calmness into her voice, wishing she had the Director's ability to influence emotion. Helen freaking out would only make this worse. "They didn't do anything to you. We've talked about this. They are not experimenting on you here. They are trying to help."

Helen barked a short, brutal laugh, devoid of humor. "That's what they told you. I thought I raised you smarter."

Mary bristled. "I've still got my gold-plated bullshit detector, Mom."

Helen swallowed noisily, opening and closing her mouth several times without speaking. At length, she lumbered back over to the observation window to look into Mary's face again, unsteady on her feet. Mary met her gaze, unflinching.

She hadn't come into this blithely. She had reason to trust the UCU would do right by her mother, and Helen needed to respect her efforts. She was neither stupid nor naive, and it pissed her off that her mother would think otherwise.

Helen blinked first. Her jaw quivered before she brought it under control to speak. "If they didn't do something to me," she said, gesturing at the disaster scene behind her. "Then why did this happen?"

Mary flicked a glance to the attendant still pressed against the wall behind her. He shrugged. *So helpful.* Mary sighed and put on her best professional tone. "So far as they can tell, you did this in your sleep."

"In my sleep?" A note of something new came into Helen's voice, something high pitched and grating. She closed the small gap between them and pressed her hands against the glass. Her eyes were suspiciously wet. "You've got to make them help me."

Mary placed her palms against the now-much-cooler glass, matching her fingers to her mother's like they were comparing hand size. "I promise."

MEANWHILE, IN INDIANA

W hen Patricia stepped off the plane onto the open tarmac and the first farm-fresh breeze greeted her nostrils, she shuddered. Cow shit, the pervasive scent of her childhood. It made her want to turn around and get right back on the plane and return to Springfield where the air smelled mostly of car exhaust, but the attendant had already rolled the stairs away. He tipped his blue cap at her, and she inclined her chin to him, taking the hint to follow the yellow arrows on the ground and make her way inside, trailing behind the other ten or so passengers who'd shared her flight.

Patricia tugged at her jeans. It had been a while since she'd worn them. Her alter ego required stretchier options, and she'd never liked denim anyway. But she wanted to blend in, at least as much as a six-foot tall city lesbian and sometimes lizard woman could blend into small town Indiana, and clothes were the easiest adjustment. Her starched white button-up Oxford still stood out among the t-shirts and knit tunics favored by the other women in the terminal. She hadn't remembered how casually everyone dressed here, accustomed as she was to corporate chic. Well, either that or spandex.

The place didn't have a proper baggage carousel. Instead, a man wearing a faded polo shirt with the word *Bedford* embroidered on the left side stood next to an orange painted wagon, handing bags to the waiting crowd. Patricia's suitcase was near the back, so she leaned against a pillar to wait and pulled out her phone, turning it back on. The buffering wheel spun for a bit, then the phone lit up with a "no signal" message.

Sighing, she tucked the useless device into her pocket. She'd forgotten the carrier she used in Springfield didn't really serve podunk Indiana—part of the seven percent of America not colored red on the coverage map, a white hole too far from any of the bigger cities to rate their own cell phone tower. Usually, when she visited, she arranged for a short-term contract with the local service, but she'd been in a hurry and hadn't made those arrangements. She'd have to check in with Suzie later on the landline at her mother's house, if necessary.

She walked up to the wagon and claimed her small green suitcase, then headed out the front door, where she hoped her rental car awaited her. The tiny airport hadn't changed since the last time she visited, some four years earlier. Even the potholes seemed sunk in the same places. She found one by stepping into it and soaking her loafer and the sock beneath. "Damn it!"

"Language!" a woman huffed, shouldering past Patricia and glaring while tossing her floral-patterned monogrammed suitcase into the back of a small, battered pickup truck.

Refraining from flipping off the disapproving woman, Patricia scanned the parking lot but didn't find any sign of a rental car stand, so she walked back into the now-empty terminal, dragging her suitcase wheels across the bumpy tiles in search of someone to ask for help. The man who had handed her the bag still stood near the luggage cart, leaning against the wall with his eyes closed.

Patricia cleared her throat. When he didn't open his eyes, she moved closer. "Hey," she said.

The man rocked back onto his feet and stretched. "Yes, ma'am," he said, sounding as if he'd actually been asleep. "You need something?"

"I arranged for a car rental, but I don't see anything outside. Where can I pick it up?"

"Ah," he said. "That'd be me. You must be Ms. O'Neill?"

"Guilty as charged."

He shot her a look that softened into a smile. "Let me grab the keys."

Patricia nodded, gritting her teeth to force herself to remain polite. Waiting grated on her nerves on a good day and this wasn't a good day. Her skin itched, making her wiggle her shoulders to keep from gouging at her back.

The man ambled out of view, his boot heels echoing in the empty room. Everyone else must have been local, with their cars parked at front or family come to pick them up. Patricia hadn't wanted to be reliant on her stepdad and sister for rides, so she'd asked Suzie to get her a rental.

She turned and dragged her bag back toward the door, watching the empty parking lot. A bird flitted down and pecked at something in the gravel then took wing again. Patricia could hear herself swallow, the room had gone so quiet. The silence made her ears hurt. It was strange to hear nothing at all.

Then the sound of those boot heels clacking returned, and the young man was standing beside her again, jangling a set of keys with a large laminated tag attached. He peered into her face, then turned his cap backward on his head, revealing a set of inquisitive brown eyes. "Are you one of Babs's kids?"

Patricia peered down at the man. He didn't look the least bit familiar. "Do I know you?"

"I don't think so. But my dad is one of Babs's ex-husbands. To be honest, I think he always carried a torch for her. I found a picture of her in his desk drawer I don't think my mother knew about, standing on the beach in a bikini. You kind of look like her. I mean, taller, and less, um…" He let the thought trail off, his cheeks reddening.

A quick examination of the man placed him in his early thirties. Patricia scrutinized him more closely. White. Clean-shaven, if sloppily. Sandy brown hair, mildly overgrown, but not yet long. Thin through the cheeks, face rather long. Squinty brown eyes. Farmer's tan visible where he'd rolled up his shirt sleeves.

He had to be Wayne's kid, given his age, but she didn't see much of the broad-shouldered, kind-eyed police officer who had saved her college career all those years ago in this man's face. "Are you Wayne's son?"

A smile split the man's face, revealing his resemblance to his father in the gap between his front two teeth. "Yep. That's my old man. He married my mom a few years after he and Babs split, and they stayed together until he died, a couple of years ago. They were very happy together."

Though sad to hear of his passing, Patricia was genuinely glad to hear Wayne had found happiness after his stint as her stepfather. Her mother had torn a swath through the marriageable men in the Bedford area in her day, as well a few already married to someone else. Wayne had been a good man, and it lifted Patricia's heart to think he made it out of a marriage to her mother intact and still able to love. He deserved better than the treatment he'd gotten from Babs.

"I'm Patricia," she said, letting her suitcase settle onto its bottom and offering her hand to shake.

"Bill. Nice to meet you."

Unsure what one said to the son of the man whose heart had been broken by one's shiftless mother, Patricia stood there, mouth running dry. The silence stretched long, but Bill didn't seem bothered. He rocked on his heels and stood companionably at her side. Finally, Bill grabbed her suitcase. "Welp, let's get you on your way. I'm sure your sister will be anxious to see you. We've all been worried about Babs."

Patricia started. She should have known her mother's disappearance would be all over town—the place was too small for a woman of Babs's flamboyance to avoid notice. Of course, everyone knew she'd gone missing. Bill probably knew more about it than she did.

He led her around the side of the building, where a bright yellow Jeep sat waiting. Patricia goggled at the color, wondering if this had been all that had been available or if Suzie had done it to tease her.

Bill popped open the cargo door and dropped her suitcase into the spotless hold. Looking into the storage area, he rubbed a hand across the back of his neck. "I know there's those that talk bad about Babs, but she's been nothing but kind that I've ever seen. I hope you find her safe and sound."

He reached for the cargo door and found it out of his reach. Patricia reached over his head and swung it closed. "Thanks," she said.

Bill dropped the keys into her outstretched hand. "Dang. I forgot how tall you are."

Patricia opted to be polite. "Makes it easier to reach the top shelf."

"Well, welcome back to Bedford." He squinted at Patricia's shoes, then swatted at the back of the car as if it were the rump of a horse.

Patricia moved toward the driver's door, then paused. "I missed lunch. Is there anything open right now?"

"You could go to Shorty's."

"Shorty's is still here?" Patricia's stomach lurched with a nostalgic desire for terrible onion rings drenched in pretty good ketchup.

Bill smiled. "Sure is. And Ed's still in the kitchen."

Patricia was startled. She'd thought Ed was on the way to old when she'd waitressed at Shorty's as a teenager. The idea that the man was still alive, let alone still working as a fry cook stunned her. He'd have to be at least eighty. "That sounds great," she said, opening the door.

Remembering her manners, she turned back to Bill. "Nice to meet you, Bill. Wayne was a good man, and it looks like he raised one in turn."

"Thank you, that's kind of you to say." He adjusted the ball cap on his head and hitched up his pants. "I'd best get to it. See you, Ms. O'Neill." He looked up into her face again and smiled. "Yeah, you've definitely got some of your mama in you."

Not too much, Patricia hoped.

WAKING IN THE GUEST ROOM

Babs Carter blinked at the ceiling, disoriented. This wasn't her bedroom. The pristine ceiling lacked the water stain in the shape of a pinup girl. The sheets smelled wrong. George wasn't snoring beside her.

She shot up with a gasp, and immediately wished she hadn't. Her head swam, and she knew with horrible certainty that she was about to throw up. She scrambled to get free of the bedding and flopped onto the floor, landing hard on her knees. Skittering across the floor like a fawn on an icy pond, she made it to the bathroom and vomited, mostly in the toilet.

Groaning, she fell back onto her bottom, skull thumping against the sink cabinet. Her head hurt, and her stomach roiled like she might vomit again. She pulled herself up and ran the water in the sink, splashing her face and rinsing out her mouth. The small effort left her exhausted, and she sat down on the edge of the bathtub, ears ringing.

Where the hell was she?

The spinning feeling in her head lessened after she sat still for a while, and she dared to turn her head and examine her surroundings. She was not in a hotel but in a well-appointed home bathroom with a deep tub in pale blue porcelain that matched the toilet and sink. Plain white tile with little blue diamonds at the corners completed the theme. The small window had a floral ruched valance over dusty wooden slatted blinds and was flanked by gold-painted sconces with clear glass cups for candles, the sort of thing she might have coveted at a Home Interiors party in the 1980s.

Supporting herself on the wall and avoiding the vomit on the floor, she made her way to the window and shoved the slats apart. She couldn't see anything useful, just the slant of a roof and a glimpse of an unfamiliar street. She'd never been in this bathroom before.

Rolling out a generous amount of toilet paper, she bent and wiped up her mess and cleaned off the toilet so she could make use of it. Her stomach continued to protest its mistreatment, though Babs couldn't remember what she might have eaten or drunk to cause the problem. She couldn't remember much, actually, and her head felt like it had been overstuffed with scratchy pink insulation.

She was dressed in soft pink pajamas. Pretty, but not her own. She generally slept in one of George's old shirts, or in the buff in the summer. Certainly never in a matched set of pointelle knits—rich lady pajamas. She peeked down the shirt and confirmed she was braless beneath. She looked at the underwear between her knees and flinched at their unfamiliarity.

Her body shuddered as it dealt with whatever moved through her system. Babs hadn't felt anything like this in years—not since she'd gotten sober. But she recognized the telltale digestive effects of substance abuse. She'd imbibed in something potent, apparently, something that left her brain fuzzy and her body in distress.

She growled at the unfairness.

If she was going to suffer these kinds of consequences, she ought to at least remember the fun that got her into this position, but she couldn't remember a damned thing, and that realization spiked panic as she tried to shove through the hazy soup of her memory.

She'd left for her Alcoholics Anonymous meeting after dinner with Annie, as usual. Had she gotten there? Had she been in an accident on the way?

She didn't seem to be injured beyond the pain in her head and gut.

No bruises. No particular soreness, other than in the fold of her elbow. Pushing back the sleeve, she found a gauze pad held there with medical tape. She yanked it off and rubbed the spot. A small bruise, like the sort she always seemed to get from an IV. Had she been in the hospital then?

That couldn't be right. If she'd been in the hospital she wouldn't have been left alone to wake up like this, with no one to help take care of her and tell her what had happened. If this was some kind of rehab facility, they were terribly negligent. Weren't they afraid she'd fall or something? She was seventy-six years old after all—even if she didn't usually let that slow her down.

Trying to remember felt like pinning down cloud fragments. They floated away without sticking, leaving greasy smears that didn't form a full picture. The YMCA sign reflected in a puddle. Her friend Daniel offering her a cigarette. The overly bright headlights of a car in the parking lot. Rough black upholstery rubbing against her face. Two men arguing—one of them cursing in German. Being carried, her feet bumping against the banister. None of it added up to anything that made sense.

When she felt like she could stand again, she cleaned herself up and went back to the mirror. God, she looked awful. Her tastefully dyed strawberry-blond hair hung in greasy waves, like it had been days since its last washing, and the remnants of eyeliner and mascara were caked into the wrinkles around her eyes, leaving her looking owlish. Digging through the drawers and cabinets, she found some soap and a washcloth and cleaned her face, the cold water sharp enough to help shake the fog still weighting her brain.

Anger grew within her. Once she figured out what had happened to her, someone was going to pay. George would be furious, and Annie must be beside herself with worry. She needed to get word to them that she was all right.

Stumbling back into the bedroom, she almost tripped over a tray left on the floor in front of the door. It hadn't been there before. An old-fashioned bed table, with a plate covered by a silver dome, a little thermos, and a fragile footed cup.

She picked the tray up and placed it on the bed—a cherry wood four-poster—then went back and tried the doorknob.

Locked.

She thumped the door with the side of her fist and called out. "Hello! Is there anybody there?"

Pressing her ear against the door, she listened for a long moment, but heard nothing. A wave of exhaustion made her unsteady on her feet, and she shuffled back over to the bed and uncovered the tray, hoping for a hint. Instead, she found a plate of pancakes, fat pats of butter melting on the spongy surfaces. She untwisted the lid of the thermos and took a whiff. Coffee. *Thanks be to God.*

She poured herself a cup with trembling hands and drank it black and scalding, not even caring when it burned her tongue. As the caffeine sparked in her brain, she poured a second cup, noticing this time that she'd been supplied with cream and sugar and then made liberal use of both. Maybe it was her hangover talking, but Babs thought the coffee heaven sent.

Only after half the thermos was gone did she wonder if it might be drugged. But the wakeful feeling pricking at her consciousness said that wasn't so. The mental fog began to lift, ever so slowly, and she took in the details of the guest bedroom and tried again to figure out whose guest she was and why they would have locked her in. Someone had some explaining to do.

JESSICA GETS THE NEWS

J essica had agreed not to fly inside the building, but nevertheless she flew down the stairs between admin and the hospital floor, nearly taking out a young man with a box in his hands as she rounded the corner at the landing. Her feet nicked his elbow as she dove from one floor to the next. She waved an apology but didn't stop to explain herself.

Sally Ann had just told her about Leonel. When she reached the hospital wing, she landed and approached the desk, tucking her clothes back into place and automatically touching the emeralds she wore at her heart for luck. "Where is he?"

The woman pursed her lips. "You can't see Mr. Alvarez right now."

"What?"

"He's sedated, and his medical team is not allowing visitors until we know more."

Jessica tried to suppress her impatience. "Can I talk to his doctor?"

The voice came from behind her. "Of course you can."

"Walter!" Jessica sprang into her fiancé's arms, knocking him back with the force of her hug. "Tell me what's happening."

Walter took Jessica's hand and led her down the hall, choosing an empty consulting room for them to talk in. He closed the door and joined her on the loveseat, taking her hands in his. "We don't understand it yet."

Impatient, Jessica prompted him. "Sally Ann said there had been an accident."

He nodded. "That's true, as far as it goes."

Walter ran a hand over his head, and Jessica noticed the dark circles under his eyes for the first time. Had he slept last night? "What's going on?"

"It's his strength."

Jessica waited, the few seconds pause seeming to stretch for days. Had Leonel lost his strength somehow? Or tried something and finally found the limits of his power? How badly hurt was he?

"He can't control it."

"What do you mean? Tell me what happened."

Walter laid out the story of what happened when Leonel returned from the bachelorette party. Jessica listened without interrupting, even as questions shot through her mind at lightning speed. When he'd finished, she found she didn't know what to ask.

"What are you doing for him?"

"Right now, we've got him sedated and are running every test we can think of. But that's not the worst of it." He dropped his head into his hands and rubbed at his eyes with the palms of his hands.

The blood rushed out of Jessica's face and her heart sped to a frightening staccato. She fought to keep her body in contact with the cushions of the loveseat. "What is it?" When Walter hesitated, she grabbed his arms, shaking him. "Tell me already."

"It's not just Leonel."

"What do you mean?"

Walter stood and walked a few steps away, hands fisted at the end of his lab coat sleeves, so hard his hands shook. "There are four cases so far."

Jessica swallowed. "Four cases of what?"

"We don't fully know yet, but there are irregularities in Leonel's blood work—additional mutations."

"I still don't understand."

"You heard about the lightning woman in the park?"

She had, of course. She'd seen the segment on the news, too, with Leonel talking to the cutest little boy. He really had a way with the public. "Did something happen to him during the fight? I thought he'd been running support. He didn't say he'd gotten hurt."

Walter waved his hand in frustration. "No, that's not it. The woman—she was a Liu-vian, on our watch list."

She had figured as much. Women didn't generally wield lightning in the natural course of events, just like they didn't fly or transform into lizards. In Springfield, these cases tended to lead back to Dr. Cindy Liu. She waited for Walter to continue.

"She had new mutations, too. We're going to have to bring everyone in for testing."

Jessica frowned. "I see." She heard what he didn't want to say, saw it in the hunching of his shoulders.

It could be all of them.

It could be her.

She felt fine, but so had Leonel the day before.

She walked over and took Walter's hands. He let his fists relax into her fingers. Jessica ducked her head so he had to meet her eyes, her gaze soft, but still piercing. His eyes were pink and streaked with red lines, attesting to his long hours without rest, but it was the downward turn of his mouth that worried her. The bleak discouragement she saw there, the dread of failure.

"I should have seen this coming," he said. "Should have kept better track." He grasped at Jessica, pulling her into a hug and talking into her hair. "I don't know what I would do if anything happened to you."

Jessica pushed Walter back so she could look into his face. She smiled, laying a hand on his cheek. "None of that, Dr. Peeples. I'm a survivor, and you're a genius. We've got this."

Walter didn't smile back. "Dear god, I hope so."

SUZIE GETS UP TO SPEED

Suzie had finally gotten back to her desk in the UCU administrative wing after a morning stuffed with meetings and lunch hour briefing. She had started opening her files and windows to organize the rest of her day when the phone rang. She hit the speakerphone option. "Good afternoon, this is Suzie."

"Where's Patricia?" The Director didn't bother with a greeting. He seldom did.

Suzie checked the time and pulled up Patricia's itinerary. "Indiana," she said.

"I see."

Suzie could tell from the man's puzzled tone that he didn't see. "Check your email, sir. Patricia had a family emergency. She filled out the appropriate paperwork and emailed you last night before she caught her flight."

There was a pause, during which Suzie made out the sounds of papers being shuffled to the side and the keyboard being clicked. The Director let out a frustrated huff.

"Is there something else?" Suzie had a to-do list longer than her whole body and didn't want to listen while the Director did something he should have done before he bothered her. She'd eventually train him out of pretending helplessness to avoid aspects of the job he didn't like. She was his assistant, not his mother.

She picked up her stylus and used it to flick through her unread emails while she waited for the man to get to the point.

The Director sighed. "You and Patricia are close, right?"

Suzie squeezed the stylus between her fingers. "You could say that."

Suzie and Patricia hadn't announced the change in their relationship to their colleagues, but the more observant among them had plenty of chances to become aware. Suzie didn't know how much attention the Director had been paying and wouldn't offer too much information until she knew what he wanted.

"Have you heard from her today?"

"Not since she boarded the plane." A few clicks and she had verified that Patricia's flight landed on time. Odd. Patricia hadn't texted to say she'd arrived. A couple more clicks revealed cell phone coverage with their carrier was spotty at best in the rural part of Indiana where Patricia grew up. Just in case, she checked her phone. No missed messages. "Were you trying to reach her?"

"It might be nothing."

Suzie didn't like the sound of that. "What might be nothing?"

When the Director didn't respond, Suzie cleared her throat and spoke more authoritatively. "Sir, I cannot perform my duties as your assistant if you do not share your plans with me."

"You'd better come to the briefing," he said. "Three o'clock. Conference Room A." And the line went dead.

Suzie didn't like being blindsided. Luckily, she had resources.

Five minutes later, she'd located the medical report on the lightning woman from the park. *Damn.*

Ten minutes after that, she'd found the incident report about Leonel. *Shit.*

After ten more minutes, she'd skimmed the security footage of Helen Braeburn's cell fire. *Fuck.*

She sent Patricia a text and waited, watching the screen. While it appeared to go through, no response came. She cursed herself for failing to get the house number for Annie, Patricia's half-sister—the one Suzie had learned existed yesterday when the kid called Patricia in a panic. Turns out Patricia had quite a few half-siblings Suzie had never heard about. She'd have to look into that when she had a moment.

Suzie pulled up police reports and news sites in Indiana and took some comfort in the lack of mention of a large reptilian woman storming the countryside. Same with the conspiracy sites and the Lizard Woman fan site. No new pictures or contact stories.

Maybe Patricia was fine. Suzie would do her damnedest to make sure she stayed that way.

She still had thirty minutes before the meeting. Plenty of time to look into the medical report and glean a deeper understanding of what "new mutations" actually meant.

SOME THINGS NEVER CHANGE

S horty's hadn't changed at all. After only thirty seconds inside the
door, Patricia felt as if all her pores had clogged with grease.
Even though the place was empty and she might have sat anywhere,
Patricia made her way to a patched and sunken booth at the back
corner. She automatically stepped over the bump in the center of the
restaurant where the foundation had sunk and been badly repaired...
in 1968. The yellow paint, added in the '70s, clung to the concrete in
bits. It didn't look like it had been repainted or repaired since.

Patricia nodded at a broad-hipped teenager leaning against the
wall as she walked by. The girl toddled over to her table as soon as
Patricia sat down.

"WhatcanIgetcha?" She said it all as one word, then snapped her
gum, and Patricia was transported in a flash back to her years of wait-
ressing. Ed, it seemed, still hired his staff based on who he thought
needed the money, rather than on who might be good at the job.

"Onion rings, tuna melt, and Cherry Coke," Patricia ordered,
handing the girl the empty squeeze bottle of ketchup from the table.
"And a refill on the ketchup."

The girl nodded and sauntered off.

"Charming girl," Patricia muttered to herself. She leaned back in her seat and took in the water stains on the ceiling. She couldn't tell if she was disappointed or relieved to find the place so unchanged after all these years. Ed had hired her as a teenager so she could pay for her field hockey gear, and he arranged her shifts so she didn't have to miss practices or games. He'd understood the sport would be her ticket out of Bedford and into a better life. He'd also understood she'd need a little money to make that happen, and her family wasn't going to be able to help her.

The kid came back and put Patricia's Coke down on the table, sloshing it a little. Patricia grabbed a couple of napkins from the table holder, plopped one down on the sticky mess and wrapped her glass in the other one.

Even though Patricia made a pilgrimage to Bedford once a year or so to check in on her mother, she'd never come back to Shorty's. She hadn't wanted to look back at the girl she'd been, too busy enjoying the life she'd built for herself. But now that she was here, she found it comforting. Shabby as it was, this place had been a refuge for her when life at home got complicated.

It still stung that Annie had waited a week to call. Worse, George hadn't wanted her to know at all. Maybe it represented pride on his part, but it felt personal. Babs might not have been much of a mother —jumping from one husband to another in a series of well-intentioned bad decisions—but she was the only mother Patricia had. What right did they have to keep her in the dark?

The teenager returned with a carefully balanced tray against her hip, scooted the plate onto the table without slopping the food, and then pulled a fresh ketchup bottle out of her apron pocket. She plastered a strained little smile on her face and asked, "Anything else?" obviously hoping there wouldn't be.

Patricia rattled her glass and the girl snatched it out of her hand to take it back over to the pop stand. Patricia caught herself imagining what the girl's story might be and smiled. Suzie's influence, no doubt. Once upon a time, she wouldn't have cared, but now she found herself considering if there might be something she could do to help. If the girl was working for Ed, she had a hard luck story. They all did.

Patricia dug into her greasy food. She'd regret having eaten it later, but that wouldn't stop her now. Some things were worth the consequences.

Back in the kitchen, she could hear the radio. Even without being able to make out the words, she could tell it was a sporting event. The tell-tale roar of the crowd and the rising and sinking patter of the commentator offered a comforting familiarity. Ed always listened to the games.

She could remember his refusal to change the station and how she always used to try to get him to try some music instead. Once, when he'd stepped out for a cigarette break, she had dared to change the dial, settling on a popular music station a little fuzzy in reception. Ed had come back to find her singing into a rolled napkin like a microphone and had nearly busted a gut laughing. It was funny now, but at the time, Patricia had wished the floor would open up and swallow her to save her from the embarrassment.

She really owed the man a great debt and shouldn't have waited so long to come back and see him. She'd spent a lot of years ignoring her past and reinventing herself. Ed had always treated her with kindness, but even back then, she'd felt the pity motivating him and hated accepting the help. She wondered now if she'd hurt his feelings by never coming around to say hello.

Guilt flavored the onion rings bitterly, and Patricia washed it away with the sweet Cherry Coke. Ed apparently still favored stirring in grenadine and cherry juice instead of buying the pre-made mixture. Patricia plucked the cherry out of the top and plopped it into her mouth.

Now that she had a moment to think, she pondered what might have happened to her mother. The obvious assumption was Babs had started drinking again, and they'd find her out at the Motel 6, hungover and breaking up another marriage. But Babs had earned her ten-year medallion and seemed genuinely happy with George in their circle of grandkids and small-town friends. Unless Patricia missed her guess, Babs had been faithful to George these past twenty years, finally settling down into a measure of respectable calm in her later years.

Nothing else made much sense. If she'd been in a car accident, the police would have found her. If she'd collapsed somewhere, they'd have heard from the hospital. What had Babs gotten herself into? A week would be a hell of a bender, even by her mother's standards.

After dipping her last onion ring into a soupy puddle of ketchup, Patricia wiped the ketchup off her fingers, dropped the crumpled paper napkin on the plate, and went to the front of the diner. The place was empty, but she knew that wouldn't last. The first dinner patrons would arrive soon, so she needed to grab the moment to talk to Ed while she could.

The teenaged waitress had disappeared, out back smoking if Patricia had her guess, so she called out. "Ed? You back there?"

No voice responded, but Patricia could make out some scraping sounds over the radio chatter, so she knew someone was in the back. Maneuvering around the cash register, Patricia slid between the pop station and the iced tea containers, bumping her hip against the door into the kitchen. She caught the door against her forearm on the return swing, and leaned in. "Ed?"

"In back!"

Patricia stepped into the kitchen, and the wave of nostalgia almost overcame the stench of old grease. She let her feet remember the way through the tiny kitchen, filled to capacity by the deep fryer, flat top grill, sinks, and refrigerators. The door to the back storage room was propped open with a dustpan and more scraping sounds came from within.

Knocking on the door, Patricia leaned her head in and saw a skinny old man bent over trying to tug a giant box across the room, his jeans so far down his hips they exposed his faded plaid boxer shorts.

"Ed, aren't you getting too old for this?"

He stood and turned to face her, the movement slower than she expected. The only sign of surprise at her presence was the lifting of an eyebrow. "Age is just a number, Patty. And you know I've never been any good at math."

Patricia balked—she hadn't expected he would recognize her after all these years. Then again, how many six-foot tall redheaded Amazons had Bedford produced in its history? Ed hadn't changed much, still broad-chested and stubborn-jawed, though he stooped more and his movements revealed stiffness in his joints. She didn't even object when he called her Patty, even though she hated it as much at sixty as she had at sixteen.

"At least let me help with the box," she said.

Ed flung out an arm and with an exaggerated bow and scooted into a corner to give her room to work.

Squatting, she lifted the heavy box into her arms. "Where are we going with this?"

Eyes wide, Ed pointed to the kitchen. "Meat fridge," he said.

A few minutes later, Patricia was wearing a long black apron and loading the freezer while Ed tried to fill her in on anyone in town she might know. She learned about the marriages, divorces, children, and personal tragedies of classmates she hadn't thought about in three decades and of some she couldn't recall at all. The litany of names and life events soothed her all the same.

She wondered what he told people about her. She still sent him a Christmas card every year letting him know what she was up to, as she promised she would when he slipped her an envelope with a hundred dollars inside when she hopped the bus to Massachusetts within days of graduation. She hadn't informed him about her scaly alter ego, of course, but she had told him she'd retired from corporate life and taken on new work "in security."

"So, I guess you're here about your mama," he finally said, having run out of people to update her on.

Patricia nodded as she grabbed the cutter and collapsed the box. "Annie called me, but she didn't say much."

Ed ran his fingers through his somewhat yellowed beard. "No one seems to know much. She went out last Thursday and didn't come back. Supposed to be at her meeting, but it looks like she never made it there. Nobody's seen her, and they haven't found her car yet."

"You think she's off the wagon, Ed?"

His mouth pulled into a thin, grim line. "No, I don't, and I'm surprised to hear you say that, Patty Jean."

"I had to ask. I haven't been back in a few years. You know her history."

Disapproval darkened his voice. "People change."

"Of course they do. And sometimes they change back." Patricia ran a hand over the back of her neck, surreptitiously rubbing the nodules rising there in the guise of massaging sore muscles. She took in a deep breath and blew it out slowly. "I didn't come here to fight. I want to help. I don't know where to begin."

"It's good you came. It's a chance to pay back some of what you've been given."

Patricia's mouth fell open, but she swallowed the retort about what she'd been given and the payback due for a lifetime supply of manure. Bedford remained something she had overcome, and nothing more. But if there was anyone to whom she owed gratitude for the life she lived now, he stood before her: a feisty eighty-something-year-old man, trying not to look like he needed to lean on the counter for support.

"Thank you," she managed, her voice shaking a little.

"I know you'll do right," he said, swatting at her arm in an awkward attempt at a reassuring pat.

"I'll do my best."

SUZIE HATES BEING RIGHT
SOMETIMES

uzie listened as the scientists argued. They'd talked around the same circle three times now, by her count, without coming to any consensus or conclusion. It ought to have been such a simple decision. In Suzie's mind, it only made sense to bring in Dr. Liu. She had, after all, created the formula that had caused all these mutations in the first place. Who better than her to analyze the new data?

"Absolutely not!" Dr. Anderson flung a folder onto the table dramatically, knocking his thick, square glasses askew. "She's a criminal. Dangerous. Reckless. Have you forgotten she experimented on people without their knowledge or permission?"

Dr. Arjun Anderson had been against granting Dr. Liu any kind of research work from the beginning, arguing that she had forfeited her right for scientific exploration with her shady ethics and lack of concern for the rights of others, no matter how brilliant her work and what they might learn from it. He and Walter had butted heads over this particular decision repeatedly in the time they'd held Dr. Liu in custody at the Department.

Walter rounded the table, exuding agitation like the exhaust trail of a diesel truck. He flung his arms wide, endangering the carafe of coffee on the corner of the conference table. "Do you think I don't know that? She kidnapped Jessica—my own fiancée! But Dr. Liu is our best chance to understand what's happening."

Dr. Kimberly Suggs spoke up, her usually lilting voice strained and tense. "Surely we can analyze this data ourselves. We give her too much freedom as it is. It's only been a few months since she tried to escape."

Suzie hadn't forgotten that incident. Cindy had managed to dose herself with a concoction that made her effectively invisible, a rash self-experiment that had nearly killed her—again.

Patricia had been a mess for weeks afterward, unable to reconcile her hurt, anger, and desire for vengeance with her need to save Cindy Liu yet again. The maelstrom of emotions Dr. Liu's little stunt had roiled up still rumbled through their lives months later.

Patricia had done the right thing—Suzie had never doubted she would. But it had cost her, had cost all of them. Bringing in Dr. Liu meant unleashing chaos into their worlds again. But sometimes chaos was a necessary stage on the way to order and understanding.

Suzie cleared her throat. "You've got to bring in Liu."

The room went silent and three startled sets of eyes fixed on Suzie Grayson. She hadn't yet spoken in the heated and protracted discussion, and her comment landed like an unexploded grenade—stopping all action and focusing the attention of the room.

Dr. Anderson blinked at her as if she were a lamp fixture that had suddenly started speaking ancient Greek, and Dr. Suggs sucked in a shocked breath. Walter Peeples widened his eyes at her, a small twitch of the head reminding her to tread cautiously.

Without raising her voice, she continued. "Who better to interpret this data than she?"

Anderson sputtered again, growing red beneath his golden brown complexion, and Suzie raised a hand to stay him. "I've listened to all of you talk in a circle for nearly ninety minutes now. I've heard seven different theories about the nature of the problem, and at least fifteen different proposals for how to approach it. Pretty impressive, given there are only three of you at this table."

Walter dragged in a ragged breath, preparing to launch another argument, but Suzie gestured at the table, calling everyone's attention back to the data before them: readings on all the Liu-vians the Department had eyes on—in house and on the streets—everyone except Patricia, alone in Indiana, a realization Suzie shoved back into a mental box for the moment.

Strange new mutations manifested in every case save one, and the ramifications were not yet clear, but they worried everyone. As well they should.

She picked up the chart on Jessica "Flygirl" Roark—the lone Liu-vian who had not suffered additional mutations—and brandished it at the trio of scientists. "You're letting your emotions blind you, and these people are paying the consequences. Leonel Alvarez is in our hospital wing right now, afraid to move. He broke another toilet off the wall this morning, trying to flush. Helen's care team monitors her constantly now to make sure she doesn't set the entire facility aflame from inside a supposedly fireproof room. Other Liu-vians are in their homes and out in the city, ticking time bombs who don't even know they might explode or how. There's no time to explore our options and test out theories. Not when the expert we need is in her cell, right downstairs. We have to take advantage of that."

Anderson exploded, his accent bending more British in his anger. "You can't be serious! You'd hand this data to that madwoman, when she's the cause of it all in the first place?"

Suzie grimaced. Sometimes it sucked to be right. They all knew "Dr. Liu" and "trust" didn't belong in the same sentence. But the scientist also understood the situation better than anyone else. If anyone could get to the heart of the problem quickly, it was her.

"Exactly. She's the cause. She developed the products that started all this. Whether you want to admit it or not, your team has been playing catchup since the Liu-vians first came to your attention. Besides, she's got a personal stake—don't forget she's a victim of her own machinations."

Suzie dug through the pile of charts, frowning when she didn't find one for Dr. Liu. "Where's the data on Liu? Didn't you test her too?"

"Why are we even listening to this girl?" Anderson pressed his hands into the conference table. "She's not a researcher or even an agent."

"No, she isn't." A quiet voice, so low as to sound more like a growl, came from the far end of the room. Everyone went silent, and the Director rose from a chair in a dark corner and came to stand at the end of the table, almost as if he were about to say the blessing over a Thanksgiving turkey. He held his broad shoulders back, his face serenely unreadable. Suzie narrowed her eyes, annoyed he'd gotten into the room without her notice. She didn't like this kind of surprise.

The Director smiled at the scientists. "My personal assistant Miss Grayson is valuable to our team precisely because she's outside the problem. She brings fresh eyes and a kind of objectivity."

Walter's gaze flashed to Suzie's, then quickly lowered to examine his own hands, now clenched in a knot on the table in front of him. They both knew she had a bigger personal stake in this case than the Director suggested. A big scaly stake, currently in Indiana.

Moving around the table, the Director rested a hand on Dr. Anderson's shoulder, who stiffened, then swayed a little under the touch. "You're not wrong, Arjun. There is risk involved. But risk is necessary to the pursuit of understanding."

The Director nodded at Dr. Suggs. "She must be supervised carefully. We can't have another incident like the chameleons."

Dr. Suggs frowned. "Why would she even cooperate? We've had her on complete lockdown since her escape attempt. What's in it for her?"

"We do have something she wants very much." The Director walked to the door, pausing with his hand on the doorknob. "Ms. Roark."

Anderson stood again, objection written all over his face, but at a glance from the Director, he faltered and sank slowly back into his seat. Suzie kept her eye on the Director, remembering the photograph she'd taken after they'd defeated the Six. There was more to her boss than she yet understood. She'd need to change that.

When the door clicked gently closed, it was as if a spell had broken. Dr. Anderson and Dr. Suggs gathered their belongings and exited without further comment. Whether they agreed or not, they knew the decision had been made. The Director had spoken, and it would be so.

After the other two scientists left, Suzie reached across the table to touch Walter's arm. The man sat statue-like, lost in cogitation. Dark circles under his eyes attested to the ridiculous hours he'd been keeping.

A moment or two later, he seemed to come back into himself and jerked his hands apart to fling them into the air, Suzie's unnoticed hand flopping onto the table.

"What about Jessica?" Suzie asked.

They were going to need her cooperation. She was the anomaly among the anomalies, the Liu-vian who had not shown additional mutations in her testing. Also the freak with the largest personal grudge against Dr. Liu, outside of Patricia.

Suzie frowned. "She's not going to agree to this."

Walter grabbed the stack of files in the center of the table, shoving it roughly under one arm. "She has to." He sighed deeply, more than one kind of weariness evident in the exhalation. "I'll talk to her."

Suzie joined him, tucking her tablet and papers into her tote. When she looked up again, Walter still stood there, looking lost. Hating herself a little for the thought, but knowing it was the truth, she offered him one piece of advice.

"She'll do it for Leonel."

PATRICIA'S HOMECOMING

Patricia parked the bright yellow, rented Jeep in the driveway at her mother's house. A dark blue pickup laden with a variety of tools took the place nearest the house. Beside it, a nondescript gray sedan with a sunflower sticker in the middle of the back windshield sat, covered in enough dust and pollen to show it hadn't been driven in days. She guessed her mom usually parked her car behind Annie's little-used sedan.

She clicked off the ignition but didn't immediately get out of the car. She considered the simple brick facade. She had never lived in this house, so it wasn't home really, but something in it still tugged at her. The longest stretch she'd ever spent here amounted to a month, taking care of her mother after her knee surgery back in 1981, the summer between her undergraduate and graduate programs.

Babs had still been married to Wayne then, and that summer shone in Patricia's memory as something special. Her brother Christopher had joined the Marines by then, and Annie hadn't been born yet, but the rest of them had all been here. Sitting on the floor with her other three half-siblings, with two parents on the sofa behind them chatting quietly through movie night was the closest Patricia had ever come to having a normal family life.

It hadn't lasted.

Babs screwed it up.

Still, George was a good man, and, so far as she could tell, a good husband. The house seemed too big now for a family of three, but the others lived close enough to visit often. Babs and George hosted grandkids often enough to make use of the spare bedrooms. Patricia wondered if she should have brought gifts for her nieces and nephews. She didn't keep up with the additions to everyone's families very well—though she sent gift cards when she received announcements about graduations or weddings, and ordering popcorn, magazines, cookies, and candy online to help fund band camp or field trips or whatever.

She'd been a bit stunned to realize Annie was eighteen already. Time seemed to be slipping through her fingers faster with each passing year.

Flinging the car door open, Patricia got out and stretched. She didn't really feel cramped, but her lizard self crawled along the inside of her skin, itching to burst through to the surface, and stretching and good, slow breaths kept her alter ego under wraps.

The living room curtains flicked to the side and just as quickly flicked back into place. They knew she'd arrived then. What had Annie told George?

The girl had said George didn't want Patricia to know, that there was no need to "bother" her. The word rankled, as if she were some random lady with no connection here, someone too distant to care and not wanting to be bothered. Sure, she and Babs weren't close, but Patricia still cared about her and wanted to make sure she had everything she needed. Would he be angry she'd come?

Maybe she should have arranged for a hotel. It had seemed like a good idea to stay at the house to follow any clues she might find there.

Patricia sauntered to the back of the Jeep, trying not to show her nervousness, and pulled out her suitcase, taking her time to close the car up and lock the doors. When she couldn't put it off any longer, she took what felt like a long walk up the short garden path, lifting her suitcase across the overgrown paving stones decorated with shiny fake gems and concrete handprints, to knock on the door.

She'd barely rapped once when the door banged open. Annie blinked at her, mouth hanging open, resembling nothing so much as an overly large toddler with her big blue eyes and pudgy red cheeks. "You came." Her voice was breathless, as if she'd run a mile to reach the door.

Patricia inclined her head. "I did. Can I come in?"

Annie shot a look over her shoulder, frowning. Then a fierceness overtook her face. "Course you can!" She grabbed Patricia's wrist and tugged her across the threshold, calling out as she did so. "Dad! Guess who's here?"

Patricia could hear the television around the corner, the familiar roar of a football game. No voice called back. Annie's lips compressed into a thin line, and she shifted from foot to foot. "Come on. You can leave your bag here."

The half-sisters looped through the kitchen, Annie leading the way. The girl walked briskly for someone so short and mumbled to herself, talking herself through a mental list. Patricia didn't interrupt. While Annie turned off the burner under a pot of some kind of soup and checked on the rolls in the oven, Patricia wandered into the dining room. She was in no rush to face her stepfather.

Pictures of the whole clan lined the wall above the table. Letting her gaze bounce across the photos, she found her own—a picture from some years ago, when she'd won an award for women in business. She'd need to send her mother a more recent picture. So much had happened since then. The stylish red-haired woman in the tasteful pantsuit looked like a stranger to her now.

She spared a glance at the family portraits of the rest of her half-siblings, gathered together in studio portraits with their kids, or, in the case of Geraldine, her cats. At the end of the row was Annie's senior portrait, in which she smiled toothily and must have been forcibly holding her eyes open. The end result left her looking crazed.

Annie still looked half unformed, but a familiar stubbornness shone in the set of her jaw. Patricia would have to look for her senior portrait while she was here. She suspected her youngest sister might look quite a bit like she did at the same age, minus the athleticism and about six inches in height. They'd both inherited their mother's red hair and the accompanying pale skin. None of the rest of Babs's kids had that combination.

Her half-sister appeared at her side and gripped Patricia's elbow. "I'm glad you came, Patty." She took a big whooping breath and tugged Patricia's arm. "Let's go talk to Daddy."

George sat ensconced in an overstuffed easy chair with duct tape over a hole in the back cushion. The television still played, but George's narrow chest rose and fell steadily. He looked frail to Patricia, and a lot older than when she'd last seen him. That might represent how long it had been since she visited, or it could be the effects of the current situation.

Annie moved to shake him awake, but Patricia caught her sleeve. "Let him rest. We can talk in the kitchen until he wakes."

Relief washed over Annie's face. Patricia didn't blame her. George wouldn't be happy she'd come and delaying confrontation was a time-honored family tactic. If Annie's luck held, she could avoid the whole conversation by going to bed before George learned Patricia was there.

Back in the kitchen, the two sat opposite each other at the gray Formica table, sipping tea. This table had been a constant as long as Patricia could remember, as far back as six step-fathers ago. Somewhere, there was a picture of her sitting on the table at her first birthday, reaching a hand toward the cake, which meant the table must date back to their very first apartment, the one she'd shared with her teenaged parents for the few months their marriage had lasted.

Struck by another memory, she ducked under the table and found the crayon dog she'd drawn there when she was six or seven, certainly old enough to know better than to draw on the furniture. Her brother Christopher had misspelled his name next to it. K-R-I-S-T-O-F-R. It pleased her to see their drawings were still there.

"What are you doing?" Annie asked.

Patricia sat back up. "Taking a trip down memory lane."

Annie looked confused and worried.

"It doesn't matter." Patricia waved her hand. "Listen, Annie. You called me to help and I'm going to do my best, but I need to know everything you know about what happened."

Annie looked toward the living room. The growl of George's snoring droned above the muffled sounds of the football game. She seemed reassured by the sound. Still, she kept her voice low as she spoke. Patricia had to lean in close to hear.

"It was last Thursday. Mama had her, um, meeting."

Patricia nodded. Alcoholics Anonymous most likely. Weird how people just wouldn't say it.

"It's at the Y, you know, out on Battlefield?"

Already wishing she could speed up the story, Patricia counseled herself to be patient and listen. Under her blouse, her skin crawled. She tried to scratch her shoulder blades against the chair back surreptitiously.

"She usually gets home by eight-thirty. Papa was out, too—bowling night—and I was watching TV. She makes me turn off *Shark Tank* when she gets home most nights, but I watched two episodes, and she still hadn't come home, so I got worried and called Papa."

Bit by bit, Patricia established the timeline of the night her mother disappeared.

Babs had left the house at six-thirty for a seven o'clock AA meeting at the YMCA, to which she never arrived. Annie had gotten worried after nine o'clock, but George told her not to fret. Annie went to bed at ten o'clock, but still lay awake when George got home at eleven. That's when they called Babs's sponsor, Olivia, and learned she hadn't been at the meeting at all.

They didn't call the police for a couple of days, so she hadn't been reported missing until Sunday after church. George looked everywhere, driving all over Bedford, even out to the hotels on the other side of the tracks. Annie hadn't been anywhere at all in the week before she called Patricia because "Papa wanted someone to be here in case she called."

"What do the police say?" Patricia asked.

Annie's red-rimmed eyes brewed new tears. "They say she ran away. But Mama wouldn't leave us. I know she wouldn't!"

Patricia knew where the police were coming from. The sheriff's office had been called out to deal with too many situations involving Babs Miller (or O'Neill, or Williams, Ryan, Smythe, Hargrave, Faucette, or Carter) over the years. Small towns had long memories. Little wonder they weren't taking the case seriously—they thought Babs was up to her old tricks, wrecking homes and boozing around. She reached out to pat her sister's hand.

"What's wrong with your skin?" Annie's whisper pitched high enough to come out as a squeak.

Patricia looked down to see a thin layer of light green scales rippling across her wrist. She pulled her hand back and yanked her sleeve over the evidence. Tamping down her panic, she forced a laugh. "Eczema. I tell you, getting old isn't for wimps. Just you wait."

Annie didn't look convinced. "You seem different."

"Well, you were still a kid the last time I visited."

She shook her head. "It's not that. Something happened. Starting about three or maybe four years ago, I think."

Patricia stared at her youngest sibling. Something had happened four years ago—Cindy Liu had changed her life forever with a skin cream that transformed her into the Lizard Woman. But Patricia had not whispered the smallest hint to her family, and it wasn't like they got the Springfield news in Bedford. How did Annie know?

"Yeah. It has to be four years. I was a freshman. You used to call every Sunday, but you stopped. When you called, you asked to talk to me, but you never remembered what I told you from call to call. I thought you didn't like me anymore."

"It wasn't that."

"I figured." The girl shrugged. "We hadn't had a fight or anything. More like you were up to something and hoping not to get caught." She leaned across the table to peer into Patricia's face more directly, her wide blue eyes curious and a little skeptical.

Patricia picked up her mug of hot tea and sipped it even though it had gone cold, stalling. Her brain spun a series of responses, but none of them were likely to get Annie to trust her, so she decided on a version of the truth. "I went through something pretty big a few years ago. I can't tell you much about it. But I'm not the same person I used to be. You're right about that."

"Are you a spy?"

Choking on her swallow of tepid tea, Patricia coughed. "A spy?"

Annie waggled her eyebrows, a childhood trick Patricia had forgotten about. The kid was teasing her.

"Sure. The government is hiring old ladies now to ferret out secrets. In fact, they sent me here. Indiana is a hotbed of international intrigue, you know."

A wide grin spread across Annie's face, and Patricia was reminded afresh of the fierce little girl who, at age six, had announced her intentions to travel the world having dramatic love affairs. Maybe the backbone hadn't been cowed out of her entirely, after all.

"Do you think you can find her?"

"I'm going to try."

DARRIN'S ON THE CASE

At his favorite coffee shop, Darrin sat outside, sipping an ill-advised late day concoction. Sleep would elude him anyway, so he might as well fuel his spinning mind in hopes that the whirling thoughts would become focused and give him a direction. The sky was a hazy orange smear, part sunset and part city lights, and a sweet sugary scent wafted pleasantly from his cup.

His footage with Fuerte and Patricia had been quite a coup. Nicole Boisseau, a more senior reporter at the *Springfield City News*, had scowled in a way that told him she regretted not holding the superhero beat for herself. Out loud, she dismissed his work as "nice" and "a feel-good segment between real news stories" and steered the conversation back to her own work, which she called "groundbreaking" and "important."

She wasn't wrong. The whole idea of powered heroes working in concert with the police and rescue forces of Springfield still played for novelty on the airwaves and in the pages of local magazines and newspapers. Other than a few op-eds complaining about property damage or speculating down conspiracy-theory lines about the origins and secret agendas of Flygirl, Fuerte, and Patricia, public reception had been positive. Most of the denizens of Springfield seemed to focus on the amazing physical feats and the flashy costumes, as pleased to see the heroes as they would be to see a Hollywood celebrity on the streets of their city.

After all, Springfield was hardly New York City. A mid-sized Southern city with no particular claim to fame beyond the nearby tech corridor, Springfield rarely attracted the broader attention of the national press, either for good or bad. It hardly seemed like the kind of place where not one, but three powerful and fascinating characters like this would appear.

Darrin felt the wonder as well. He found it impossible not to be awed when Fuerte picked up a car and Patricia...well, Patricia boggled the mind. It delighted Darrin that she refused to use a catchy moniker, but instead used an ordinary first name, like someone who went to college with your mother. "Patricia" was such a ridiculously normal name for a six-foot-tall bulletproof lizard that it made Darrin smile every time he heard it.

He suspected the Lizard Woman of Springfield didn't always look so terrifying, though. In analyzing film clips the day before, he'd seen her at a variety of levels of armor and imagined she might be a very human-looking woman beneath her dinosaurian aspect. That would explain the tuft of bright red hair, so incongruous against the scales and spikes.

A soft cry went up from the table next to him, and Darrin followed the pointing fingers and mouth-open gazes to spot Flygirl soaring through the air just above the streetlights on her evening patrol, red hair glinting in the reflected light. She waved as she flew, a broad smile lighting the part of her face visible beneath the cowl.

While Darrin and the other onlookers watched, she bent her athletic body and spiraled into a turn around the bank at the corner and disappeared from view. Despite being such a tiny woman, barely over five feet tall and slender, Flygirl was definitely larger than life.

Darrin listened to the excited chatter around him, one of his favorite information-gathering techniques. You could learn a lot about what people thought by being quiet in a crowd. An older woman told a story about seeing Flygirl at a hospital charity event, and a young man talked about the children she'd helped save when a semi overturned on an overpass. Delight and joy bubbled from their excited voices.

Flygirl made a great frontwoman for the mysterious UCU. Solidly professional, the master of a quotable soundbite, and perfect at projecting a balance between confidence and humility that made her a media darling. He'd love to get an extended interview with her. Even better would be to get all the heroes in a single conversation.

But the UCU limited access to their flashier officers, a decision that frustrated Darrin, even as he understood it. These heroes were people after all, and they had to come from somewhere. He respected the need for secrecy even while he longed for insight, understanding, and the lead spot in the nightly broadcast.

Having finished his coffee, Darrin decided to walk through the city park. The police had cleared the crime scene tape earlier that afternoon, and he could now examine the site of the fight with the lightning woman from the other day.

This case bothered him. It felt different than other battles against criminals he'd covered for the *City News*. The lightning woman hadn't seemed to want anything.

Fuerte had insisted the woman needed help and had not intended harm, despite the hour or so she'd spent hurling lightning in the middle of the city. Quite likely, that was the truth. In fact, she might have gone into the park out of a desire to get away from more populated areas, to make sure she didn't hurt anyone.

He'd kept her name out of the story for now, until they knew more, but he'd been looking into Marietta Cooper, a sixty-four-year-old Black woman who lived near the park. With no history of violence, Ms. Cooper had a particularly boring backstory including nothing more exciting than an ex-husband and somewhat contentious divorce.

Darrin knelt to touch the seared earth where the lightning woman had struck. Yellowish-brown branching scorch marks drew a ghostly winter tree shape in the lawn, beautiful and frightening. Poking at it with his pocket knife, he found some of the sand in the soil had petrified into gray coral-shaped glass. Eerie. He snapped some stills with his phone. They might be useful for the channel's website. It amazed him to imagine the electricity had emanated not from the sky but from a retirement-aged woman.

Ms. Cooper had retired from a career as a schoolteacher about four years ago after an impressive thirty-eight-year stint teaching middle school English. Nothing in her earlier life suggested she had any unusual powers or gifts beyond the infinite patience it must take to deal with a classroom full of thirteen-year-olds on a daily basis.

Strolling nearer the water, Darrin approached the destroyed park bench. He'd already seen images of the destroyed fixture on social media and news sites. The wooden slats had cracked and splintered, leaving long shards scattered across the lawn. The shards had been cleaned up now, and caution tape cordoned off the scorched and splintered bench.

The metal structure beneath remained mostly intact, though the wrought iron had discolored in spots. His drone footage of the fight had captured the moment when the metal glowed bright with heat. Darrin considered Marietta Cooper again as he snapped a few more pictures for his files.

Sixty was a few years shy of the sixty-five age mark the punitive new state retirement program required for full benefits, but plenty of people took the financial hit to start enjoying their sunset years while they were still healthy enough to do so. But Ms. Cooper had turned sixty and retired from teaching four years ago. Four. That number kept coming up—much too often for coincidence.

Four years ago, right after Darrin moved to Springfield to take the job at City News, there had been a fire at the college. The official story had been that a disgruntled student had threatened people with a flamethrower until he had been subdued by authorities, but stories circulated about a woman who had thrown fireballs with her hands. Others claimed to have seen a flying woman that night.

The Lizard Woman fan site posted blurry pictures of what appeared to be Patricia, alongside the famous first image of her at the fire over in the Riverside neighborhood. Early theories suggested that she could breathe fire herself, like a dragon, though Darrin hadn't seen anything promoting that idea in a while, and it had been more than a year since the Lizard Woman had been involved in a fire of any kind.

Darrin's personal theory involved another powered person who could wield fire. There had been a few blips on the news scene in the last couple of years—a woman threatening a doctor at the Urgent Care and a fight over by City Hall when the gang of jewel thieves had been apprehended. True, there hadn't been any recent sightings, but maybe the mysterious fire-wielding woman connected to Ms. Cooper somehow. If Springfield was home to three powered people, it only made sense to consider the possibility more of them might be out there.

The more he thought about it, the more Darrin believed something significant had happened in Springfield four years ago, something the city still saw fallout from today. He aimed to find out what it was.

SUZIE MISSES THE CALL

S uzie pounced on the phone, sending it flying across the bed. It
bounced against the dresser and skittered across the floor. She
flung herself after it, but it had gone dark by the time she grasped it.
She clicked over to the missed calls. Patricia. *Damn it.* The one call she
had not wanted to miss. Before she could click to call back, a text
message popped up.

"Arrived safe. Signal bad. Wi-Fi not much better. Will call tomorrow. Exhausted. Good night."

Suzie's finger hovered over Patricia's name. They needed to talk.
But it was late, and Patricia had plenty to deal with already—back
among the family she never even talked about, dealing with her mother's disappearance. Surely if something were happening, she'd
reach out.

Before she'd quite decided to do so, Suzie clicked and called.
Straight to voicemail. She hung up. Patricia had probably turned off
her phone after sending the message. When she declared herself done
for the night, she meant it. No sitting there playing solitaire for an
hour after she intended to go to sleep, like Suzie.

Suzie would have dialed the house phone, even not knowing
what can of worms her calling might open for Patricia, but she

didn't have enough information to find it. Presumably, "Babs" was short for Barbara, but the woman had married six more times after Patricia's birth, so Suzie didn't know what last name to look for, and an initial search had picked up 1,300 women in the right age range, and a disappointingly large number of them had been divorced at least once. She'd track her down eventually, but it would take a little time.

In the whirlwind of their romance, Suzie hadn't realized how little she'd actually learned about where Patricia came from—who she'd been before she became the Lizard Woman of Springfield. Embarrassing, especially for someone who prided herself on information management.

From helping with the wedding plans, she knew more about Jessica's fiancé's family than that of her own girlfriend. That had never bothered her before.

Still, she didn't want to be *that* kind of girlfriend—the clingy one unable to trust that their partner knows what she is doing and is capable of taking care of herself. Patricia's fierce independence and self-assurance were half of what attracted Suzie to her in the first place. Women her own age never quite seemed to have it together, but Patricia knew what she wanted and would fight for it.

Everything must be okay. Patricia wouldn't send such an innocuous message if she were unexpectedly scaly or in any kind of crisis. After arguing with herself for some minutes, Suzie settled for sending a text. "Glad you are safe. Some news here. Call me when you are alone tomorrow."

Then she flung herself into the bed and lay there staring at the ceiling, one hand still wrapped around the phone, in case it buzzed again.

She replayed the Director's comments from the afternoon's meeting in her head. He'd praised her insight, but the words rang hollow in her memory. He'd said her insight was valuable because she had objectivity, but Suzie felt anything but objective now.

What if these mutations affected Patricia, too? She thought back to Patricia's first transformations, back when she'd been the unwanted intern foisted on Patricia by Uncle Mike. She'd heard Patricia O'Neill was a bit of a dragon lady, but Uncle Mike didn't know the half of it.

That day in her office four years ago, when Patricia's scalier self emerged for the first time, the Lizard Woman tore through a silk blouse and Suzie's notions of what might be possible.

When the Director had shown up at her grad school a few days before her graduation, she'd understood he was recruiting her, in part, as bait for Patricia, though he never said it directly. They'd become close when she'd been Patricia's intern and had helped see her through her transformation. Her presence in the organization made it more likely Patricia would sign on with the Department, alongside Jessica and Leonel, despite her mistrust of covert organizations. Loyalty was one of Patricia's finest qualities.

And it had worked—Patricia had joined the UCU, and Suzie's presence on the staff had been part of why. Would the Lizard Woman of Springfield still be an urban legend instead of a member of the crime-fighting team if Suzie hadn't been there? Maybe not.

But maybe so. Though Patricia denied it, she had a hero's heart and her desire to help improve the world they lived in almost matched Suzie's. Patricia needed someone to help her see past her cynicism to the possibilities, to remind her that caring didn't equate with weakness.

Someone like Suzie.

Falling in love had complicated things. That hadn't been part of her plan.

A combination of guilt and ambition swirled in her guts as she pondered her position, making a hot soup of mixed emotions. Suzie had allowed the Director to use her to influence Patricia's decision. She'd wanted the job that badly. How many opportunities did a recent graduate in business administration get to do something that really mattered?

Sure, she could work for a nonprofit, but she'd die still in debt for her degrees and any change she wrought would come at a glacial pace. Suzie didn't want to wait.

Working for the UCU gave her the chance to make a difference now, to see the impact of her work on the lives of people in need of help immediately instead of waiting decades to get into a position that let her see the fruits of her labor. She told herself those ends justified the means, and most of the time she believed it. Intentions had to count for something.

She wished she understood the Director's intentions. Working with the man drove her crazy. He was secretive—on the verge of outright deceitful—and Suzie preferred straight-shooters to manipulators. Making decisions with incomplete information nearly always led to disaster, but getting full information from the Director was like wrestling an eel—a handsome eel used to getting his way with flirtation and who didn't know what to do with a pretty blond lesbian immune to his charm.

He seemed immune to hers, as well. Despite her work over the past few months—taking his antiquated systems and bringing them into the twenty-first century, tracking assets and agents, creating a new system for the dispatchers that kept them all on track, and taking his vague plans and turning them into workable endeavors—he still didn't seem to trust her.

Everyone said her behind-the-scenes work on the hospital case had made it possible for Jessica and Leonel to get the Earthquake Woman under wraps safely without civilian casualties. And where had the Director been when she and Patricia had been nabbed in the park and Suzie had thwarted their would-be-kidnappers by throwing her shoe into the works? She'd proven herself over and over again, and yet she still didn't even know her employer's real name.

Or his real face for that matter.

Picking up her phone again, she went to the subfolder where she'd hidden the photograph taken in his office when they were celebrating the capture of The Six. There he was, sandwiched between Leonel and Suzie, a man she'd never seen before that day—or since.

The man she knew as the Director appeared tall and straight-backed, elegant with a streak of gray at the temples of his raven black hair and a lantern jaw. He reminded Suzie of a thinner version of her own father. The man in the photograph stood at least a head shorter than Patricia, with brown hair in need of cutting and an almost heart-shaped face. Could she trust a man who didn't show his true face to the world? Or had she done something foolhardy, signing on without understanding what she was getting into? Or, worse than that, for taking Patricia with her.

Bouncing out of bed, Suzie grabbed her keys and headed for the parking garage. No one else would be there in the admin wing. If she wouldn't be sleeping tonight, she might as well get something done.

WHAT WALTER ASKS

Across town, Jessica sat across the kitchen table from her fiancé, arms crossed over her chest and face still red from the heat of the past hour's arguments.

Walter had been uncharacteristically terse during dinner but had refused to talk to her about what was bothering him until the boys and Eva had gone to bed. Now she understood why.

"I can't believe you'd ask me to do this," she said. Anger and disappointment fought in her guts. Of all people, Walter should understand why she wanted to keep as wide a berth as possible between herself and Dr. Cindy Liu. Not only had the woman kidnapped Jessica herself, she had threatened her *mother*. Eva, Jessica's mother, still bore a scar from where Helen had burned her elbow, and it had been a matter of luck the boys hadn't been home the day Dr. Liu brought her fire-throwing henchwoman to Jessica's door. If they'd been there, who knows what might have happened.

Knowing Cindy Liu and Helen Braeburn were in custody at the UCU was one of the great comforts of Jessica's life. Locked away and unable to hurt anyone else. As they should be.

And here was Walter, her intended—the man who ought to protect her and her boys just as she would protect him—asking her to work with Dr. Liu.

Walter dropped his glasses on the table and rubbed his hands over his face, ending with the heels of his hands pressing into his eyes. "If we had another way, I wouldn't ask it. I know how you feel about Dr. Liu, and I don't blame you. I feel the same way. But we need her insight if we're going to help the others."

Jessica rose, stalked over to the refrigerator, opened it, and stood staring at the contents, as much for the chance to cool the heat of her cheeks as out of any desire for a snack. She grabbed a yogurt, then rattled through the silverware drawer, trying to think of anything she could say. As she always did when worried, she sought the shard of emerald she wore around her neck, gripping the cylindrical gem through the thin material of her shirt and running a thumb over its familiar terrain.

Her fingers shook. Confronting an earthquake-causing woman or a psychic jewel thief was one thing. Confronting your future husband was something else entirely. She'd take a super-powered villain any day over the turmoil burning in her guts now.

When she came back to the table, Walter had replaced his glasses and smoothed down his hair. When his gaze met hers, his eyes were bleary with exhaustion, his face puffy, the soft brown irises of his eyes nearly lost in the bloodshot whites. He hadn't slept in too long, and it showed.

"Surely our researchers can figure this out on their own."

Walter flung his hands in the air. "Sure, given enough time and resources, we might be able to figure this out, eventually—months or years down the road. But meanwhile, Liu-vians around the city are exhibiting dangerous symptoms. The lightning woman in the park is just one of the calls we've taken this week."

"But you could get there, without relying on her. It's possible."

"We've beaten this horse to death, Jessica. Time is everything. People are going to get hurt if we don't figure this out quickly. People have already gotten hurt."

"But…" Jessica chewed her lip. "Why me? Didn't you say my blood-work doesn't show these new mutations?"

Walter nodded. "That's exactly why—if we can figure out why it's not happening to you, we'll be a step closer to finding a treatment for the others."

Jessica looked away, a maelstrom of lava seemed to eat through her stomach, part fear, part guilt, part anger. Walter came to kneel at her side, taking her hand into his and searching her face.

"You're the bravest woman I know. Every day you take risks in your work, putting yourself in danger to keep others out of it. Why is this different?"

"It just is." How could she explain it to him? None of the criminals she had helped capture and detain were after her in particular. But Cindy Liu was—the woman had been fixated on her since the start, determined to get her under the microscope and rend any secrets from her flesh. Jessica met Walter's gaze. "Those risks aren't personal. This one is."

"I see." Walter rocked back on his heels, letting her hand slide out of his. He spoke to the tiled kitchen floor in front of his knees. "And what about Leonel?"

Jessica's chest ached. She gasped wordlessly.

"We have to keep him under heavy sedation now. His room is half-destroyed, and David is beside himself. I'm sure the risk feels pretty damned personal to them, too."

Walter rolled up onto his feet. "I'm the one who has to weigh the good and bad and decide what's best in this situation. That's my job. Just like yours is to face down the bad guys in the streets."

He waved a hand, as if their entire conversation were smoke in the air between them and he could disperse it with the gesture. "Do you think it makes me happy to bring in Dr. Liu?" He shook his head. "But we need answers—fast answers. We'd be fools not to use all our resources." His voice thickened, full of emotion. "I would never let her hurt you, Jessica. I love you. We'll protect you every step of the way. But you have to do this. For Leonel. For all of them."

Taking in a long, slow, shuddering breath, Jessica stood and walked to her fiancé. She stood looking into his eyes for a long moment before dipping her chin in a quick nod. "All right then. For Leonel."

SATURDAY

SUZIE'S ALL-NIGHTER

Suzie's hand buzzed, and she groaned, disoriented. She tried to roll over and jolted awake when her desk chair wobbled and nearly spilled her out onto the floor. Blinking groggily and peeling off a piece of paper that had stuck to her cheek, she realized she had fallen asleep at her desk at the UCU. Exhaustion must have finally beaten worry last night and let her drift off.

Pins and needles ran up her slender arm, and she rubbed at it absently for a moment until she realized the buzzing had not been within her flesh, but coming from her phone, still vibrating angrily against the surface of her desk. She swiped to answer without checking who called. "Suzie here."

Static assaulted her ear. She pulled the phone back and stared at the screen. Patricia's winking visage looked back at her before the phone beeped and tossed up a message about a lost call. She called back and was sent straight to voicemail, again.

Ridiculous.

This was the twenty-first century, and she held a computer in her hand, more powerful than the ones that had sent the first astronauts to the moon, but she could still be stymied by the distance between cell towers in rural Indiana.

Anger boiled under her skin. Only a recognition of the futility of destroying her phone kept her from throwing it against a wall. Sighing, she checked the time. Six-thirty. Patricia never had lost the habit of rising early, despite her late hours. The woman hardly seemed to need sleep at all.

Suzie, on the other hand, needed her full eight hours, and a six-thirty wake-up call full of frustration left her rattled. She stood up and stretched. Her neck and back popped, and she stumbled to the nearest bathroom, waiting for her brain to come back online.

A few splashes of cold water made her alert enough to remember the danger Patricia was in. Tugging her blond hair into an awkward little bun on the top of her head and arranging her comfy, at-home clothes back into place, she hurried back to her office, grateful no one else had come in this early to see her looking so unprofessional and haggard.

Clicking on the coffeepot, Suzie stood, thinking. The thoughts swirling through her head were simultaneously frantic and foggy, half-formed and confused. As she tried to organize the storm into a checklist, every third item lit up red in her mind screaming, "Patricia!" in tall neon letters. She needed to get focused or she'd be worse than useless, and Patricia needed her at the top of her game. She gulped the coffee as soon as it was ready. Ignoring her tongue's complaint about the temperature, she poured another.

Returning to her desk, she pulled up the document she'd been working on the night before and deleted the half page of nonsense letters she'd apparently typed with her cheek. The proposed retrieval mission plan needed a bit of tweaking before it was ready to send to the Director. Even exhausted, she knew the necessary logistics: transport, personnel, equipment.

In case he argued the Department's resources shouldn't be squandered on a personal rescue, she'd prepared a list of arguments from staff loyalty to the danger to the public image of the UCU should Patricia lose control in a public setting.

While the document printed—the Director was old school when it came to these things—Suzie clicked through updates and emails. Three additional Liu-vians from the watch list were now housed in the medical wing, brought in overnight. She'd need to talk to the Director about adjusting the shift rotation. The usually quiet night shift wouldn't be able to manage with so many potentially dangerous patients under their care. She moved the message from Dr. Suggs about supplies of sedatives to the Director's priority inbox, ensuring he'd see it as soon as he arrived.

Clicking to another system and logging in with the Director's credentials, Suzie ascertained that Leonel and Helen were stable for now. The night nurse had noted that Mr. Alvarez required a double dose of tranquilizer before he could rest, and he remained quite emotionally agitated.

Suzie frowned. Had anyone checked in with David? Having his husband there could help keep Leonel calm, and they needed him calm until they figured out what was happening to him and the other Liu-vians. Someone should check on Mary as well. She added the phone calls to her to-do list, for a little later in the morning when it was reasonable to expect people to be awake on a Saturday.

The coffee helped. So did the work. Setting wheels in motion helped settle the restless worry jangling her nerves.

She slipped the proposed rescue mission to Indiana into a folder and tucked it under her arm, then pushed open the door that adjoined her office to the Director's. Early Saturday morning, the light poured in through the floor to ceiling windows, and Suzie winced at the brightness, crossing to pull the blinds. In the more comfortable, dimmer light, she examined the room.

Littering the small table next to the opulent leather sofa were two scotch glasses, ice melted and intermixing with the leftover alcohol to make a light amber liquid. The cleaning crew had apparently not been through yet to take away the evidence of a late-night meeting. She glared at the door she'd just entered as if it were responsible for a level of distraction that kept her from noticing. Who had the Director been talking with?

A sheaf of papers lay strewn across the imposing dark walnut desk, tell-tale wet rings revealing that the man drank while reviewing reports. Setting her own folder in the chair, Suzie sorted the papers into neat stacks: medical reports back in their folder, incident reports in another, and a loose stack of "other."

"Other" was an interesting pile.

Among the documents, she found a paper planner. She smiled to herself, finding the idea of a paper calendar in the twenty-first century amusingly quaint. Glancing at the week as she closed the book, two things caught her eye: "lunch with mother" and "shrink." Disconcerting to realize the man had a mother and a therapist both of whom she knew nothing about. She filed the information away for later, to think about when she had more time.

"You're in early, Miss Grayson."

Surprised, Suzie nearly threw the pile of papers she'd gathered. Instead, she whirled on her heel toward the doorway to glare at her boss.

"I could say the same to you, sir." Refusing to show that he had ruffled her, she gestured at the piles of paper. "Looks like you had a late night, too."

The Director slipped his hands into the pockets of his well-tailored slacks, jingling something inside one of them. "Yes. It's been an interesting few days." Joining her beside the desk, he looked her over for a moment. "You look...casual," he said.

Suzie looked down at her leggings and tunic shirt, quite the departure from her usual business attire, especially the sneakers. When she'd decided to come into work the night before, she hadn't bothered to change from her cozy at-home clothes. "Well," she said, "It is Saturday."

"Which begs the question why you're here at all." The Director raised an eyebrow at her.

Suzie reached behind her and retrieved her folder from the Director's chair. "I came in overnight to work on this."

The Director accepted the file and sat on the desk, scanning through the document quickly. "You're right, of course," he said.

Suzie's mouth fell open. She'd expected to have to fight with her boss to save Patricia, and his quick capitulation threw her off balance. "I'm glad you agree. Should I start building an away team?"

"Let me see to that," he said, tossing the file back onto his desk. "But, since you're here, perhaps you can help me with something else?"

"Of course, sir."

"It's about Dr. Liu."

DARRIN EXPLORES THE OLD
NEIGHBORHOOD

An orange stripe of color began to spread into the still-mostly-dark sky as Darrin parked his car outside the destroyed house in the old Riverside neighborhood. He sat for a minute, watching the sunlight spread before he got out.

The street was quiet, as one might expect at six o'clock on a Saturday morning. Across the street, a traditional two-story house showed signs of recent construction, but otherwise, the houses looked like they might not have been touched since they were built in the 1950s. Simple, square houses, small by contemporary standards but pleasing in a nostalgic way. From the look of the gardens, additions, and outbuildings, he'd guess some of the denizens had lived here all their lives. The whole street looked settled, permanent, and loved.

Darrin's grandparents had lived in a neighborhood like this one, with old-growth trees shading a quiet street where kids could play soccer in the road with only an occasional time-out to let a car go past. Peaceful. Sleepy. Not at all like the sleek high-rise Darrin himself lived in, centrally located in downtown Springfield with easy access to food, fun, or trouble depending on the night.

This quiet, old-fashioned neighborhood with the river running behind it didn't seem like a likely hotbed of activity, but there had been that fire four years ago, where the Lizard Woman had been sighted. Darrin wanted to see it for himself, see if he could find any more pieces to the puzzle of what happened four years ago in Springfield, and what it has to do with the lightning woman in the park.

He walked up to the gate and stared at the fire-blackened husk of a house, with boarded-over windows and caution tape blocking the damaged porch. The owner of record was Cindy Liu, who took possession a few months before the explosion and fire.

Though a neighborhood group had repeatedly asked the city to intervene and tear the place down for the sake of safety, the house remained. The bank and insurance company had still not settled responsibility for the conflagration and made a financial reckoning—longer than usual for insurance games, which is why the house still sat here rotting, four years later. The two institutions might circle around each other for years yet to come.

The wrought-iron gate screeched as he pushed it open, scraping against the broken cement of a walkway profuse with weeds springing up in the cracks and gaps. Darrin circled the house, staying well away from the crumbling structure as he explored.

Once upon a time, this had been a charming home, with a wide, inviting porch shaded by the branches of an impressive oak tree. The remnants of a large flower bed lingered, now mostly overgrown with weeds, but a few tenacious flowers bloomed in the soft morning light. Large windows lined the upper floor of the house and had probably afforded a nice view of the treetops.

Around the back, the damage was worse. Broken glass and pieces of a window frame rested some feet from a gaping hole that revealed a sagging floor falling into the basement. Crouching to peer inside, Darrin could make out broken tables and more glass. He shined a flashlight inside and caught glimpses of what looked like aquariums and cages as well as a tank of some kind at the back of the basement room. What kind of laboratory had it been?

The news reports about the fire said flammable materials stored in the basement had ignited and caused the explosion and ensuing fire. That could mean anything from a meth lab to poorly stored garden fertilizer. This didn't look like the kind of neighborhood for a meth lab.

After four years, Darrin wasn't sure what he'd expected to find, but looking at the house raised more questions than it answered. He'd definitely need to look more deeply into Cindy Liu, the owner of the house. Very little had come up in his initial searches, beyond a notice of a talk she had been scheduled to give at Our Market, a local co-op store.

As Darrin shined his flashlight across the destroyed ground, something glinted green, catching his eye. Afraid he'd lose track of it if he stood, Darrin duck-walked across the ground, holding his crouch and keeping the light on the spot where he'd seen the glint. Prodding the soil with his fingertips, he felt something hard beneath the top layer of dirt. He poked at it, and a long, slender rock unearthed itself, flipping up out of the dirt like a see-saw. Darrin picked it up and wiped it off with his other hand, revealing something green and crystalline. Quite lovely, it glowed like a gem against his palm.

"Whatcha doing, Mister?"

Rising quickly to his feet, Darrin slipped the crystal rock into his pants pocket and turned to face his unexpected audience. Two boys stood there, fishing poles over their shoulders and buckets and boxes in their hands. One Black, one Hispanic, both around ten or twelve years old. They must have been cutting through the yard on their way to the river.

Darrin shrugged, trying for friendly and non-threatening. His clothes were a little rumpled after his night's wanderings, but hopefully he still looked reputable. "Just poking around. I was curious about the fire and thought I saw something in the dirt. You guys live around here?"

The shorter boy, bare-shouldered in a black muscle tee with Fuerte's picture on the front, piped up. "You gotta stay out of the house, Mister. It isn't safe."

The other kid spoke up. "Besides, the spacesuit guys already took everything good."

Spacesuit guys? Interesting. Darrin nodded. "Thanks. Do you guys know anything about the lady who used to live here?"

The Hispanic boy cocked his head curiously. "The old one or the really old one?"

Darrin smiled. "Either one."

"I liked Miss Evangeline, but she was super-old, like a hundred or something. My big brother raked her leaves and shoveled her snow, and she'd send home these fruit sticks for all of us. I forget what they were called, but they were Chinese candy." The boy's face lit up as if he were tasting the sweet treats all over again. Looking back at Darrin, he frowned, "I don't know about Miss Cindy, though."

The Black boy nodded. "Miss Cindy was grouchy. She'd yell at us when we cut through her yard to get to the river." He pulled a face, looking like he smelled something rotten.

"She was kind of scary," the shorter boy admitted.

"What happened to her?"

"Nobody knows. My friend says he saw her the night of the fire, but no one has seen her since."

Missing? Darrin hadn't seen a missing person's report on Cindy Liu or signs of an investigation to find her. What had happened to her?

"Come on." The taller boy pointed with his head at the path ahead. "We'd better get going before it gets too hot."

"Thank you, gentlemen." Darrin inclined his head. "Good fishing!"

PATRICIA'S PYRAMID

When Patricia flexed her arms toward the sky, sunlight glinted off her scales. A run in her old stomping grounds had done her a world of good, as had letting her scalier self off the leash for a while. The feeling of formication that had plagued her the past few days had faded as soon as she'd shifted, and the small physical relief made the rest more manageable.

It looked like kids still used the area for partying. Liquor bottles and beer cans littered the landscape, and the remnants of fire pits blackened the earth. Saplings and weeds sprang up between the stacked limestone blocks. The idea, back in the 70s, had been to celebrate the limestone industry in Bedford by building a one-fifth scale replica of the Pyramids at Cheops. The project had barely begun when funding was yanked, leaving some cleared land and the right kind of desolation to attract young people who wished to go unobserved.

The sun hadn't yet fully risen, but in case someone else in Bedford enjoyed an early morning ramble by the abandoned limestone pyramid ruins, she slowed her breathing to pull her scales and spikes back in. The yellow spikes on her shoulders slid back into her flesh at her mental command, but something felt off—the movement hitched and hesitated, like a machine needing oiling. When she ran a hand over her shoulder, she could still feel small nodules bubbling the flesh, hard as bone shards.

Lowering herself to the rocks, she folded her legs in front of her, ignoring her still-taloned toes, and took in a long slow gulp of air. Her scales looked odd—too pale, like they were sheathed in a membrane. Panic's sharp, hot breath panted in her mind, making it even harder to rein in her inner monster. It hadn't been like this in a while—she had mastered the art of slipping from her human skin to her reptilian armor and back again. She could usually manage it with ease, the way other women changed shoes.

But now wasn't the time to worry about it, not if she hoped to regain her pale, lightly freckled flesh by the time the furniture store opened and she could go talk to Olivia, her mother's AA sponsor and her best lead in the search for her errant progenitor.

She lay on her back, the warm stones of the would-be pyramid comforting in their familiarity. Watching drifting clouds, she counted off her breaths and tried to force her mind down calmer paths. She thought about Goldie, the dog who used to pace her heels as she tried to outrun her demons. The golden retriever's soft brown eyes had always conveyed such sympathy, like Leonel's. Unlike Leonel's gaze, Goldie's hid no judgment or expectations. They'd spent a lot of hours out here together, Patricia and Goldie, staring at the horizon and trying to breathe.

Warmth rippled down Patricia's body, shifting like sand in the wind, and she felt her scales slide back into hiding. She sat upright and ran her hands across her arms and shoulders, relieved to feel the papery dry skin she had grown accustomed to and only the ordinary bumps any sixty-year-old woman might have. Her feet and legs, too, had returned to normal.

The stress must be getting to her more than she realized. Transforming shouldn't be this difficult.

Pulling her running shoes out of her bag, she slid them back on and rose to her feet, turning to look over the surrounding tree-covered hills. She'd seen a lot more impressive views in her time, but none of them calmed her like the rolling miles of green and the rocky outcroppings of home. She ought to bring Suzie to see it.

BACK AT HER RENTED, bright yellow jeep—zero points for subtlety, but bonus points for legroom—Patricia picked up her phone again. Still no signal. She'd gotten through for a moment early this morning, but the call had gone dead before she could hear anything beyond Suzie's sleepy hello. If she were honest, she'd been relieved to avoid talking about her feelings a bit longer.

Life with Suzie brought her joy, even if Patricia doubted it could last. Patricia had long assumed romance had passed her by while she'd been busy chasing a career. She certainly never expected Cupid to strike when she was nearly sixty. Even more surprising was that love arrived in the form of a pocket-sized blond woman half her age. At last she'd found someone who understood her bitter-edged humor but still believed in her—someone as driven and determined as Patricia herself, if in different directions.

Patricia prided herself on her pragmatism, and the realist in her predicted the end with Suzie almost at the beginning. The gulf between them spread wider than the age gap. Suzie's optimism sparkled against the dark background of Patricia's cynicism, but eventually Suzie would realize how much trouble Patricia was and move on to someone simpler, someone easier to share a life with.

The conclusion left her sad, and Patricia shoved her maudlin train of thought into the backseat with her running bag, dropping behind the wheel again. Suzie made her want to be a better woman, to find her inner hero and do the right thing, even when it hurt. From the beginning, Suzie had been the impetus for her forays into heroic action, pushing her to save the beauty queen at the mall. She'd also been a large part of the reason Patricia had agreed to sign on with the Department and work with the UCU.

Even coming to Indiana had been as much to please Suzie as out of worry for her missing mother. Would she even be here right now if not for her? Maybe not. That was the awful thing about young people —they cared. And they thought you should care, too. Exhausting.

Last night, Patricia had fallen asleep at the kitchen table, waiting for George to turn off the TV and come talk to her. She'd awakened at two in the morning in a darkened room of a silent house, disoriented and annoyed, as well as stiff in the neck and sporting an imprint of the edge of the Formica tabletop on her cheek.

George had to walk right past her to get to the stairs and the bedroom he shared with her mother, but he didn't wake her. That stung afresh. She'd known he didn't want her there, but it hurt when he didn't even acknowledge her presence in the house.

She'd come, hadn't she? That should count for something.

Frustrated, she'd brushed her teeth, gone to the spare bedroom Annie had suggested, rolled around on the too-small mattress in the too-hot room for another couple of hours. Her disjointed sleep was plagued by disorienting dreams until she gave up and went for a run.

A quick glance at the clock in the car told her it wasn't yet seven o'clock. Good. She'd have time to shower and corner her latest stepfather before she started her investigation in earnest.

WHEN SHE PULLED BACK into the driveway not thirty minutes later, George's truck was gone. Patricia cursed. After the late hours he'd kept the night before, it seemed unlikely George's absence could mean anything other than that he didn't want to talk to her. Avoiding her like this struck her as childish, especially for a man of his age, and she struggled against her desire to track him down and scream at him, maybe with her scales out for added effect.

Instead, she took three long breaths and let herself back into the house, calling out softly, "Annie?" No one answered, so Patricia figured Annie still snoozed. Fine. Patricia would be more human after a shower and coffee anyway. Pausing in the kitchen, she set up the coffeepot and then went upstairs.

After retrieving her necessities from her room, Patricia made her way to the bathroom at the end of the hall. As she passed Annie's room, she was amused to see the girl still displayed the sparkly plaque they'd made together ten or so years ago at one of those paint-your-own pottery places. Annie's name scrawled unevenly across the rainbow, the puffy paint they'd used having expanded so the second N and the I merged into a purple blob, now looking more like an O with a heart over it.

Patricia really should have kept up with Annie better. Annie had been a neat kid, and she'd probably been pretty lonely these last four years, with all of the rest of Babs's kids grown up and moved away. Patricia promised herself she'd stay in closer contact when this was over and see what she could do to help the girl get a good start in life. She realized she didn't even know if her youngest sister had plans to go to college, or what she would study if she did go. Suzie would chide Patricia for being a bad sister, and she'd be right.

It hadn't been easy, growing up with Babs...for any of them. Patricia could have made it better for Annie, if she'd tried. Maybe it wasn't too late to remedy that.

Feeling a renewed sense of purpose, Patricia shut herself into the bathroom and turned on the water. She'd have to ask Annie about doing some laundry. She'd only brought a few changes of clothes, and the ones she'd worn running smelled less than savory. The pipes shuddered and groaned, signaling the arrival of hot water, and Patricia slipped past the slightly mildewed curtain to stand in the clawfoot tub.

The bathroom had clearly been designed with children in mind—the deep tub was perfect for a bath, but the shower had been a later addition, rickety and too short for a woman of Patricia's stature. Annie and Babs would probably be fine. They were both a more average five and a half feet tall, but George would struggle. Maybe the shower in the master bedroom was taller.

Steam filled the tiny room and Patricia automatically shifted her vision, taking advantage of her reptilian alter ego's third eyelid to keep everything in focus in the humid atmosphere. She moved quickly, suspecting the size of the water tank wouldn't support the marathon showers she liked to indulge in at home, and made it back downstairs before the coffee had finished brewing.

Clean and presentable in specially designed slacks that could flex with a transformation in case the day demanded a scalier version of herself, she waited for the last gurgles of the machine to cease.

Behind her, the shuffle of slippered feet announced the arrival of her kid sister. "Hey there," Patricia said, pulling down a second coffee mug. "You a coffee drinker?"

"Yes, please." Annie replied through a yawn and settled heavily into a kitchen chair.

Patricia played waitress as she poured in a little milk and brought the sugar bowl to the table for the girl. She stood looking out the window at the backyard while they sipped from their respective cups. The outside of the window was overgrown with spiderwebs laden with dead bugs and plant debris. Not Patricia's favorite part of Indiana life. She might miss the open spaces, but she didn't miss the prolific insects.

Figuring Annie had gotten a few sips of coffee into her and would be coherent by now, she joined her at the table. "Got any big plans today?"

"Daddy wants me to stay here in case anyone calls, or Mama comes home."

Patricia frowned. It wasn't healthy for the girl to stay cooped up, and the chances of anyone calling after a week were slim. "Don't you have voicemail?"

"You mean like an answering machine?"

"An answering machine? Who's the senior citizen here?" Patricia poked her sister in the arm. "Get with the program. This is the twenty-first century."

Annie smiled. "Not in Indiana, it isn't."

The smile slid off of Annie's face, and she set her coffee mug down too hard, chipping the bottom rim against the table. "What is wrong with your eyes?"

Patricia froze. She hadn't looked in the mirror when she finished her shower. Had her eyes remained transformed? She blinked. Everything felt normal. "What do you mean?"

Annie stuttered, pushing her chair back from the table like she might flee the room. "The-the-they're yellow. A-a-and the pu-pu-pils are wrong."

Patricia closed her eyes, shielding her face with her hands. She concentrated hard, ignoring the rapid sound of her sister's panicked breathing, and visualized her human eyes. After a few seconds, she felt a sort of settling, a kind of click.

She pushed her hair back from her face and spoke softly to Annie, who had shoved her chair back and gripped the armrests like she had to hold herself against the cushion by force. "It's okay, Annie."

A silent tear spilled down the girl's cheek and splashed on her t-shirt, but she looked into Patricia's face again. She must have seen human eyes again because she loosened her death grip on the armrests and let her face fall into her hands. The two women sat in silence while Annie pulled herself together, sucking in great whooping breaths.

When she could breathe again, she glared at Patricia. "I'm not crazy."

Patricia shook her head. "No. You're not."

"I saw what I saw—it was real." The girl thrust out her chin, daring anyone to contradict her.

"I know."

New tears welled up in Annie's eyes. "You mean, it really happened —your eyes..."

Patricia laid her hands on the table and looked seriously into her sister's face. She had yet to lie to any of her siblings about anything more serious than Santa Claus, and she certainly wouldn't start now. Sometimes her honesty hurt, but Patricia believed some kinds of pain were preferable to others.

"When I stopped visiting four years ago...I really was busy, and then dealing with retirement. I didn't lie about anything. But it wasn't all. Something happened to me. Something that changed me."

Annie stood, picking up her cup and walking over to the sink. "I'll make a fresh pot of coffee. You'd better start at the beginning."

DARRIN GETS TOO CLOSE

Someone shook Mary's shoulder. She jolted upright, immediately grabbing the hand that touched her. She pulled it up and to the right, forcing the nurse to twist her body to stay on her feet.

"Hey!" the woman shouted. "What are you doing?"

Mary released her hold. "I'm sorry. You startled me."

The nurse rubbed her shoulder. "Next time, I'll poke you with a stick from farther away." The words were joking, but the woman's face remained serious.

"I'm really sorry. I was having a tense dream. Did I hurt you?" The medical staff had been so kind to her and more patient with Helen than her mother probably deserved. She owed them thanks, not injuries.

"It's all right." She rolled her shoulder a couple of times. "No serious harm done. You should go home and get some real rest."

The nurse looked through the observation window. Mary joined her. They had cleaned up the detritus from Helen's flareup a couple of days ago and moved her to another bed. Helen lay on her back, face slack in unconscious oblivion. Her gentle snores rumbled through the sound system. Nothing was on fire.

"See? Your mother will be all right. The new sedatives are keeping her far enough in that she's stopped starting sleep fires. We'll call you if anything changes."

Mary slid out of the armchair she'd spent the night in, wincing when the upholstery stuck to her lower back and pulled at her flesh. She could definitely use a little air and a shower. "You're probably right. If she asks for me, you'll tell her I'll be back later?"

"Definitely. It's good to see you two getting along better."

"Thanks."

A few minutes later, Mary had made her way through the tunnels to street level. Her boots clicked across the concrete and echoed in the deserted parking garage where her rusty Honda Civic sat alone between two columns. She checked the time. Barely six-thirty.

She texted Jorge, her on-again, off-again boyfriend and fellow wage slave at Our Market. "Tell Trish I'm coming in. I'll be there by eight. Just need a shower first." Money and distraction would do her more good than sleep.

MARY MADE IT BY SEVEN-THIRTY. Once home, the undisturbed quiet of her apartment jangled her nerves and sent her hurrying through her morning ablutions, anxious to get to work and have a taste of normalcy. The people at Our Market were weird in their own way— hippy-dippy-artist-types, as her mother would say—but none of them threw fire or read minds, and no one there expected Mary to do anything besides stock shelves and talk shit. Just what she needed.

Jorge was working the coffee stand, and when he spotted her among the group of customers waiting for their frothy concoctions, he slipped her drink into the queue between a chai tea latte and an iced mocha, winking at her when he called her name. She saluted him with the cup, unable to garner the energy to flirt.

After checking in with Trish, the day manager, she headed to the back room and spent a half-hour or so breaking down cardboard for recycling. The work might have been dull, but it kept her body moving, and at the end of it, she felt a sense of satisfaction seeing the pile of boxes reduced to a flat stack on the ground. Slipping out to the yard, she lifted her face to the sun and stood listening to the morning chatter of customers sipping coffee at the tables.

Someone grabbed her arm and tugged her backward, but Mary didn't resist. She knew the feeling of those long, strong fingers on the flesh of her elbow and allowed Jorge to spin her into the shadowed corner—out of view of customers and security cameras—and press her to the wall for a kiss. A long, lovely kiss.

"I've missed you," he said. His voice had gone husky and breathless.

Mary adjusted the scarf holding her long dreads back. "Me too."

Stretching an arm over her to rest it on the wall, Jorge lifted her chin to look into her face. His eyes searched hers. "You look tired. You doing okay?"

"They've got mom stabilized." Jorge knew the fuller story, but he also knew better than to discuss it publicly. She'd fill him in fully later on.

"And?"

She pressed her lips into a thin line. "They don't know what's causing it."

Jorge shoved his hands into his pockets and rocked back on his heels. "They'll figure it out. They did so much to help my brother Miguel over there. I know they'll help your mother, too. We have to have faith."

Mary wasn't quite the believer Jorge was, but she had to admit the Director had kept his word so far, keeping her informed and involved with her mother's care. She hated that she'd had to put her mother in protective custody, but especially now, when Helen suffered uncontrolled and quite literal flareups, she was grateful to have the resources of the Department on her side.

"Mary!" A somewhat strident call came from around the front of the building. Trish.

"I better go." Squeezing Jorge's hand, Mary hurried to the front of the building in the direction of the summons.

She called out as she rounded the corner. "Right here, Trish."

Trish waved her over. She stood next to a tall, handsome Black man who looked a little familiar. Mary slowed her steps, giving herself an extra moment to observe. When he smiled at her, she recognized him: the guy from *City News*. A spike of worry jabbed her in the gut, but she returned his smile and joined her manager.

Resting a hand on the man's arm, Trish introduced them. "Mary, this is Darrin, with the *City News*. Maybe you've seen his work? He had that interview with Fuerte a couple of days ago." Trish made no secret of how much she admired well-muscled masculinity, so it was no surprise she'd pay special attention to coverage of the Hispanic hero and to the handsome reporter standing before her. A catty part of Mary longed to tell her Leonel was married...to a man, but she kept her connection to the UCU and its heroes on the down-low.

Instead, she nodded to Darrin, shaking his proffered hand briefly. "Nice to meet you. I'm afraid I don't watch much TV." It wasn't true—she followed all the UCU coverage religiously—but the lie gave her a layer of distance she might need, depending on why he was there.

"Darrin was asking about Cindy Liu for an article he's working on, and I remembered that your mother had been close with her, so I thought maybe you could help?"

Mary kept her face placid, even though her heart had leapt into her throat. "I never met her myself, so I don't know much, but I'll try to help. We can talk at the table under the big tree, if that's okay?"

The last had been directed to Trish, who frowned, probably disappointed she'd miss out on the conversation and the opportunity to flirt with the handsome reporter a little longer. But she agreed, waving a hand. "Sure, sure. We're not too busy right now. Take your time."

Mary gritted her teeth, annoyed that Trish had taken away her easiest escape by making it sound like she could talk all day if needed. "Thanks."

She turned to Darrin. "Shall we?"

Choosing the seat that gave her the best view of the yard and all the people in it, Mary sat. Darrin tugged back the other chair and sat opposite her. They sat in silence for a moment and Mary felt Darrin's gaze on her face, taking in the details of her appearance. A prickling sensation raised the hairs on the back of her neck. She didn't like this attention. This man noticed things, and she had things to hide.

"So," she said, plastering a banal smile on her face. "How can I help you?"

"What can you tell me about Cindy Liu?"

Mary sighed, trying to sound bored. "She and my mother were friends. Kind of a grumpy old lady, but they got on well." She pushed a lilt into her voice, trying to sound young and disinterested. "I guess you'd call her an inventor? We used to carry a few of her products here at Our Market, and my mom was a fan."

"I see. What kinds of products?" He had pulled out a small notebook and rested it against his thigh.

"The usual things—tea, soap, skin cream. All organic and natural, of course." The question seemed innocuous enough, but it brushed up against some touchy subjects. She decided to push back. "What's gotten you interested in her?"

"A hunch," he said, shrugging. "I don't know yet if it will go anywhere."

"I'm afraid I don't know much about her."

"Maybe I could talk with your mother, since they were close?"

A cold trickle ran down Mary's spine, but she shook her head as if sad to refuse him. "My mom isn't well," she said. "She's under medical supervision, and I'm afraid she can't really handle visitors." Especially not reporters.

"I'm sorry to hear that." He sounded genuinely concerned. "I hope she's receiving the best of care."

Mary nodded curtly. "She is."

The man bit his lip and looked around as if he were concerned someone might be listening in to their conversation. Scooting in his chair, he leaned across the table. "Listen. I know this might be touchy for you, but I'm looking into Dr. Liu's disappearance four years ago. There are some strange things going on in this city, and they all seem to circle back to a couple of fires in the area, one at Cindy Liu's house and the other at the college campus. The clues keep bringing me back to Dr. Liu, but the trails all die out. I want to understand what happened."

Mary stood, shoving back her chair. "I'm afraid I can't help you." She gripped the back of the chair. "I should get back to work. No matter what Trish says, I do have work to do."

Darrin's gaze dipped to Mary's fingers, gone white-knuckled with the intensity of her grip on the chair. She forced herself to relax her hands and smile at the reporter.

He stood and pulled out his wallet, fishing out a business card and laying it on the table. "I understand. If you think of anything you can tell me, please reach out."

Mary had no intention of speaking to the man again if she could help it, but she slid the card across the table and slipped it into her back pocket. "I will," she lied, then turned on her heel and forced herself to walk slowly back across the lawn, even though she wanted to run.

She had to talk to the Director right away. This wasn't good.

TEA AND BRIBERY

S uzie sat on a chair, legs crossed and a dangling foot bouncing impatiently, while a very sleepy sixty-nine-year-old woman in the body of a teenager blinked uncomprehendingly at her.

"Who are you again?" Cindy Liu stretched and yawned.

Good. This would go easier if Dr. Liu didn't remember her. After all, their last in-person encounter involved Suzie injecting her with drugs. This time she had come to recruit her to solve the mutations problem for the Liu-vians. She'd refused Walter flat-out when he'd made the offer.

Suzie hadn't forgotten this woman wreaked havoc across the city of Springfield. Sure, Patricia, Leonel, and Jessica had built something positive out of that chaos, but it didn't excuse Dr. Liu's reckless endangerment of others. It could as easily have resulted in their funerals. But just now, the UCU needed a bit of Liu-vian recklessness. She kept her personal feelings to herself.

"Let's go." Suzie stood and opened the door.

Cindy's eyes opened wider. "Go? I haven't even had breakfast."

"Research is better than breakfast." She tapped her foot on the hard tile floor and gestured at the slippers on the floor. "Now," she said. "Xiànzài."

Shrugging, and ignoring Suzie's attempt at Chinese, the seeming-girl swung long slender legs out from beneath the blankets and slid her toes into the slippers.

Patricia always said Cindy was never more interested in something than when she affected complete disinterest. If that was the case, Suzie really had her attention. She noticed the girl followed closely at her heels as they traversed the quiet halls of The Glass House. Good. She needed the doctor's interest.

When Suzie took a sudden left, Cindy's slippered feet slid on the tile, and she had to pinwheel to keep from falling. Keeping her face neutral, Suzie scanned her keycard and held the door open for the mad scientist.

Cindy shuffled through the door, moving slowly, but Suzie didn't miss the way the woman's gaze bounced around, taking in details, gathering data every second, observing.

It was how she'd managed her escape attempt a few months earlier —learning the guard schedules and procedures, finding a weakness to exploit. Just like Suzie was doing with Dr. Liu.

Know your enemy. She brushed away the thought that maybe she and Dr. Liu had a few things in common at the core. Expediency mattered more than consequences to either of them.

Closing the door behind them, Suzie flipped on the lights, revealing a small laboratory. At the sight, Dr. Liu's eyes narrowed.

"I already told Peeples to screw himself," she growled.

Suzie smiled sweetly. If Dr. Liu knew her better, she'd know the saccharine expression for a sign of danger. Luckily, she didn't seem to remember Suzie at all.

"Sit," she said, pointing at the chair behind the worktable at the center of the room.

Dr. Liu complied, feet flat on the floor, hands clasped demurely in front of her, imitating an attentive schoolgirl. The image was somewhat undercut by the unkempt hair and the baggy uniform that combined the demoralizing, ugly simplicity of prison-wear with the utility of scrubs. Suzie noted a streak of gray running through the woman's otherwise raven-dark hair, incongruous with the pimple-dotted adolescent face. *Good. She was affected, too.* Self-interest would be a good motivator if Suzie needed additional ammunition to garner the woman's cooperation.

Pretending difficulty with the door security, Suzie gave Liu a moment to take in her surroundings. Suzie herself didn't fully understand what all the equipment in the room did, but Walter had ensured her that any tool the woman might need stood at the ready. Dr. Liu's placid demeanor began to give way to signs of curiosity.

Lifting a covered tray from the rolling cart that had been left inside the door, Suzie delivered it to the table. She pushed the tray in front of Cindy and raised the lid with a flourish, revealing a stone teapot and a small, bowl-style cup. Steam wafted from the spout and filled the small room with the scent of jasmine tea.

Cindy's face lit up, and she reached for the pot eagerly. She poured a cup and held it to her mouth, closing her eyes and inhaling the steam. A groan of pleasure escaped her lips as she took the first sip. As she served her second cup, she gazed curiously at Suzie, who stood, arms crossed and face carefully impassive.

Breaking the silence, Cindy said, "Do you know they've been serving me Lipton tea in a styrofoam cup full of lukewarm water the entire time I've been held here?"

She did know, of course. Even though supervising Cindy's captivity was not her purview, she had a vested interest in the woman who had been her girlfriend's best friend for forty years then betrayed her violently. She knew a lot of things about Cindy Liu, everything in her UCU file and quite a few things that weren't. She'd use them all to get what she needed.

Only after she had emptied the pot did Cindy speak again. "What do you want?"

"Nothing you don't want yourself." Shoving the tray to the side, Suzie reached under the table and emerged with a cooler, placing it in front of the scientist.

Cindy stood and carefully slid back the lid, peering inside. Shooting another look at Suzie, she reached in and removed a tray of vials, setting it on the table in front of her. "Am I supposed to know what this is?"

"What you've been asking for."

The scientist had already removed the lid and begun examining the vials. Each had been labeled with the date it had been taken and a code indicating the subject. "You might know J32 as Jessica Roark," Suzie said.

Cindy almost fumbled the vial she held in her fingers. "What?"

"H60 is Helen Braeburn."

"Helen?" Cindy took a step back from the vials, as if Helen might burn her through a blood sample.

She still feared facing the woman who'd tried to kill her a year ago. *Good*. Suzie could use that.

"P58 is Patricia O'Neill."

Cindy folded her arms over her chest and glared at Suzie. "What is this about? Who are you? What do you want?"

Suzie crossed to the end of the table and sat down, pulling up a chart on the laptop she'd left there. "A few days ago, your victims began to show anomalies."

Out of the corner of her eye, Suzie caught the grimace at the use of the word "victims." Keeping the pleasure in seeing her barb score a hit from her face, she spun the computer around so Cindy could see the charts comparing earlier levels of various hormones, enzymes, metabolic functions and other data points Suzie understood less well. "The latest blood work suggests new mutations are occurring."

The doctor's gaze scanned the chart, a furrow growing between her brows. She reached for the computer, and Suzie let her take it, watching carefully as the woman changed some parameters and the data rearranged itself on the screen. "Who is L17?"

"You don't know them, but they're one of your victims, too."

"Victims?" She nearly spat the word.

Suzie raised an eyebrow, affecting the iciest disapproval in her arsenal. "What else would you call people you experimented on without permission and whose lives you irrevocably changed?"

The woman-girl's lips puckered as if she tasted something sour, but she didn't argue. She turned back to the data in front of her, pointing at the tall point on a line graph. "This spike. Do we know what happened?"

Suzie shook her head. "No. That's why I'm talking to you."

Quick calculations transpired on the woman's face: intent to refuse, realization of the offer on the table, an examination of her opponent. Dr. Liu studied Suzie's face for a long moment, making her wonder if the scientist did remember her after all, from the night on Springfield campus, when Helen had attacked to try and free the doctor and Leonel had thrown the fire-wielding woman into a wall.

After a long silence during which the two women stared into each other's faces, each making their own plans, Cindy spoke. "I'll need a few things."

Suzie put a piece of paper and a pen in front of her. "Make me a list."

BRAWL AT THE MALL

S ally Ann Rogers stared at the man in the surveillance footage clip that Dispatch had forwarded to her phone. She paused it and rewound, stopping on the moment when he tossed off the third security guard, hurling the woman across the mall and through the plate glass window of the store opposite. He'd brushed her off like someone might shake off an annoying cat, even though he stood barely taller than she. Sally Ann zoomed in on his face, freezing the frame before he took off at a run into the heart of Springfield Mall.

Forty-ish, light-brown skinned, possibly Hispanic or Indian—hard to tell with his face distorted by rage. Short hair, slight beard. Plain blue t-shirt and gray joggers. No visible tattoos. Nothing very helpful for identification.

Still, the man was something more than merely human. He had to be, to exhibit such strength, but he wasn't on any of their watch lists, and the system didn't recognize his face. He couldn't be another Liuvian. Wrong gender. "Who the hell is this guy?"

There'd be time to figure that out later. Right now, she needed to get her team on the scene before anyone else got hurt. Evacuation of the mall was already under way, and when security had called the police, the police had called the UCU in turn. The timing couldn't be worse. If ever there had ever been a moment for the services of Leonel "Fuerte" Alvarez, this was it—between his cool head, approachable demeanor, and seemingly bottomless strength, he would have been her first-choice agent to bring in on this case.

But Fuerte huddled in the medical wing, struggling not to break things while the eggheads worked to understand why his powers had suddenly surged again. He was in no condition to help. Patricia, her other heavy hitter, had taken a flight to Indiana of all places to deal with a "family matter." Sally Ann hadn't even known the woman had any family—she'd always seemed like a complete loner. And Flygirl had just finished a night shift of patrol.

These past couple of years, Sally Ann had gotten spoiled by having super-powered colleagues to put into play when the circumstances got weird, but once upon a time, not so very long ago, she'd handled situations like this without their help. Using her wits, her epic fighting skills, and the occasional hint gleaned from her small psychic gift, she'd worked behind the scenes to bring down impossible criminals, back before the UCU had an official name and a public face.

Looked like she'd be remembering how it used to work today.

While Dispatch put out the call for her team, Sally Ann suited up, donning the flexible, lightly armored suit she utilized when she expected hand-to-hand combat, and grabbed her baton and a set of tranq darts, affixing them to her gear. Their best bet would be to knock the guy out and bring him in. They'd figure out who he was, what happened, and what he wanted afterward. Safety first.

By the time she made it to the motor pool, Agent Driver had already pulled up one of the smaller armored vans. Two new agents, faces bright with anticipation, stood by the doors, waiting for orders. She recognized them from the last round of training but didn't remember their names. At least they were serious, capable young men. As she remembered, the taller one had been a little hot-headed, but the shorter, stockier man followed orders well.

They awaited only Agent Lester, who'd been with the UCU almost as long as she had. She grabbed her phone to check his status, then put it back away again when she recognized the heavy sound of his boots on the concrete behind her. "Load up," she said. "Springfield Mall."

While Gabe Driver, the silent agent with an uncanny ability to make machines perform beyond their abilities, hurried them through downtown traffic toward the outskirts of Springfield, Sally Ann quickly briefed her team. The two rookies exchanged a look of excitement, and Sally Ann suppressed a sigh. She hoped they were ready for this. Actual battle never ran like it did in simulations, and the perpetrator wouldn't pull his punches, even if all the reports suggested he was otherwise unarmed.

"Hey," she said, as the van door slid open to eject them at the side entrance to the mall, "Don't get hit."

She ran into the building, leaving the others to keep up. The strong man had last been seen in the food court, so Sally Ann followed the smell of French fries and Szechuan chicken. Signs of the man's rampage littered the wide walking avenues in the form of toppled kiosks, shattered glass, and broken furniture. Security guards directed the remaining shoppers who had not already evacuated the mall down the two sides, while Sally Ann and her team vaulted up the middle.

She heard the man before she made it into visual range. Heavy thumps and clatters of broken glass came intermittently from the floor above them, along with howls of rage or pain. It sounded like the man was tearing the place up.

Then, all went silent.

Having reached the atrium below the food court, Sally Ann froze mid-stride, the three other agents coming up short behind her. "I don't like this," Sally Ann hissed, scanning the upper ring for signs of danger.

Signaling her team to wait, Sally Ann took a zigzag path toward the fountain at the center so she could finish her observation of the upper ring. She spotted the danger moments before a large, dark object came hurtling her direction. She flung herself into the air, tucking into a backflip and landing in a crouch a few yards away in time to watch the fountain crumble under the weight of the sculpture of the heavily muscled Bulldog that usually graced the food court, minus its sneakered feet.

Still holding his stone football in his stone arm, the college mascot now lay flat on its back in the middle of a busted fountain, baring its sculpted teeth at the upper ring where a man stood, hands on the railing, glaring down at Sally Ann.

"Sorry, Butch." Sally Ann offered the quiet apology as she directed her team over the headset and skirted the growing puddle surrounding the fountain.

The statue had to weigh a good two hundred pounds, and their opponent had lifted it over his head to hurl it at her. The landing force hadn't all been gravity. She prayed the fountain and mascot would be the worst casualties of the fight. She missed Fuerte all over again. They'd have to find a way to subdue this man without getting too close.

Her team scattered, seeking other ways to access the upstairs and surround the rampaging strongman. Sally Ann kept her eye on the man upstairs. Her hand automatically sought the specially-designed baton clipped behind her. The best thing about leaving regular law enforcement for the UCU, besides the acknowledgment that weird things were real, was the toys. The seemingly simple baton on her back could expand into bo staff length and featured a few surprises. Sally Ann had a feeling she'd need them today.

She and the strong man stared each other down for long seconds, until he turned away, spinning to face whatever he'd heard behind him. If it was one of the rookies, Sally Ann prayed he'd remember his training and proceed with caution. Otherwise, he might well become the next flying object in the room.

While her opponent's attention focused elsewhere, Sally Ann made her move, hurling herself at one of three long banners dangling from the top level of the mall to the lower. The long blue cloth became her gym rope as she made her way up from the D to the S in "Springfield," until she could reach the railing where she'd last seen the man of the hour.

Achieving the top of her climb, she dangled a moment, listening.

Hearing nothing, she pulled her legs up beside her, changed her grip, and leapt for the top bar, swinging over it as if she played vertical leapfrog. She landed as softly as her velocity would allow. Jessica, or "Flygirl" as she was known in the field, wouldn't have had to touch the ground at all, but Sally Ann had trained her, and even bound by the limits of gravity, she could still maneuver in unexpected ways.

She touched down next to a pair of boots attached to the taller rookie, the hothead. He lay sprawled on the ground, unconscious, but his chest rose and fell steadily, and a quick examination revealed no obvious life-threatening injury, though she thought one of his arms might be broken. Sally Ann clicked on her headset. "Driver, man down. Near the food court." Three clicks on the microphone indicated his understanding.

Staying low, she worked her way around the circle of railings overlooking the atrium she'd climbed up from, and sought the rest of her team. She could make out the muffled sounds of fighting over the soft strings version of something meant to be rock and roll blaring from the sound system. "Sweet Child O' Mine" in Muzak? Was nothing sacred?

Daring a peek over the railing, Sally Ann rose enough to allow her to see the wider scene. Almost directly across from her, the assailant fought. Lester and the shorter rookie stood at his two sides, working in tandem to keep the man off-balance. Sally Ann noted with pride that the new agent had learned the triangle pattern perfectly, always remaining out of arm's reach and moving in at different heights with each attack. His attacks weren't as effective as Lester's yet, but they were definitely keeping the strong man off balance.

Spotting the opening she needed, Sally Ann rose to her feet and ran around the circle, going wide around the fight to approach the strongman from the back. Cueing her intentions through the headset, she drew within throwing range and flung the first of her tranq darts into the meat of the man's shoulder. The small dart stuck there, waggling when the man moved, but other than eliciting a roar of anger and pain when it pierced his flesh, made no effect. He lunged for the other two agents in turn, never quite getting his hands on either man.

Lester kept him focused on the fight in front of him, and Sally Ann threw another dart. This one sank into the man's triceps. He didn't seem to feel it, but kept flailing and yelling incoherently. Trying to track her movements in addition to that of their opponent, the rookie lost his timing and a wild swing from the strong man clipped him hard on one shoulder, sending him stumbling backward and into a display of stuffed animals wearing clothes.

The strongman roared and stomped toward the young agent, the two tranq darts embedded in his shoulder wobbling with his movement. Sally Ann expected a man this size to drop like a stone with that much sedative in him, but he hadn't even slowed. Whatever ran within this man's system must give the endurance of a horse and the metabolism of a hummingbird.

Lester planted a swinging kick in the man's lower back that should have sent him to his knees, but the man kept moving, focused on the young agent who was struggling to get back to his feet, holding one hand to the injured shoulder. Probably dislocated. She'd told him not to get hit.

Unable to get a clear shot to try another tranq dart, Sally Ann snagged her baton from its clip on her back and expanded it. The metallic thwack brought a grin of satisfaction to her face. Planting the end against the remains of the Bulldog statue and using her staff like a pole vault, she flung herself up and over the strong man, landing between him and the young agent, and swinging the weapon in front of her.

Startled, the man stopped. Confusion shadowed his face, and he stumbled. Sally Ann wondered if the darts might finally be taking effect. But then he sprung at her. Luckily for Sally Ann, the man proved clumsy and inaccurate, untrained as a fighter. She easily dodged his attempt to grab at her and used the opportunity to get her staff between his calves and sweep his legs out from under him.

On his knees, the man huffed at the ground, then pulled himself into a crouch, balanced on the balls of his feet. He pawed the tile floor like an angry rhinoceros and ran at her, head and shoulders low. Sally Ann braced, ready to dodge him like a matador in the bullring. Instead, Lester barreled in from the side, pushing the man with his shoulder like a defensive tackle, which indeed he had once been not so long ago in his college days. It wasn't enough to knock the strongman off his feet, but it gave Sally Ann a moment to get her staff into position.

She thrust it at the strong man as if she intended to stab him with it. As she hoped he might, he grabbed the end of it, pulling to tug it out of her hands. She let him have it, but not before she pressed the button sending a shock of electricity through the metal pole, similar to the punch of a taser. An entirely separate kind of "letting him have it."

The man went stiff, then fell to the ground, Sally Ann's staff rolling out of his hand. She spun it onto her foot and kicked it back to her hand, collapsing it and affixing it to her belt with a smooth, practiced gesture. Approaching slowly, she observed the man still trying to rise and reached for another tranq dart. But he slumped to the floor, unconscious at last.

Flopping into a nearby bench, miraculously still intact, she assessed the scene. She hoped the mall had good insurance, because the place was a mess. Two injured agents, maybe three. Lester lay on the ground, probing his leg and testing the movement. He hadn't escaped unscathed either. Her cheek stretched tight with a swelling bruise, and Sally Ann realized she'd taken an impact she hadn't registered at the time.

Not a disaster. But it definitely could have gone better. It *would* have gone better, with Fuerte or Patricia.

She kicked at a shard of broken glass resting near her foot and rose. "Come on, boys," she called. "Let's get this guy out of here."

STANDING in a cluster outside the mall, a news reporter and crew awaited, the big familiar daisy logo of *Springfield City News* wrapped around the plastic microphone cover the reporter held at the ready. Sally Ann recognized him—Darrin Berger, the handsome go-getter who usually reported on the superhero stories. He'd been present a couple of days earlier, when the lightning woman attacked in the park.

A tall, well-muscled, tawny-skinned man with a with a tapered fade that pulled her eyes along his square jawline and to his full, generous lips, Darrin was stunning, and very aware of it.

The reporter's gaze bounced across the group of agents, looking for someone. After a moment, he let the mic drop to his side, his disappointment evident. No powered heroes. He recovered quickly, pushing the mic out in front of him and shouting, "What happened in there?"

Sally Ann left the other agents to secure the prisoner and see to their injuries while she addressed the news crew. She'd had some practice addressing the press, though she always thought she looked stiff and nervous when she saw herself on the news. She didn't have a gift for it like Jessica, but she'd have to do.

Touching her bruised cheek, she stalked over to Darrin's side, offering what she hoped appeared to be a professional and friendly smile and not a crazed grin and wondering how large her cheek had actually swollen. It felt huge from the inside, but maybe it wasn't so bad yet.

After greeting her with a knee-melting smile and thanking her for her time, the reporter asked a couple of perfunctory questions, which Sally Ann dutifully answered, making sure to credit the hardworking men and women of the mall security team and the Springfield police force who ensured all the civilians made it to safety, leaving the UCU team free to handle the strong man without endangering the public. "Share the credit, take the blame," as the PR team always said. Positive press mattered, but good relations with the rest of the rescue and law enforcement teams in the city were more important.

While the news crew packed the equipment back into their van, the reporter lingered on the sidewalk, Sally Ann standing awkwardly by his side. When Sally Ann finally turned to walk away, Darrin reached out and touched her arm, the light touch making Sally Ann wish she weren't buried under layers of armor and protective gear. She'd like to have felt those fingertips on her skin.

The man spoke softly, like the two of them were sharing a secret. "So, where's Fuerte?"

Sally Ann shrugged to hide her consternation, looking back at her own team to avoid losing herself in his dark, almost black eyes. "He's dealing with something else right now."

A troubled look crossed Darrin's face as he puckered his lips and furrowed his brow. He probably worried he'd missed a bigger story while wasting his time on ordinary UCU agents like Sally Ann when he could have had some camera time with Fuerte somewhere else in the city. Reporters hated getting scooped, and *Springfield City News* was always in fierce competition with the city beat at their competing station to get there first.

Not sure why she felt the need to do so, Sally Ann added, "Something top secret. Not public yet."

The gleam in the man's eye made a flutter in Sally Ann's chest. *Down, girl,* she counseled herself. *The gleam was for Fuerte, or the promise of a story, not for you.*

"You know," Darrin said. "We should talk sometime, the two of us."

Sally Ann froze and stood, unable to respond. Did he just ask her out?

Darrin smiled at her. "I bet a woman like you has some stories to tell." He slipped his slender fingers into the pocket at his hip and pulled out a business card.

"This is my personal cell," he said, holding the card out to Sally Ann, who managed not to snatch at it, but to take it gently from his fingers.

He smiled again, with a slow slide of his lips that had her fighting the urge to lick her own lips in response. He pushed his voice low, so it came out almost as a purr. "Call me. I'll buy you a drink."

Sally Ann slipped the card into her back pocket and dipped her head in a kind of bow before making her way back to the UCU van, the back of her neck steaming with the feeling of the man's gaze on her.

Lester shot her a look as she got in, then cocked his head at her, curiosity lighting his face. Sally Ann crossed her eyes at him, and he shook his head, but she was left wondering what he'd seen...and if there had been anything to see.

As the van rolled away, Sally Ann looked out the window, but Darrin Berger and the news crew had already gone.

PATRICIA AND THE SOFA QUEEN

"Maybe you should wait in the car," Patricia suggested.

Annie crossed her arms over her chest, in a very familiar stubborn stance. "Uh-uh. No way."

Patricia sighed, wondering what had possessed her to agree to bring her little sister along. She never used to have trouble saying no, even when it hurt someone's feelings. Was she going soft?

But after the morning of confessions, it hadn't felt right to leave her at home, moping by the phone, even if she couldn't figure out why the girl wanted to come along.

Having Annie there placed limits on what she could do, even now that the girl knew about the Lizard Woman. Knowing your big sister can transform into a giant bulletproof reptile is different than seeing it in person. Patricia would have to play nice, even if intimidation might be more effective. Since when did she start shooting herself in the foot by being too nice?

"All right," she said, opening the door. "But let me do the talking."

Annie didn't promise, but she gave a curt nod before stepping out of the car.

Furnitureland filled three joined shops of the strip mall, smack in the middle, with a fried chicken place on one side and a hair salon on the other. Part of the A had fallen off the sign, so it read "Furniturelond." Patricia imagined a Scandinavian spokesmodel wearing a patterned red sweater inviting them to come on down and get a "Swede" deal.

The parking lot was nearly empty at ten a.m. on a Friday. Apparently not prime time for sofa shopping. Good. They'd be able to talk to Olivia uninterrupted.

A bell rang as they entered the store, and the two women lingered by the entrance. Annie feigned interest in the red plaid living room set while Patricia scanned the store, looking for Olivia Hutton for a good three minutes before she realized she didn't know what she looked like.

Whoever she was, she must not get many customers at this hour because the bell hadn't brought anyone to investigate.

"Come on," Patricia said, pointing toward the back of the store. "Looks like the offices are back there."

Annie followed, chewing on her thumbnail and peering around at the furniture displays. Patricia followed her gaze toward a fussy four-poster bedroom set, complete with a red velvet coverlet and heart-shaped pillows. It looked like it belonged in a honeymoon suite from 1954. Nothing at all like Patricia's king-sized platform bed, dark wood and sleek lines.

"What does Olivia look like anyway?" Patricia asked as a short, slightly chubby woman with bushy brown hair emerged from the back room, wiping her hands on a paper towel.

She started at the sight of them standing there, then smiled broadly, grabbing a clipboard off a coffee table shaped like a stack of books as she made her way over. "What can I show you ladies today?"

"That's her," Annie said, then stepped behind Patricia like a shy toddler who'd been asked to say hello to a stranger.

Patricia pushed her shoulders back and walked toward her. "Olivia, right?"

"Yes, ma'am. That's me." She tilted her head to one side and peered up into Patricia's face. "Do we know one another?"

"No, but you know my mother, I think."

The woman looked confused for a moment, then spotted Annie and nodded. "Ah. You must be Babs's other girl—the one who lives down in Springfield. Patricia, right?"

Patricia nodded, offering her hand to shake.

"Nice to meet you," she said, squeezing her fingers. Her hand was still faintly damp, and Patricia fought the urge to yank her fingers free and wipe her hand on her pants.

Turning to Annie, the woman's smile widened. "Annie-girl, it's good to see you. Are you holding up okay?"

Annie swallowed and ducked her head.

Olivia pursed her lips and turned her attention back to Patricia, keeping her hand still trapped in a damp handshake. "It's been hard on all of us, but maybe harder for the young ones, huh? Is there any news? About Babs, I mean?"

Patricia took back her hand and pushed her fingertips into the front pockets of her slacks. "Not so far. I was hoping I could talk to you, see if you know anything helpful."

"Of course, I've already told the police everything I know, but sure, we can talk. Come on, let's try out the new leather set."

Olivia led the way to a dark brown set of den furniture, two recliner chairs, a giant ottoman, and a sofa all posed in a circle surrounding a rope braid rug, like the one that had graced the living room in most of the houses Patricia could remember living in as a kid.

Olivia flopped into one of the recliners and yanked the handle, tilting herself backward. "I'd buy this one myself, if I had the money. Feels like the lap of luxury." She ran a hand over the armrest, caressingly.

Patricia and Annie perched on the sofa, the new leather creaking beneath their collective weight. Annie wiggled back against the cushion, leaving her feet dangling a few inches off the floor. Patricia leaned forward, resting her elbows on her knees and considering the pattern of the rug.

After a few moments of silence, she cleared her throat. "Annie tells me our mother was on her way to AA the night she disappeared."

126

Olivia nodded, folding her hands across her soft midsection. "That's what they tell me. But she never got there."

"What did you think when she didn't show up?"

Olivia smacked her lips, letting out a slow chirping breath. "Well, I worried, of course. I'm her sponsor, and not showing up without sending a message is a bad sign. But I'm an optimist. I hoped she might be sick or something. I figured I'd call the house if I didn't hear from her in a day or two, you know, to check in?" She shook her head. "But George called me later that night."

Patricia considered her questions carefully, wishing she had Sally Ann or even Leonel by her side, someone better at asking indelicate questions without scaring people off.

Annie surprised her by piping in. "Did Mama usually talk to anyone special at the meetings?"

"You mean, like a friend?"

Annie shrugged.

Olivia kicked the recliner back into an upright position and leaned forward, a strange mixture of sadness and excitement on her face—the look of an inveterate gossip with sad news they were bursting to share but had been holding back for fear of appearing insensitive. "Well, there had been a new man coming to group these past few weeks. They did find a lot to chat about."

Annie shifted in her seat, and her arm squeaked against the upholstery.

Olivia blinked, seeming to reconsider what she'd been about to say. Color rose in her cheeks as she focused on Patricia. "Babs has a way with strangers," she said. "She's very...approachable, if you know what I mean."

Ah. Patricia understood now. Babs had been flirting with the new guy, but Olivia didn't want to talk about Babs's reputation in front of her daughter...at least not the youngest one. "I see. What can you tell me about this new guy?"

Olivia grimaced. "Well, I really shouldn't say. One of the A's is for anonymous."

Patricia waited. Sally Ann had been training her on the value of silence in an interrogation. She had to admit it was effective, even if it went against her nature.

Olivia looked around though the shop remained empty, then tilted further forward, bringing her head nearer Patricia's. "Between us, I didn't like him much. You know how some people rub you wrong? Like they put out a weird vibe? This guy—Daniel—he was like that. Friendly enough. Never did anything wrong. But something about him put me off."

Patricia's hackles went up, along with nodules along her shoulders, rubbing against the thin material of her blouse. She hid a calming breath by shifting in her seat, working to keep her lizard-self under wraps. "Daniel, huh? What does he look like? Do you think I could talk to him?"

"Come to think of it, he didn't attend last week, either. Took me a while to notice. He didn't talk much. Quiet fella. Maybe about forty or forty-five. Dark hair. Round glasses."

Patricia went cold, a sick feeling rising in her gullet. It couldn't be the same man who had kidnapped her and found a way to suppress her powers. Could it? "Do you know his last name?"

Olivia shook her head. "No. It's a small town, so sometimes I know the names of the people who come because I already know them from somewhere else, like with Babs—she taught my Sunday school class for a while, when Reverend Johnson was still there, before the scandal." She paused again, shooting a sideways look at Annie that said all Patricia needed to know about what kind of scandal and who had been the other involved party.

Olivia cleared her throat. "But I'd never seen this guy before he showed up for the first time, about a month ago. Said he was new to the area."

Annie had pulled her feet up onto the sofa with her, leaving her small flowered sneakers on the rug. She tapped Patricia's arm. "I think I might have met him. A couple of weeks ago, Mama's car wouldn't start, and someone gave her a ride home." She turned to Olivia.

"Did he talk kind of funny? Like slow, and kind of scratchy?"

Olivia rubbed her chin. "You know, come to think of it, he did. I guessed him for a smoker, but he never joined the other nicotine addicts during the break, so maybe not."

"It must be Mr. Price," Annie said. "Mama invited him in and gave him coffee. I remember because she showed him all the pictures in the dining room, even the awful one of me where I look like something scared me."

Patricia slid her suddenly clammy hands across the cloth of her pants. Daniel Price. It couldn't be a coincidence. "Did you tell the police about this guy?"

Olivia blinked at her in confusion. "Well, no. I mean, they didn't ask, and I didn't think..." The woman's eyes widened, and her hand sought the buttons of her shirt, settling over her heart like someone's maiden aunt expressing shock. "Do you think he had something to do with Babs's disappearance?"

She didn't think so, she knew.

Daniel Price, Cindy Liu's father, the man who'd kidnapped Patricia, drugged her, and kept her captive for days. The madman who had outlived his natural lifespan by killing other men and stealing their bodies...the villain who had disappeared without a trace when they captured Cindy and hadn't yet been found.

Until now.

In Bedford, at Patricia's mother's AA meeting.

It could be no coincidence. Daniel Price had her mother.

"Patricia?" Annie bumped her arm, her eyes wide with alarm. "Are you okay?"

Shaking her head, Patricia blinked. "I'm sorry. I got lost in thought." She stood up so suddenly Olivia had to scoot back in her chair to avoid clocking heads with her. A roiling feeling trembled beneath her flesh, like something was about to burst out of her.

She shifted uncomfortably, gritting her teeth as she fought for control. She forced a tense smile. "Thanks for your time, Olivia."

Annie worked at the laces of her sneakers, struggling to unknot the tangled strings in her hurry.

Olivia pushed herself to her feet, taken aback by Patricia's abruptness, but masking it with practiced salesman politeness, following her to the door. "Of course, of course. I do hope the police find a lead soon. Babs is a fine woman, and I know this has got to be hard on her family."

Patricia mumbled something she hoped sounded properly grateful. Beneath the sleeves of her blouse, her scales shifted, and she rubbed her arms, picking up the pace and leaving Annie to catch up. A moment or two later, she heard the sound of Annie's sneakers smacking the shiny white flooring. Patricia didn't linger for polite goodbyes. Instead, she tossed a wave over her shoulder and walked so briskly toward the car Annie had to jog to keep up with her.

"Patricia," Annie hissed. "What's wrong? Why are you going so fast?"

She held out the keys. "You better drive."

Annie looked worried, but she accepted the keyring and jogged around the car to get in the driver's side.

Patricia flopped into the passenger seat and leaned it back, sucking in long breaths and pushing them out slowly, imagining her scales sliding back into hiding. Beside her, Annie started the engine and fussed with the seatbelt. Her breathing had become almost as ragged as Patricia's.

"It's okay, Annie. I just need a minute." She hoped that was true.

Annie tapped her fingers on the steering wheel, but she didn't say anything. After another minute or so, she put the car into gear and started driving.

Patricia's eyes fluttered. "Where are you going?"

"Nowhere yet, but Olivia is still standing at the front of the store watching. It's going to look weird if we don't leave, so I'm going to drive around until you tell me what the hell is happening."

The Lizard Woman writhed beneath Patricia's skin, and it took all her concentration to keep her scalier persona from bursting out in broad daylight. Her brain spun with the realization that Cindy Liu's madman of a father had likely kidnapped her mother. It didn't make any sense. Why take her mother? Babs didn't even know about Patricia's super heroic life. She couldn't tell him anything. No demands had been made for ransom or even information.

Unless they had and the UCU hadn't told her. But no. Suzie would never have allowed the Department to hide something like that from her.

Patricia's blouse grew tighter, and Annie gasped as the seams popped, failing to constrain her broadening arms and shoulders.

"Get us someplace hidden," Patricia grunted from between gritted teeth. She'd have to puzzle out what Price wanted later—when she wasn't in danger of transforming in front of Bedford's morning shoppers.

Annie spun the wheel hard, throwing Patricia against the window. The car bumped against a curb, but Patricia kept her eyes closed, straining to control her transformation. She felt it when the road changed from pavement to gravel. *Smart girl. Taking us out in the country.* Finally, the car stopped with a jerk as Annie threw the car into park.

"What should I do? How do I help?" The girl's voice had spiked high, coming out as a squeak.

"Call Suzie." Patricia groaned.

Annie reached across and snagged Patricia's phone out of her pocket. "What's the unlock code? Who's Suzie?"

Patricia gave her the numbers.

"No signal." Annie sounded on the verge of tears.

Growling the words, Patricia ordered, "Use your phone. Her number is in my contacts."

While her sister juggled two phones with trembling hands, Patricia shoved her back against the seat, trying to counter the pressure of her shoulder spikes and keep them from bursting through.

SOMEONE'S IN THE LAB WITH CINDY

S uzie's phone buzzed against the table. Dr. Liu raised an eyebrow at her, then turned back to her microscope. Suzie had been watching her work for hours now, which managed to be both dull and fascinating. Lots of thoughtful grunts and scribbled notes, with little explanation.

Suzie understood. She didn't like to talk about her in-progress work either.

The phone didn't identify the caller, so it came from someone not in her contacts. 930. Why did that area code seem familiar? As she was about to click "decline," it hit her: *Indiana*. She answered, moving to a far corner of the room for some semblance of privacy. "Hello?"

The line crackled and broke up, but a young woman's voice came through, sounding barely this side of hysterical. "Is this Suzie?" There was a sort of dip in the U reminding Suzie of the way Patricia said her name if she'd had too much to drink.

"Speaking. Who's this?"

"An-Annie. I'm Patty's sister?" It wasn't a question, but she said it like it was.

Suzie shot a look back to the table where Dr. Liu didn't seem to be paying attention to her. In fact, she looked so completely disinterested that she had to be listening.

Curving her body around, Suzie lowered the volume on the phone, neither willing to leave the doctor unsupervised, nor to allow Cindy Liu to eavesdrop on what might be a very sensitive conversation. "What's the matter?"

"It's Patty. She told me to call you."

Images of Patricia transforming into the Lizard Woman in the middle of a strip mall in Indiana flashed through Suzie's mind. "What's happening? Is she all right?"

The signal crackled again. Suzie thought she heard Patricia groan in the background, but it could have been her imagination.

"She says it will be fine, but I don't think so. She told me to call you."

The girl had already said that, but desperation approaching hysteria shook her voice. Suzie still needed more information, so she'd need to keep the girl calm. "I'm going to help, Annie. It's going to be okay, but you need to tell me exactly what's going on."

Suzie listened as the girl rambled on for some minutes. Something about a furniture store and someone named Olivia, then about how Patricia got upset and how she had to drive because Patty was changing. They were parked on a side road right now, and she didn't know what to do.

"Can you put me on speakerphone?"

"My ph-phone doesn't do that. It's Mama's old fl-flip phone, and it only kind of works," she said. "I only have it for emergencies."

Suzie dropped her voice to a near-whisper. "I take it Patricia cannot hold a phone now?"

"I don't think so. Her h-hands."

Pressure gathered under Suzie's ribs, a knot of worry she had to force her words around. "Can she talk?"

"Kind of. I think it hurts her."

A pang spread across Suzie's chest, as if someone had punched her. If Patricia hurt enough to let it show, this was serious. She pressed her palm to her forehead and rubbed it toward her temple as if she could rub out interference stopping her from solving the problem.

"If she gets out of the car, can she stay hidden?"

"Y-yes. There's nobody here. Just a cornfield."

Suzie hissed out a sigh of relief. "Okay. Tell Patricia to get out of the car and stop fighting her change."

While Annie relayed her directions, Suzie spared a glance for Dr. Liu. The scientist no longer pretended not to listen, but stared openly, mouth hanging agape. With the blotch of acne spiraling across her cheek, she looked like a teenager who had walked in on her parents having sex. Suzie shook her head but gave up trying to protect the privacy of her call. Her greatest ally might well be squatting on a stool across the room anyway.

Suzie returned to her seat, setting the phone on the table and bumping the speaker option. They both listened to the rustling sounds Suzie assumed represented Patricia's exit from the car and continued transformation. Suzie dug her nails into her forearms to keep herself from biting them. Dr. Liu scooted her stool nearer, ignoring her samples and microscope, fixated on the phone.

At last, a familiar growl called out, "Suzie?"

Suzie could have wept from relief, but she kept her voice even. "I'm here."

"It's Price."

"What?" What did she mean? The price of what?

A hiss of anger or pain. Static. Then the growling voice again. "Daniel Price."

Suzie still didn't understand. Daniel Price had nothing to do with the uncontrolled spikes of power affecting the Liu-vians.

She shot a look at Dr. Liu who had gone very still, her face stony with control. Daniel Price was the name Cindy's father used when he'd abandoned her to the UCU—the name of the dead scientist he now wore as a skin suit, the latest in a long and macabre history of mad experiments transferring his brain and consciousness into the bodies of others.

Suzie still didn't understand what this had to do with Patricia's transformation problem. "What about him?"

"He was here. He took her." Patricia's voice stretched tight and crisp, as it became when her temper grew short.

Suzie put on her most soothing tone. "I'm not following."

An angry burl rasped in Patricia's exhale, making her sound like a rhinoceros considering charging. "My mother. Daniel Price took my mother."

Cindy smacked a hand over her mouth, only a whimper escaping her attempt to silence herself. Sliding off the stool, she came to stand nearer Suzie as if proximity to the phone could make the situation clearer.

"I need help." Patricia's voice cracked.

Suzie knew how much it cost her to say it aloud. A fierce glow filled her chest and spread up her face. She closed her eyes to keep the passion out of her voice. "And you'll have it. We've got a team working now to stabilize your condition."

"Screw my condition. Don't worry about me. I need to find Price. Now."

The UCU had spent minimal resources seeking Daniel Price in the months since the capture of Cindy Liu. The Director had deprioritized the case, focusing instead on building the reputation of the crime-fighting forces and strengthening relationships with other police and rescue forces. The new public face and public relations were at the forefront of his thinking. There had been no significant leads in months.

Suzie didn't know how to tell Patricia she had no information on the location of Daniel Price. The stubborn woman had asked for help for once in her damned life, and Suzie didn't have it to give her. She let out a slow breath, preparing a diplomatic answer—something that would keep Patricia from doing something rash but wouldn't be an outright lie.

Cindy Liu's slender brown hand shot out, muting Suzie's phone. "He's in Ohio," she said. "I have an address."

Before Suzie could respond, Cindy tapped the button again and sat back down, pulling out the slide she'd been examining and digging through the samples to look at something else, as if nothing had happened.

While Suzie sat speechless, Annie came back onto the line. "What do I do?"

Shoving aside Cindy's shocking information and the thousand questions it raised, Suzie focused on the problem at hand. "Can you get Patricia back to your house unseen?"

The girl agreed, and Suzie told her to go home and to stay there, giving Suzie time to gather information and resources. "I'll call in two hours. Make Patricia wait to hear from me."

Annie laughed, or maybe cried. "You really think I can make my sister do anything?"

Suzie coughed dry agreement. "Try saying 'pretty please,' and tell her Suzie will kick her ass if she goes off half-cocked."

The call ended, and Suzie saved the contact. She sat staring at the now-dormant device like it might burst into flame.

Beside her, Cindy Liu moved through her samples at lightning speed, making notes in a mixture of cryptic English and Chinese. Suzie's Chinese wasn't strong enough to help her parse the likely highly technical scientific information, but she spotted "metastasis" and "metalloproteinase" among the English notes, words she recognized from her grandfather's fight with cancer.

"What do you want?" The words blurted from her mouth before Suzie had decided to speak.

Cindy didn't bother to pretend to misunderstand. She met Suzie's gaze levelly, eyes full of experience and distrust, at odds with the seeming youth of the face they looked out from.

"Take me with you. I want to be there when the UCU takes him down."

SALLY ANN LOVES IT WHEN A
PLAN COMES TOGETHER

hen Sally Ann arrived at Leonel's hospital room on the UCU
W medical floor, she found she wasn't alone. Jessica sat on the
floor, knees pulled up to her chin. From a distance, she looked more
like a sulky teenager than the fearless agent they had dubbed Flygirl,
but Sally Ann knew better than to assume any weakness. She'd trained
Jessica. The woman had a will of iron and a work ethic to match it.

Plopping down beside her, she patted Jessica on the knee. "Rough
night?"

Jessica looked at her with pink-rimmed eyes. "You could say that."
Her eyes grew wide. "What about you? Your cheek!"

Sally Ann touched a hand to her cheek. It had continued to swell.
"I didn't duck fast enough, I guess. Don't worry, though, I've already
applied Dr. Suggs's healing accelerant. It'll be back to normal in a few
more hours."

Jessica pulled out her phone and checked it. "I didn't get a call."

"Naw. I left you out of this one. Figured you had enough on your
plate. Plus, you'd just done night patrol. We had it covered." Sally Ann
let her head fall back to look at the ceiling. "So, how's the big guy?"

"Don't know." Jessica glared at the locked door beside them. "I
can't get in."

"Well, that's bullshit." Sally Ann bounced back up to her feet and offered a hand to Jessica to pull her up.

Jessica ignored the hand and arched into a backbend, walking her hands up the wall until she stood back on two feet.

Sally Ann snorted. "Showoff."

As she swiped her card at the door, a musical tone sounded, and a faint buzzing signaled the release of the locking system. Sally Ann pushed the door with her shoulder. "Come on. Let's see if he needs anything."

Against the far wall, Leonel sat on the floor of an empty room, resting his head against the wall and tugging his lion's mane of hair out around his haggard and exhausted face. The whoosh of the door mechanism attracted his attention, and his eyes flew open.

"Hey there." Sally Ann said, stepping in front of Jessica who had let out an indelicately shocked gasp at the sight of their friend and colleague. "Holding up okay?"

Leonel tried to smile, but the tension of the past couple of days showed in the tightness of his jaw. "Better than the furniture," he said, pointing at the neatly stacked pile of chair, table, and bed parts by the window. A large handprint had been impressed in the chair back, now detached from the crumpled seat reduced to a ripped cushion and bent metal sticks. A side table appeared to have been mostly reduced to sawdust. Sally Ann couldn't tell what kind of furnishings the rest of the pile had once been. No wonder he was sitting on the floor.

Elbowing Jessica in the ribs, Sally Ann widened her eyes. Jessica took the hint and affected an easy smile, shoving her shock and dismay out of view. "I hear you might be getting that kitchen remodel you wanted."

"David won't be happy about it. We just paid off our mortgage."

Jessica's voice went soft and wistful. "I don't know about that. He likes to spoil you."

Leonel's cheeks trembled, and Sally Ann worried tears were imminent from one or the other of her companions, so she changed the subject. "You missed quite a fight today, man."

"Oh yeah?" Interest sparked in Leonel's soft brown eyes.

"Yeah. You should have seen the new recruits, though. Way faster learners than you were."

Ignoring the teasing, Leonel looked down at his hands. "No one got hurt, though, right?"

"Well, I did get a shiner," Sally Ann admitted. She definitely wouldn't tell Leonel about Mike's knee or that those new recruits were being looked after by Dr. Suggs now. Guilt didn't make much of a palliative. "We got the bad guy, but it would have been more fun to watch you take him down."

Jessica took Sally Ann's arm, tugging her back toward the door. "We better let you rest, Leonel."

Nodding, he let his head fall back against the wall, the light impact sending cracks spidering through the drywall. A tear ran down his cheek as Sally Ann closed the door.

Back in the corridor, Jessica slid down the wall, stretching her legs out in front of her, the same shock Sally Ann felt mirrored in her face. "What the hell is going on?"

"You probably know more than I do. They said it's some kind of new mutation."

"It's not fair. He's already been through so much."

Sally Ann reached up and pushed down on Jessica's shoulder, bringing her back to the floor. She always got flighty when upset. "These things are never fair. And all of you have been through a lot."

Jessica burped into her elbow, a trick that always seemed to help keep her grounded when her body wanted to float. "I want to help. I can't just sit here."

Sally Ann cocked her head. "What could you do? I mean, isn't this more a job for the eggheads than our resident high-flying crime fighter?"

"Walter says I'm the only Liu-vian not affected."

Sally Ann's throat went dry. She hadn't heard that tidbit. "Do they know why?"

Jessica shook her head. "No. They've gotten Dr. Liu working on it."

"Is that a good idea?" Sally Ann didn't like the idea of Liu back in a lab. Last time, she'd nearly escaped. If her plan had worked, she'd have been on the streets again trying heaven-only-knows-what.

"Walter says we have to risk it. No one knows what's going on with us better than she does."

Sally Ann heard the hollow ring to Jessica's words, the doubt. She had mixed feelings about it herself. "That makes some sense, I suppose."

"I'm so scared," Jessica said. "What if she can't help Leonel? What if we're playing right into her hands, and it's all another ploy to escape?"

"None of that now. Nobody's going to let that happen."

At that moment, both their phones lit up with an urgent text from the Director. Sally Ann read hers. "Conference A. Now." When she looked up, Jessica had already flown halfway down the hall.

"No flying in the hospital wing!" Sally Ann yelled, leaping to her feet and bolting after her airborne colleague.

SALLY ANN BURST through the door seconds after Jessica and found most of the chairs taken, excepting one reserved at the head of the table for the Director. Glancing around the room, she took in the crowd and tried to prepare herself for what might come. This didn't look like a simple debriefing from the incident at the mall.

Peeples, Suggs, and Anderson, the three top eggheads, had pulled their chairs together to hold an intense discussion. Jessica had taken a chair behind Walter and leaned in to listen. Had they learned something about what was going on with the Liu-vians? If they had, Sally Ann guessed it wasn't good—the three were deep in problem-solving mode, all gesticulation and red-faced spittle.

Suzie sat at the end, ignoring the chaos in the room, and focused on the small laptop in front of her.

Agent Driver sipped a cup of tea, watching everyone else with an air of bemusement. The ever-silent Gabe was hard to ruffle. Sally Ann flopped down in the chair beside him. "What's up?"

Driver shrugged but made the sign for flight.

"A mission, then?"

The door opened and closed, and the room fell silent in an instant, all eyes turning to the Director. To Sally Ann's surprise, Mary Braeburn stood beside him. She leaned against the wall, arms crossed over her chest and a troubled expression on her face.

"Thank you all for coming," the Director said, jumping in without his usual chatty preamble. The situation must be serious if he wasn't taking time to schmooze the room. "We have a multi-faceted problem before us this afternoon." Stretching a hand toward the other end of the table, he dipped his chin. "Miss Grayson?"

Suzie stood, perfectly poised as always, but dressed in leggings and a soft knit top rather than her usual tailored suit and heels. Sally Ann noticed she had dark circles under her eyes and unusual signs of tension in the position of her shoulders. Whatever had happened had flapped the unflappable Suzie Grayson.

Nevertheless, in a few concise sentences, she conveyed the situation with Patricia. Watching her dispassionately describe her own girlfriend's inability to control her transformation, Sally Ann was amazed anew at the levels of self-control in the petite blonde.

Sally Ann had been surprised to learn Suzie and Patricia were a thing, but romance wasn't an arena she pretended any knowledge about. The cobwebs on her date-night clothes attested to her lack of expertise in matters of the heart. Heck, she'd barely managed to have a regular conversation with that gorgeous reporter this afternoon. If Patricia saw love-life material in this young woman, then she must be made of sterner stuff than her current appearance suggested.

"That's not all, though." Suzie ran a hand across her head, pulling loose several long strands from her ponytail in the process. "She's in Indiana. With her sister. Out of signal with intermittent communication. She flew there early Friday morning when she learned her mother had gone missing."

Sally Ann goggled for a moment at the realization that infamous loner Patricia had a mother and a sister in Indiana, but her jaw dropped completely at the next bombshell. "It appears her mother was taken by Daniel Price."

The room reacted with quiet groans and mumbles—everyone remembered the macabre story of Cindy Liu's father. Even among people accustomed to dealing with the strange, that story had tapped out the freak-o-meter. Suzie ignored the reaction and continued. "Dr. Liu claims to know where Price is and will share that information with us—but only if we take her along on the mission."

Walter stood and slapped the table. "That's insane! We can't actually be considering letting that madwoman leave the facility."

Jessica laid a hand on Walter's, and Dr. Suggs chimed in, more calmly. "I agree that seems foolhardy. What's to stop her from manipulating the situation and attempting another escape?"

The Director turned to Jessica. "That's where Flygirl comes in."

Jessica let her hand slip off of Walter's and blinked at the Director. "Me?"

"No one understands the risk better than you—you know what she's capable of and won't underestimate her or be fooled by her current appearance. I'm sending you on this mission to ensure Liu does not have the opportunity to wriggle out of our grasp. You'll be on guard duty."

The colored leached out of Walter's face even as Jessica nodded, her mouth gone thin and grim with determination. "Of course," she said.

Nodding to Suzie, the Director continued. "Miss Grayson is sending you all the mission parameters now." The room's noise settled into clicks, mumbles, and the odd gasp as everyone read the details and ascertained their individual roles.

Gabe Driver pushed back his chair so fast that he nearly knocked it over as he leapt to his feet. The grin on his face nearly made his eyes disappear into his ball cap. Scrolling through the information, Sally Ann saw why: they'd be taking the Dact! Their new state-of-the-art jet hadn't yet gone on a mission, and Gabe had been chomping at the bit to get it into the air.

The Director smiled at their resident technopath. "You can go get started, Gabe. You leave at 0600." Turning back to the room, he sent everyone in different directions to work on preparations. This would be the first mission outside of Springfield for the fledgling organization. Excitement buzzed through the group as they made their exits.

Sally Ann spotted Walter and Jessica in deep consultation and stood to follow them, but the Director stopped her. "Stick around for a moment, please."

After the others had left, the Director sat down at the table opposite Sally Ann, Mary taking the seat beside him. A shimmer of light seemed to wash over him, and then Sally Ann could see Steven, the Director's true face.

Far less handsome and imposing than the broad-shouldered and lantern-jawed image he generally projected, Steven was a slight man, with muddy brown hair over an unprepossessing face. If she worked at it, Sally Ann could see through the facade on her own, but it strained her limited psychic gift and mostly she chose not to put in the work, letting his perspective manipulation work on her. Mary, on the other hand, could always see through his psychic manipulations, a skill which had made her invaluable in fighting the Six last year.

When he'd begun training her, during that mission, they'd talked about how his own power worked. When he'd first learned he had the ability to push his will onto others, as a small boy, he'd imagined his eyes spinning in hypnotic rainbow spirals, like they did for Kaa the snake in the old cartoon version of *Jungle Book*. Over the years, he'd used his Kaa voice to deflect blame and gain advantages in every arena.

In real life, he'd said, the work was subtler than in cartoons, requiring finesse and restraint. Too much too fast and the subject felt the influence and fought. If he tried to force it, he could do lasting damage, something he didn't ever want to do again. Sally Ann tried to trust in her own perceptions, but whenever the Director was around, she had to question every impulse to see if it originated from within or without her own mind. It made it harder to trust her boss than it had been a year ago.

"We've got another problem," the Director—Steven—said.

"Darrin Berger came to see me at Our Market today," Mary said.

A jolt went through Sally Ann at the mention of the reporter's name. "What did he want?"

"He came poking around about Dr. Liu, asking questions about her products." Mary's hands were folded on the desk in front of her, clasped hard enough it seemed she had to fight to hold them in place.

Sally Ann nodded. That wasn't necessarily a problem. It could be coincidence. There must be more to the story for it to affect Mary so visibly.

Mary went on. "He asked to talk to my mother."

That was a bigger problem. Helen Braeburn had rather publicly demonstrated her pyrokinetic abilities, wreaking violence on the city on more than one occasion in her quest to get to Dr. Liu. She'd been in custody for more than a year now, but rumors about her still popped up in the UCU's data monitoring. Her missing person's case had gone too public to sweep completely under the rug.

Sally Ann frowned. "What did you tell him?"

"I said she was under medical supervision and couldn't see visitors."

Good dodge. But it wouldn't hold him forever, not if he had already connected Helen and Cindy. "I see." She turned to the Director. There had to be a reason she had been invited to the table, but she didn't yet understand what it might be. "What do you want me to do?"

A shimmer moved across the Director's face, and his features started to morph. Sally Ann felt a tickle at the back of her mind, a suggestion she should trust in the man in front of her. The feeling cut off abruptly, when Mary poked him hard enough to make him grimace. "We've talked about this—no manipulation. Just ask her."

Looking somewhat sheepish, the Director shifted in his chair before meeting Sally Ann's gaze. "I want you to go talk to him. Convince him to bury the story."

Sally Ann laughed. "You've got to be kidding." The Director's continued steady gaze silenced her giddy response. "Wait. You're serious?"

He nodded.

"I don't get it. This isn't what I do. I punch things, remember? You want Jessica for finessing the press. Or better yet—you go. Do your thing and give him a push."

"I could. But then I'd have to keep on doing it. My suggestions are not permanent. I saw the interview from outside the mall this morning. I also heard from Mike that this reporter is interested in you. You could use that to our advantage. Convince him through more lasting forms of coercion."

Sally Ann looked down at her bruised knuckles and pictured Darrin Berger, slick and beautiful in his fashionable suits and expensive haircut. She thought again about the spark she'd felt when they'd spoken that morning. Imagining herself as the Mata Hari in this scenario had her fighting laughter, but she wasn't one to turn down a challenge.

"I kind of doubt I'm his type, but sure I'll talk to him. It's not every day a girl gets paid to flirt."

The Director nodded, pleased. "Suzie can get you his contact information."

Sally Ann fished a slightly crumpled business card out of her pocket. "No thanks. I've already got his number."

GODZILLA IN THE KITCHEN

Waiting made Patricia restless, but she was trying not to do additional damage to her mother's house, so she forced herself to be still. She'd already broken a mirror and skewered the upholstery on the loveseat before Annie suggested the best place for her might be in the kitchen where the furniture was durable and the passageways less crowded.

The old-fashioned diner style chair groaned a little under her fully transformed bulk, but it held. She tried to relax. After what felt like several hours, she gave in and asked, "How long has it been?"

From where she stood at the counter, stirring something in a mixing bowl, Annie pointed at the clock hanging above the kitchen window with a dough-encrusted spoon. It was a goofy clock—one that sang out a different bird's song when the hour struck—that had to be a gift from Geraldine, their sister with all the cats. "Not even an hour yet. You have to give her a little time."

Patricia sighed again, staring at her taloned hands resting on the Formica. Flecks of pink paint still stained a couple of the nails. Strange to think it had only been three days since she'd danced with Suzie at Jessica's bachelorette party.

She replayed the conversation in her head. Suzie had promised to call in two hours. It hadn't sounded like that long until she was faced with sitting quietly in the kitchen, waiting to see which bird would call out when the hour clicked over.

Still, she owed it to Suzie to give her a little time to mobilize. She didn't doubt for a moment her girlfriend would find the information. What else had Suzie said? Something about a team working on her condition. What did that mean? There was nothing new about her condition, other than a little control issue—and that could probably be attributed to the stress of dealing with her mother and learning about Daniel Price's role in things.

"Annie, can you get my computer for me? It's in my bag, upstairs."

The girl nodded and wiped her hands on a kitchen towel. "You stay put."

Patricia growled. She'd stay put, even if it killed her, and it felt like it really might. Her skin itched, but she knew better than to try and scrape her back against the chair when her spikes were out. She already owed her mother some replacement furniture.

She closed her eyes and tried to imagine the surf running out endlessly on the long pristine beaches of the Virgin Islands, where she'd spent a holiday with Suzie not too long ago. She'd need to let go of this stress to get control of her transformation.

Eyes still closed, she ran her hands over her arms. She knew she was still covered in scales, but they felt wrong—papery and thin instead of smooth and glossy. Rubbing them felt nice, though. Soothing. Stretching an arm out to the side, she rubbed her hand down it, shoulder to wrist in a long solid motion. The crawling formication sensation under her skin lessened, so she repeated the motion with her other arm. Turning her head in a slow circle, she breathed out through her nose, trying again to pull the spikes on her shoulders in.

A gasp behind her brought her out of her attempted meditation. "Thanks, Annie. You want to be my secretary? I don't think I can type with these." She waggled her talons.

"Patty Jean?"

A man's voice, a panicky, rasping man's voice.

Patricia sprang to her feet, knocking the chair over as she pivoted to face her stepfather. The man grasped the doorframe, his face going pale beneath his gray and white beard. He slumped.

Patricia reached for him, then pulled back her hand, not sure how to help without hurting him "Annie!" she yelled. "Annie, come help!"

Heavy steps sounded through the ceiling while George's mouth opened and closed like a fish dying on the shore.

"It's okay," Patricia said, knowing how ridiculous that had to sound coming from a lizard woman standing in your kitchen.

George blinked slowly, then looked down at the floor, "Is that your skin?"

Patricia lunged for the doorway, managing to catch the man before he collapsed and to lay him down gently. When Annie arrived in the doorway, huffing and red-faced and clutching Patricia's laptop to her chest, she found Patricia sitting on the floor and her father propped up against the wall.

"What did you do?" Annie flung the computer at Patricia, who managed to pin it against her chest without slicing it open. Kneeling, Annie picked up her father's hand and held it between hers, patting it. "Daddy? Daddy, are you okay?"

Scooting back to give them some more space, Patricia brushed her hand across something on the kitchen floor. It crunched under her fingers, pulling her attention.

While Annie continued to fuss over George, Patricia gathered the long, semi-translucent object and held it to the light to examine it. Too big to be an onion skin but with a similar sheen. A long tube, like a discarded stocking made of paper. No, not a tube, exactly. Something jagged, irregular. She draped the item across her lap, seeking the other end.

When she found it, she understood what her stepfather had meant. The tube ended in the shape of a taloned hand, like the one that now held it. Patricia held an ecdysis—her own shed skin.

She shot a look at her sister and stepfather, relieved to see George coming around. She rolled the cast-off skin into a ball and gathered the other one up, shoving the wad of jettisoned flesh into her pocket. She'd need to get this to the science team.

A couple of feet away, Annie helped George to his feet while he complained that he didn't need help. At least she hadn't given the old man a heart attack.

As Annie helped her father round the corner and led him toward his easy chair, she looked back over her shoulder and mouthed "Stay there." She needn't have worried. If Patricia could have made herself invisible, she'd have disappeared entirely.

According to Annie, George was usually gone until six or seven at night, even later depending on how many handyman jobs he had taken on. They should have had hours yet before he arrived.

Still seated on the kitchen floor, Patricia did her best to still her breathing. She strained to pick up any clues about what was happening in the other room but heard only the ticking of the clock on the wall behind her and the thumping of her own heart.

Seeking control, she held her taloned hand out in front of her and concentrated on the nails alone, pulling with her mind to draw them in. She imagined them retracting, sliding back into her fingers and revealing normal, well-manicured nails beneath. A shuddering feeling jolted up her wrists and forearms, but nothing changed, and Patricia let her still-taloned hands fall to her knees. Unable to make out words from the murmuring voices in the living room, she got to her feet, carefully avoiding gouging the floor tile or skewering any appliances.

She stood looking out the back window, the sun-whitened glass reflecting her own face back at her—scales traced her cheekbones, and alien, yellow eyes blinked back at her. She'd made her peace with her alter ego in the past few years, even reveled in the abilities her reptilian form gave her, but the idea of living like this forever left a burning feeling in her abdomen.

"Come on, Suzie," she whispered. "Call."

LOVE AND DUTY

Jessica paced outside the lab where Dr. Liu worked. She hadn't been expecting the Director to put her on guard duty, and the bubbles of acid promulgating in her stomach attested to the uptick in her stress.

It hadn't helped that Walter had freaked out, too. He'd pushed her to cooperate with Liu's research in hopes of helping Leonel and the other Liu-vians, but neither of them had anticipated this kind of direct interaction with her erstwhile kidnapper. When they'd parted ways, Walter was muttering about taking it up with the Director.

She wasn't the gullible child she'd been four years ago. She'd been through stringent training and faced down dangerous situations with ease now; but walking into this room felt like walking into a trap, and talking herself into turning the knob proved difficult. Gripping the handle again, Jessica touched a hand to the emeralds sewn into the lining of her bra, where she'd kept at least some of the gemstones since she'd taken them from Dr. Liu's laboratory after her kidnapping. As always, the reassurance of their presence and the promise of control they offered calmed her. A surge of confidence blossomed in her chest, and she flung open the door.

Inside the newly created lab, a diminutive Chinese-Hungarian girl paced from machine to machine and back to a notebook filled with scrawled notes. She didn't look up when Jessica entered, intent on her work. After a few moments, she called out, "Did you bring my samples? And I could use another pot of tea."

"I think we've had about enough of your tea, haven't we?"

Dr. Liu set down the pen she'd been holding, jerking her head up at the sound of Jessica's voice. The two women watched each other warily for a long moment. Finally, the scientist broke the staring contest. She picked up a test tube and popped it into a machine, hitting a button that made it whir and spin.

Her face carefully neutral, she looked back at Jessica, who hadn't moved from her spot a few feet inside the room. "You're looking well," she said.

Such an ordinary greeting, like something she might have said four years ago, when Dr. Liu had merely been Jessica's mother's friend, coming by for tea and conversation instead of the chaos agent that had altered so many lives.

Jessica blinked, stupefied. No thanks to you, she thought, but chose to remain silent.

"I thought you were the blonde."

She had to mean Suzie.

"She got called away." Jessica vaulted across the room in one bound, landing neatly on a tall stool in the corner. "I got babysitting duty."

Dr. Liu's shoulder twitched, the only sign Jessica's catty dig had found its mark.

"It looks like you've gotten control of your flight. That's good." Her eyes were bright with interest.

Feeling sick, Jessica didn't respond, feigning interest in the condition of her fingernails.

"Your cancer is still in remission, I take it?"

It was, but Jessica bristled at the idea of sharing such intimate information with Dr. Liu. The doctor took her silence for confirmation.

"I wonder why."

"Lucky, I guess."

"I don't believe in luck." The doctor took the sample back out of the whirring machine and crossed to another device in the room, a kind of microscope, Jessica guessed. As she spun the dials, Dr. Liu mumbled to herself. "Why not her?"

That was the question of the hour, the entire reason Dr. Liu had been released from her cell and allowed back into a lab, despite her questionable track record when it came to cooperation with her captors. Jessica's thoughts turned to Leonel, remembering the wall cracking behind his head from the simplest of movements, how exhausted he had looked. If there was anything she could do to cure him, she'd do it, even if it meant opening up to Dr. Liu.

She let herself drift up, hovering near the ceiling tiles where she could see Dr. Liu working. Most of the time, Jessica didn't worry about fully understanding the science behind what had happened to her. She enjoyed working on her speed and altitude, but her eyes glazed over when Walter and the rest of the science team theorized about the physics behind her powers. Even when she'd gone through radiation and chemo, she hadn't wanted to know all the details—the how hadn't mattered to her as long as the process worked and her body stopped trying to destroy itself from within.

But watching Dr. Liu work, she wished she understood more fully —could assess for herself whether what she was doing had legitimate purpose and would likely to lead to a cure. From where she watched, though, Cindy Liu could have been doing anything from making soup to building a bomb.

The door opened again, and Jessica spared a glance for the interloper. Sally Ann stood with her hands on her hips, Suzie behind her.

Dr. Liu lifted her chin and examined them briefly. Her eyes narrowed when she met Sally Ann's gaze, but she ignored her to address Suzie. "Did you get the new samples?"

Suzie held up a medical case, and Dr. Liu practically vaulted the table to come and take it. Sally Ann stepped between them and brought the scientist up short with a flat hand wielded like a traffic cop who might also be a ninja.

"First, tell us some more about dear old Daddy," she said. "We need to know your information is good."

"Not until we're in the air. If I tell you now, you'll leave me here." Dr. Liu screwed her face into a sneer that had probably looked a lot more menacing when she'd had some lines around her eyes. As it was, she looked like a judgmental teenager turning up her nose at the broccoli on her dinner plate.

Jessica watched in silence as the two women stared each other down. The hair on her arms tingled beneath her sleeves, the burst of static electricity in the room a cue that Sally Ann had activated her gift. Before last year, Sally Ann had been able to read emotional resonances and occasional psychic imprints of memories on paper, somewhat unreliably. When the UCU faced the Six, she began working on strengthening her small ability to fight the team of psychically powered thieves and now could sometimes pull information straight from the minds of people.

It frustrated Sally Ann that her gift wasn't stronger or more dependable, but Jessica remembered that Sally Ann had pulled information from Dr. Liu before. When she talked about it afterward, she'd said some people were easier to read than others, like their internal radio broadcast louder than other people's. Dr. Liu's mind apparently screamed especially loudly.

A little bead of sweat dripped down Sally Ann's cheek. She wiped it away, smiling. "That's all right. I got what I needed."

Dr. Liu stuttered a protest, but Sally Ann ignored her, nodding to Suzie who crossed the room and set the case on the table. The scientist pounced on it like a half-starved tiger, then glowered at Sally Ann.

Grinning, Sally Ann put her fingers in her mouth and whistled, drawing glares from all three of the other women. "Hey, Flygirl, peel yourself off the ceiling and come talk to me."

Jessica rolled into a spiral and dove for the floor, startling a gasp out of Cindy Liu and spinning around Sally Ann twice before landed neatly on her sneakered feet beside her former trainer.

"Outside," Sally Ann said, squinting at the other women.

"Don't go far," Dr. Liu called out, the imperious tone to her voice reminding everyone she was not only older than she appeared but used to giving rather than taking orders. A few months' imprisonment hadn't changed a lifetime's habits.

"Yes, Mother," Sally Ann said, using her most nasal tone to amp up the sarcasm. When she was rewarded with red-faced rage on Cindy Liu's face, she smiled broadly and put a wiggle in her hips on the way out of the room.

In the hall, Jessica let out the laugh she'd been holding back. "That was amazing. You really made her squirm. Did you get the address out of her?"

Sally Ann grimaced. "No. But I did get enough to feel sure she really does know where he is. She isn't yanking our chains. Be careful, though—she's definitely up to something."

"Obviously. It'll be worth it, though, as long as it works. How's Leonel? And Patricia?"

Sally Ann smirked. "Oh, you know Patricia. Big, green, angry. Another day ending in Y."

"And Leonel?"

Sally Ann's expression softened. "He'll be all right. We'll figure this out."

Jessica bit her lip. She didn't like the idea that their best hope lay in the hands of a petulant narcissist with a history of subterfuge. "I better get back in there," she said. "Suzie shouldn't spend too much time alone with her."

"Suzie will be all right for a moment," Sally Ann said. "I want to tell you something." She shifted her feet like she didn't want to say what came next.

Jessica froze, afraid to ask. Sally Ann generally blurted out whatever she had on her mind. Something that made her circumspect would probably have anyone else running away in fear. The few seconds pause was more than Jessica could take. She grabbed Sally Ann's shoulders and shook them. "What is it? Tell me already."

A slow smile slid across Sally Ann's face, and she lifted her gaze to Jessica's, mischief sparkling in her eyes. "I've got a date tonight."

For a second, Jessica forgot everything else. She clasped her hands at her heart. "With who?"

Sally Ann groaned. "Clearly I need to get out more if you're this excited I have a date. His name is Darrin."

"Darrin Berger? From *Springfield City News?*"

Of course, Jessica would know him. In her role as Flygirl, she served as spokesperson for the UCU all the time, even more often than Leonel did as Fuerte. The press loved her, and she had proven a natural at spinning the story and keeping the UCU more popular than maligned by the citizenry of Springfield. Sally Ann kicked at the edge of the wall, leaving a scuff. "That's him."

"Where? Who asked who? Details, woman!"

Sally Ann laid out the story and for a few moments, Jessica lost herself in hopes of romance for her friend and mentor. Even the revelation that the Director expected Sally Ann to use the date as the means to get Darrin to squash a story didn't diminish her enthusiasm —she understood mixing work and love better than most. She'd first met Walter when he taught her to use an air pack to control her flight.

The more she thought of it, the more she loved the idea of Darrin and Sally Ann together. If it went well, they could double date! Maybe David and Leonel would come, too. Pulling herself out of her daydream, Jessica gave Sally Ann a gentle shove.

"Get out of here. You need to get the swelling in your cheek the rest of the way down and figure out what you're going to wear. That man is capital-H-hot." She leaned in closer, then grimaced. "And take a shower. You smell like a gymnasium."

"Thanks. Fighting crime will do that, you know."

Jessica grabbed the door handle and yanked it down, pausing before re-entering the room. "Wear yellow," she said. "It sets off your skin."

SOMEWHERE IN OHIO

By the second day of sitting around waiting for something to happen, Babs was going out of her mind. After the coffee had arrived, she spent the morning watching the door, expecting someone to arrive any minute and explain what had happened to her. But no one did. Two more meal trays appeared that day, for lunch and dinner, both arriving when she was in the bathroom, giving her no chance to find out who brought them.

Another breakfast tray awaited her when she woke the next morning. Eggs and bacon this time. She stacked the trays and dishes on a small table near the door, not knowing what else to do with them.

The guest room would be quite nice if Babs really were a guest and able to come and go as she pleased. The queen-sized bed featured a pillow-top mattress and a lovely thick comforter. It had been made up with Egyptian cotton sheets, something with a high thread count by the luxurious feel. The furnishings were a little fussy and old-fashioned for her taste, but obviously expensive.

Bored and worried, she'd finally foraged through the drawers, desperate for something to distract or inform her. She found a television remote, and by checking in on a news channel figured out she was in Ohio of all places, some place that got Cincinnati stations. She also learned it was Saturday, more than a week after the last day she could remember with any clarity.

After that shocking revelation, she'd spent a half hour banging her fists on the door and crying and yelling. All she gained for her efforts were some new bruises on her forearms and a hoarse throat.

She'd found some clean pajamas in her exploration of her well-appointed cell and decided she might as well get clean. Running a hot bath, she sat on the edge of the deep garden tub, swirling in lavender-scented bath salt with one hand while the room filled with steam.

She did her best thinking in the tub. Something about the humidity opening up new connections in her brain, maybe. Or perhaps it had to do with the way the water made her feel weightless. Maybe she'd come up with an idea.

Keeping half an ear cocked for the sound of the door opening, she slipped into the warm water and let her mind drift. She replayed last Thursday night in her mind, trying to understand, to find some kind of clue as to what was going on.

She'd had supper with Annie, some fancy Mac-n-cheese with breadcrumbs on top and a very nice chicken breast. The girl was getting to be quite a good cook. She'd left her late-life-surprise daughter watching her annoying *Shark Tank* show and driven herself to the YMCA where her AA group met.

Daniel, a newcomer to the group, had stopped her in the parking lot, saying he needed to talk to her. Babs hadn't hesitated to follow him to his car. Not every seventy-six-year-old woman still got propositions, but Babs regularly did, and often from men quite a bit younger than she. Lucky genes and confidence, she guessed.

When she'd followed Daniel, she'd expected to indulge in a little flirtation over coffee somewhere, and then let him down easy with a rejection that suggested she would say yes if she were free. She'd have gone home to her husband, her vanity flattered by the attention, and reminded him why he married her. No harm done.

But that wasn't what happened, apparently.

Had she been kidnapped? By Daniel? He seemed so harmless. A

bookish little man, bespectacled and slight. But they did always say to watch out for the quiet ones.

She explored her body under the water but couldn't find any signs of trauma beyond the IV site and the new bruises she'd given herself by banging on the door. Surely, she was too old to be kidnapped for the sex trade at this point, and if Daniel wanted to kill her, why would he drug her, pack her off to Ohio, and lock her in a nice guest bedroom? It didn't make any sense.

Clean and clad in dark blue, silky pajamas that looked like something a mom on a soap opera might wear, Babs returned to the bedroom. She checked the door again. *Yep*, still thicker and stronger than a bedroom door had any reason to be, and more importantly, still locked from the outside. By her count, she'd been here nine days.

They had to be frantic back home, but Babs had no way to get a message to her family. She wished she'd let Patty buy her that fancy watch thingy she'd offered last Christmas. They could have used it to track her. She'd looked, but her purse and the phone inside it were not in the room with her. They were probably still on the seat of her car in the parking lot of the YMCA.

Poor George. He would think she'd run off. She wouldn't blame him for thinking so, given her history, but she had changed. She really had. In twenty years, she hadn't cheated on him even once...even though she'd had more than a few opportunities, some of them more than a little tempting. George was the best thing that ever happened to her, well, except her kids, of course. Her kids were both the best and the worst things that had ever happened to her, especially Patty Jean.

While she sat on the bed staring at the door and willing it to open, to her amazement, it moved. A buzzing click sounded, and the door pushed slowly and evenly inward, like it moved along a track. Babs tensed, trying to decide if she should take shelter within the room or bolt for the opening and take her chances with what awaited her in the rest of the house. She planted her bare feet on the rug and wondered how to keep the slightly too-long pajama pants from tripping her up if she made an escape attempt. The soft material wouldn't stay rolled up.

But when the door opened enough to let her see the hallways, it was clear there would be no point in trying to escape, at least not that way. As she'd expected, Daniel Price stood in the doorway, but a surprise stood behind him—a rather imposing and kind of handsome surprise, holding a gun. Babs pulled her feet up into the bed and scooted back, nearly pulling off the silky pajama pants in the process.

Daniel *tsk*ed at her. "Now, now, there's no need to be afraid. I'm not going to hurt you."

Babs looked pointedly at the Black man holding the gun in her direction, and Daniel shrugged.

"Yes, I'm sorry about that. We'll call this man my insurance policy. But I'm sure you're going to be a good girl and cooperate, won't you?"

Narrowing her eyes, Babs did her best to seem imperious and fierce despite the fact that she confronted him from bed while wearing someone else's pajamas. "That depends. What do you want? Where am I?"

"Of course you have questions."

Behind Daniel, Babs thought she saw disgust in the broad face of the bodyguard or henchman or whatever he was. Maybe she could evoke his pity, get him to take her side and get her out of this. She let tears pool in her eyes. It wasn't hard. She'd been fighting crying all morning—tears of angry frustration. It wouldn't hurt to let Daniel and the big guy misinterpret them as tears of fragile femininity.

"Please," she said, lips trembling. She wept. Not too much, of course. She wanted to gain sympathy, not garner disgust. Puffy eyes and trembling cheeks, but no red nose or snot. One of her husbands had called this tactic her Blanche Dubois. "I want to go home."

"And you will, *Schatz*. I need a few more samples from you, now that the drugs are out of your system. It's for my research."

"What kind of research?"

"Don't you worry about that," he said. "It's for a good cause." He set down the tray he'd been holding, shoving her dirty dishes over on the small table. He opened something on the tray, and when he turned around he was holding a phlebotomy kit. "Roll up your sleeve, please."

Babs hesitated, shooting a look at the gunman whose lips had compressed into a thin line of disapproval.

Stepping closer, Daniel smiled at her. "I assure you it will not hurt. I am skilled with a needle. Relax, *Schatz*."

Though she shrank back into the pillow when he gripped her arm, it didn't stop him from filling a series of small vials with her blood. Sweetheart, indeed. She'd *schatz* him when she got the chance.

When he finished, he took the vials back over to the tray and ferried the samples and the dirty food dishes out to the hall. The big man stood impassively, a small twitch in his cheek and jaw hinting at his discomfort with the goings-on. Babs rubbed at her elbow and looked pleadingly at him.

Daniel returned with a new food tray and set it at the foot of the bed. "See? I told you it would not be that bad." Reaching into a pocket, he pulled out a wide plastic jar and set it on the bed next to the tray. "I will also need you to provide a urine sample. You can leave it with your food tray this afternoon, and I will return for it when I bring your dinner."

Blood and urine? What kind of research? Babs began to feel like she was at her yearly physical.

She reached out a hand, and Daniel let her hold his hand. "Please," she said. "Let me call home. I'm worried about my daughter," she'd said, rubbing his strangely cold fingers with hers. "She must be worried sick."

"Patricia?"

Weird he would bring her up. There had been a sharpness in his tone when he said Patricia's name, and his hand tightened on her fingers. Did Daniel know Patricia? Why would he be interested in her eldest daughter? Surely, it couldn't be romantic.

Truth be told, he was too young for either of them, and Babs was pretty sure Patricia was dating a woman now anyway. She'd seen a few pictures of a tiny young blonde. Awfully young, but really what room did she have to judge? A woman's got to take her pleasures where she can get them, and love is love, even if it looks pretty weird from the outside.

When she'd said "daughter" Babs had been referring to Annie, hoping to play on his sympathies by suggesting that the child suffered without her. Patricia could certainly take care of herself.

Trying to remember if she had ever told Daniel about her eldest daughter, Babs went on, hoping to get him talking. "All my girls: Patricia, Geraldine, Jenny. My youngest, Annie." She sniffed, wiping at imaginary tears since her real ones had already dried. "Do you have any children, Daniel?"

He drew in a breath. "One. A daughter. Cindy. She's a scientist, like me." Something like pride rang in his voice, pride and something darker: anger, or maybe regret. Or maybe it was the German accent that kept creeping into his voice. How had she never noticed that when they talked at AA?

Daniel sucked in his cheeks and blew a frustrated huff through his nose. "Our relationship has been...difficult. My Cindy, we are very much alike in some ways."

Strange coincidence, that.

Cindy had been the name of Patricia's college roommate. A Chinese girl. Patricia had brought her with her once on a visit. Babs hadn't liked her much. Too haughty and full of herself. But the two of them had stayed friends—they'd even gone to Paris together a few years ago. Babs had seen the pictures.

"Daughters can be like that." She decided to push for more information. "Cindy, did you say? What a pretty name. What's she like?"

"Brilliant, in her own way. But stubborn. If she'd listened to me she wouldn't be in the trouble she is now." He spoke to the wall, avoiding her eyes or maybe reliving memories he didn't want her to observe in his face. "In a way, she saved my life. I'm trying to return the favor. If I can understand her research . . ." Returning to himself, he spoke with renewed strength, a fervor lighting his eyes. "I'll do whatever it takes."

Babs didn't have to fake the troubled feeling that wrinkled her brow. "I don't understand. How does keeping me here help your daughter?"

"It's complicated."

She laid a hand on his arm, leaning in a little closer and ignoring the slightly sour scent emanating from his flesh. "I'm a good listener."

He patted her hand and removed it from his arm, placing it back in her own lap. "It's better you don't know too much. It will all be over soon."

"So, you'll send me back home?" Babs smiled brightly, keeping her eyes round and guileless. Sometimes all men needed was to believe you thought the best of them.

He retrieved a bundle from the door. After snapping on a pair of latex gloves, he pulled out a long swab from a tube. "I'm going to need to swab your cheek this time, as well."

When she demurred, he smiled at her, a pleasant enough expression, even if it didn't reach his eyes. She didn't miss the cold condescension in his next words. "Your cooperation will end this sooner."

A chill ran down her spine. He had no intention of letting her out of here. Not alive, anyway. What had she gotten herself into?

PATRICIA AND THE CRYPTID
CLUB

G eorge squinted at Patricia, mouth compressing into a line of grim satisfaction. "I knew it."

Patricia stood in her mother's living room, in her full scaly glory, feeling like a sixteen-year-old who'd been caught in the liquor cabinet. George, ensconced in his battered armchair, unfolded his hands from across his belly, and pulled the handle of the La-Z-Boy to fling the footrest floorward and push him up onto his feet. He crossed the few steps between them to stand next to Patricia and leaned in close, examining the spikes protruding from her back.

"Are these bone?"

Resisting the urge to pull away from her stepfather, Patricia shook her head. "Not exactly. Osteoderms, so they tell me."

"Like a stegosaurus?"

Patricia shrugged, though she'd been surprised George knew what osteoderms were. Walter had to explain it to her. Then again, science had never really been her thing. Maybe it had been George's. Other than being happy that he made her mother happy, Patricia hadn't really gotten to know the man.

"Can I?" He reached a hand toward the yellow spikes rising from her right shoulder.

She nodded, and he gingerly poked one of the protuberances with a finger. Patricia tried to catch her little sister's eye, but Annie had curled up in the cushions on the sofa and wasn't looking.

George barked a short laugh. "I knew it had to be you."

"What do you mean?"

"The Lizard Woman of Springfield. My cryptid club talked about you." George shook his head, waving a hand at her scaly arms. "Benny swore you were some kind of mutated crocodile, like those pet alligators in the sewers of New York. Won't he be surprised!"

Patricia didn't know whether to be relieved she hadn't actually given her stepfather a heart attack or annoyed that he seemed to think he'd be bringing her to the library for show and tell at his little group of conspiracy nuts.

"Your red hair, like your Mama's used to be. That's how I knew."

"I'm hardly the only redhead in Springfield, George."

"True enough, but I remember you from your field hockey days. My daughter Crissy played, too, you know, about the same time as you."

Agitation shook through Patricia, and her spikes jutted out an additional inch or so. George stumbled back, falling into his chair with a thud that scooted the heavy furniture back a few inches.

"Was this why you didn't tell me Mom had gone missing?"

"What? No!" George shot a look at Annie. "Is that what Annie told you?"

Annie grimaced, squeezing a pillow to her chest, and Patricia rushed to her defense. The last thing the girl needed was tension with her father. "Not really. She said you didn't want me to know."

"I thought we could handle it without you. No need to pull you away from saving people in the city if Babs backslid." He wiped at his eyes with the back of his hand. "If I'm honest, I was embarrassed—I'm ashamed to say now what I thought had happened. I was wrong not to call you. She's really missing."

Annie moved to sit on the arm of George's chair and wrapped her arms around her father's neck. He patted at her arms.

Patricia cleared her throat. "Does Mom know? About me, I mean."

George shook his head. "I don't think so. If she did, she'd have told everybody. She's always bragged about everything you did. The entire town knew when you made Vice President, and I think the amount you negotiated for your early retirement got bigger every time she told the story."

Annie emerged from the hug, looking a little paler than usual, her cheeks damp. The afternoon had demanded a lot of her. "It's true. Mama always talks you up, especially when the other kids are here. It's super annoying."

Shifting from foot to foot, Patricia considered what to say in response and came up short. Pride and embarrassment swirled through her in equal measures, leaving her nauseated. She wanted to sit down, but she didn't want to risk any more of her mother's furniture, so she stalked back to the kitchen. George and Annie followed her, and Annie put the tea kettle on while George peppered her with more uncomfortable questions about her life as the Lizard Woman.

After fielding a few of the less embarrassing ones, she cut him off. "George, I came here to find Mom, and in case you can't tell, I'm having issues of my own right now."

"I did wonder about that. You can't change back?" The words were probably meant to convey his concern, but curiosity made his eyes bright.

Patricia laid a hand on top of her head and squeezed, trying to contain the headache pushing at her scalp and maintain her patience. It ought to have been a relief, talking about her transformation instead of explaining again why she'd never gotten married or produced any progeny, but nosy, personal questions about the way her body worked raised her hackles.

Keeping secrets could be difficult, but she'd take that over the pain of confession any time. Letting her head fall back, she focused on the ceiling. George nattered on, running theories about why she might not be able to transform—from government plots to biological weapons, sunspots to chemicals in the groundwater. She tuned out, imagining the arrival of aliens who would beam her through the ceiling and take her some place quiet and still and lonely and dark.

Her attention jumped back to the conversation when she heard Daniel Price's name. Annie was telling George about their morning visit to the furniture store and asked if he remembered Daniel Price. Patricia refocused in time to hear George discounting the idea that the man could be dangerous. "Him? Such a frail little man. Babs could take him out with a wallop of her purse."

"He's more dangerous than he looks," Patricia growled. "I've had a run-in with him before."

George looked at her, waiting for her to say more, but she didn't offer the story. Her head hurt so much it made her vision blur.

"Patty Jean?"

She tried to tell him she'd always hated that nickname, but the words seemed trapped in her throat. Somewhere, far away, a phone rang, or maybe the ringing was in her head. It echoed strangely, like she listened from underwater.

And her head.

She'd never felt anything like this headache—was this what people meant when they talked about migraines?

Something grew inside her head, something with razor nails trying to shove its way out through the top of her skull. Needles of pain seared her eyes, and she closed them against the heat.

Somewhere, someone called her name, but she couldn't respond. Too busy falling in a spiral. At least it was dark and quiet at the bottom.

MIXING BUSINESS AND
PLEASURE

Sally Ann arrived at the agreed-upon bar ten minutes early, then stood indecisively on the sidewalk for two or three minutes. She was out of practice on the whole dating thing. Did arriving early make her look too eager? Maybe she should walk around the block first and arrive exactly on time, or even a few minutes late—to make sure he had to wait for her and not the other way around. Or maybe she should go on in and get herself a drink, showing her independence and lack of concern about being alone. The drink might help her nerves, too.

Checking her reflection in the glass of the window, she was glad she had taken Jessica's advice about what to wear. The canary-yellow blouse hung off her shoulders, dipping low enough to give a glimpse of her tattoo without fully revealing the phoenix that flew across her chest and torso. The tip of the wing peeked out above the gathered material at her bosom.

The blouse wasn't her usual style, but something Jessica had talked her into buying one languid summer afternoon. Shopping with Leonel and Jessica had been more fun than she admitted to either of them at the time, and they'd been right about this blouse. Sexy without verging into slutty, and loose-fitting enough around her torso to easily hide the baton clipped to her jeans at the small of her back. She looked good, if she did say so herself. And with these boots, she stood nearly five-foot-four.

She pushed open the door and stepped inside, then paused to give her eyes a moment to adjust to the change in light. To her surprise, Darrin stood up and waved her over to a booth across from the bar. He'd been early, too, and must have been watching the door.

Sally Ann gulped, drinking in his appearance and realizing it had been much too long since she'd spent time with a man who wasn't a colleague. Dressed down from the suit he wore on-air, Darrin wore expensive jeans and the light blue t-shirt fit like it had been tailored for him. Maybe it had. Sally Ann's pulse quickened.

A waitress approached the table as she settled into her seat and, after a quick glance revealed Darrin had ordered a classy-looking cocktail she didn't recognize, Sally Ann opted for a Manhattan instead of her usual basic beer. As soon as the waitress stepped away, Darrin leaned across the table and squeezed Sally Ann's wrist, resting his palm against hers. "I haven't been able to stop smiling since I got your text this afternoon. Everyone over at *City News* thinks I've lost my mind."

She arched an eyebrow at him, suppressing a desire to laugh giddily. "Thanks so much for coming. I wasn't sure you would." Sally Ann slid her hand from his grip and pulled it across her body, resting her fingertips on her bare shoulder.

Darrin's gaze followed her hand and lingered on her exposed skin for a moment before he pulled his gaze back up to her face. "Hey!" he said. "You're not even bruised. I thought sure I'd be catching the fish eye from people who thought I gave you a shiner."

Sally Ann smiled, sending silent thanks to Dr. Suggs and her healing accelerant. The woman could have made a fortune with it if she'd gone corporate instead of government. "I heal fast."

"I'm glad. It would be a shame to spoil that face, even short term."

The waitress brought her drink, and Sally Ann made herself take only a sip, resisting the urge to down it in a gulp for the jolt of courage. It would be awfully easy to forget this man worked as a reporter. For him, flirtation was a pleasant method of interrogation, and she'd be wise to keep her guard up. If he was smart, he'd be careful about her in turn.

The two sized each other up for a long moment before Darrin finally broke the silence. "You'd think I'd be better at small talk, but all I can think of is: so, how was your day?"

Sally Ann lifted her glass and swished the ice around. "Well, I could tell you, but then I'd have to kill you."

"Touché."

"You were there for part of it, anyway. I didn't watch the news tonight. Did I play well?"

Darrin's face lit up. "You were amazing. Are you sure you don't have superpowers, too?"

"Not so far as you know," she said, winking.

"The mall security camera footage isn't great—grainy and glitchy. But you might start getting some fan mail from our viewers for those moves."

A short silence fell, and Sally Ann rolled her glass around between her hands, considering. The Director expected her to leverage this conversation to get Darrin to shelve the story on Dr. Liu before it led to uncomfortable public revelations for the UCU, but she couldn't figure out how to get the conversation to flow that direction.

Darrin's stomach growled loudly, and he thrust a hand over it, embarrassed.

Sally Ann laughed. "Did you skip supper?"

"Guilty as charged."

"Okay then." Sally Ann stood up.

Darrin sat there looking confused.

"You better pay for our drinks so we can get out of here."

"Where are we going?" He tossed a couple of bills on the table. Sally Ann noticed the generous tip with appreciation. You could tell a lot about a man from his tipping habits.

She walked toward the door and caught him checking out her backside when she turned to talk to him over her shoulder. She grinned at him. "With the noise your stomach was making, we're going to need some serious food. I'm taking you to Giovanni's."

He sped up so he reached the door at the same time as her. Reaching over her to push it open, he asked, "What's Giovanni's?"

Sally Ann laid a dramatic hand over her heart. "Are you telling me you haven't yet experienced the best meatballs in the city of Springfield? Come on, mister, have I got something to show you."

Giovanni's, two blocks over, buzzed with activity on a Saturday night, but Sally Ann was a regular, so the pair scored a cozy table in a back corner in short order. The corner pressed a little tight for the tall, broad-shouldered reporter, and the place was noisy with the chatter of happy customers, but he didn't complain. Especially not when the waitress arrived with a bruschetta board and two glasses of water.

"Your usual, hon?"

"My friend here hasn't tasted your wares, Miss Jenny. I think we're going to need one of each and a couple of ciders."

"You got it, sugar."

Darrin laughed as the waitress walked away. "I can never get used to all that 'hon' and 'sugar.' Nobody talks like that where I'm from."

"Where's that?" Sally Ann deftly separated sections of the brie and apple bruschetta, dropping a piece on a small plate and handing it to him.

Darrin shoved it in his mouth. "Cincinnati," he said, still chewing. "You?"

"Durham."

Eyes rolling back in his head, Darrin groaned. "This might be the best thing I have ever eaten."

"Oh, just you wait," Sally Ann teased. "You'll need to loosen your belt before I'm done with you."

Darrin froze—stuck halfway between a smile and an expression of shock. Was he blushing? Sally Ann snort-laughed. "Oh, honey. If you're this easy to embarrass, I am going to eat you alive."

Leaning forward, Darrin stared into her eyes. "Promise?"

"Oh my!" Sally Ann fanned herself, pleased that he played along. "Is it hot in here?"

The waitress interrupted with a plate of meatballs so large it barely fit on the small round table. The scent wafting off the food made them both groan with pleasure, and the waitress laughed at them. "Is it safe to leave you two alone with these balls?"

"Don't worry, Miss Jenny. We'll behave."

Two hours later, the pair waddled out of Giovanni's and back onto the streets of downtown Springfield.

"That was amazing," Darrin said. "It'll mean extra gym time this week, but it's worth it."

"I could use the chance to walk some of that off. You have time for a stroll?"

"With you? Definitely."

He jutted out an elbow like a gentleman in a play, and Sally Ann looped an arm through his and let him lead her down the street toward the park. The downtown dinner crowd had thinned, and a younger clientele had filtered in to start the late-night party scene. Strains of music drifted to them as doors opened and closed.

She was enjoying this way too much. It would be hard to switch gears into more mercenary purposes.

"Got any interesting stories coming up?" she asked, after they had walked in companionable silence for a few blocks.

"Well, I'd tell you, but then I'd have to kill you," he said.

"Touché."

He slowed his steps. "Actually, there is something I'd like to ask you about, if it's okay to talk business on a date."

Though part of her heart deflated, Sally Ann kept her expression bright. "Shoot," she said.

They were passing a church, with a small rose garden that offered a few benches. Darrin steered her toward one and pulled out his phone as they sat down together.

"So, here's what we're seeing." He held the device out between them and Sally Ann scooted closer to him to look. In the picture, a woman stood on a rainy street corner, a raincoat pulled tightly around her, her posture screaming misery.

"May I?" Sally Ann took the phone and zoomed in on the woman's face, revealing yellow eyes that weren't a trick of the light. She felt Darrin watching her, so she kept her expression stolid. No need to let him know she recognized this woman: another Liu-vian, one with low-level powers the UCU had been keeping an eye on for the past few months. She'd been able to pass off her freak-factor as a skin condition up until now, but clearly things had accelerated.

She handed the phone back to Darrin. "Interesting."

He raised an eyebrow at her. "All right. What about this?" He brought up another picture—a sixty-six-year-old White woman with eyes as white as her hair staring into the distance. Another: a short dark-eyed woman, Indian, whose hair appeared to be on fire. All in all, he showed her ten pictures, all of them women the UCU kept tabs on, all of them exhibiting levels of ability heretofore unseen in them.

Two trains of thought circled in Sally Ann's mind: disappointment that this date had turned out to be more business than pleasure after all and worry about Liu-vians across the city seeing escalations in power. Did the eggheads know how bad it had gotten? Would they find a treatment before something terrible happened?

She needed to think and found it hard to do with Darrin Berger sitting near enough to allow her to feel the heat of his body and smell the sweet-clean scent of his soap. She'd have taken him for a fancy cologne sort of guy. The more natural, simple choice surprised her. She liked it.

Pocketing his phone, Darrin turned toward her, angling his body so their knees touched and he could look into her face. An earnest sincerity out of pace with his line of work lit his amber-brown eyes.

"Listen. My boss wants to run with this story—he figures we can probably get at least one of these poor women to have a breakdown on camera and our ratings will go through the roof."

Sally Ann drew in a breath to object, but he stayed her with a shake of his head.

"The thing is—I think there's more to this. All these displays of strange powers? They started three or four days ago. Three or four days ago is also the last time anyone saw Fuerte, Flygirl, or the Lizard Woman in public, and if there's something like this happening to people who are already powerful, that's a crisis for our city."

Sally Ann looked into Darrin's face for a long moment, trying to decide if she could trust him or if she only wanted to because he was so good-looking.

Almost as if he heard her doubts, he went on. "If our super-powered citizens are going through something, it doesn't do anyone any good to announce that on the nightly news. It's going to invite the worst element to come out of the woodwork while Springfield is unprotected."

"It's not."

He looked puzzled. "Not what?"

Sally Ann jutted out her jaw. "It's not unprotected. Springfield. It's got me."

Darrin regarded her, seeming to weigh her words. "So, what do I tell my boss?"

"What would it take to keep this quiet for a while?"

"I'm sure I could stall him if I offered him something shiny, some-thing to skyrocket our viewership...something like a group interview."

Sally Ann shook her head. "That would be...difficult right now. But I might be able to get you some airtime with Flygirl in the next few days—with a pre-approved list of questions. And we could talk about a group interview down the road."

Darrin grinned like he had won the lottery. "Done!"

"I'll see what I can do." Sally Ann stood, the romantic bubble of the evening broken by the negotiations. Hoping to recapture the glow to some degree, she reached for Darrin's hand, tugging him back to his feet. "Walk me back to my bike?"

"Your bike? Did you ride a Schwinn to our date tonight?"

The incredulous expression on his face made Sally Ann want to tease him further with a story about her matching pink helmet and elbow pads, or make up an imaginary cross-country bicycle tour, but she relented. "Not quite. You'll see."

As the two meandered back toward the bar where they'd started their evening, they stayed near enough to bump hands and occasionally hips as they moved. Once, when Sally Ann stretched out an arm to point out another favorite place to eat, she bumped her breast against his elbow, and they'd both gone silent for a long moment. An electric spark that had nothing to do with superpowers ran through Sally Ann at each touch, and she was pretty sure Darrin felt it too.

Sally Ann's apartment waited two blocks away and as she considered whether or not to mention that titillating bit of information to the man sauntering by her side, her phone buzzed. Reluctantly pulling her fingers from Darrin's, she took a few steps away to check the offending device. A text from Jessica, in all-caps: "NEED YOU. NOW."

Shit. No time for love, Dr. Jones. She texted back. "OTW."

The slump in Darrin's shoulders told her he'd picked up enough from her body language to know their date was over. He shoved his hands in his pockets as she came back to his side, a charmingly boyish posture that stoked Sally Ann's fire a little hotter.

"Phone," she said.

He handed it to her, eyeballing her warily. She unlocked it—his eyebrows rising at the realization that she'd already learned his unlock code. *Well, that's what you get when you date a secret agent.* Scrolling to his contacts, and noting that his ICE contact appeared to be his mother—good sign—she pulled up an empty form and filled in her digits, the personal ones this time, then passed it back to him.

"My hours are strange, but I suspect yours are too." She stepped closer, near enough to feel the heat of him, and looked up into his face, her voice dipping lower. "But I'd like to see more of you."

Looping a hand around his neck, she pulled his face down to hers and pressed her lips against his. His response was gratifyingly fast, arms wrapping around, pulling her close.

His hands started at her waist, and Darrin paused when his fingers brushed against the baton at the small of her back, but he moved his hand higher and deepened the kiss until someone shouted at them from a passing car, making them both laugh.

Sally Ann settled back onto her heels and touched a finger to her tingling lips while she waited for her vision to go back to normal. Then, giving a smile and wave, she turned around and ran around the block to where she left her Harley.

A minute later, she rounded the same corner, yellow blouse flapping around her body as she sped down the street. Darrin hadn't moved. Showing off, she hit the button to jolt her speed even higher— a modification Driver had installed for her. She half-expected to leave a streak of fire on the road behind her.

WEARING OUT WALTER

Walter fell asleep at his desk while poring over the data again, hoping he'd spot something he had overlooked the first three times. One minute, he'd been reviewing a report on biomarkers for cancer among the Liu-vians and the next, he jerked awake to find Suzie Grayson standing in his office, pale as a ghost and calling his name.

Groggy, he had to make her explain the situation twice before he could grasp it. It was the most rattled he had ever seen the unflappable young woman—she couldn't stand still and talked a mile a minute, waving her hands one second then wrapping her arms tightly around herself in the next. Patricia. Unconscious. Indiana. Skin. Skull. Cure. Daniel. Finally, he understood that their scaliest agent had passed out in her sister's kitchen, and Suzie wanted to know what to do.

He understood how she felt—helpless panic could be paralyzing. He could all too easily imagine Jessica suddenly losing her hold on gravity and floating off into the atmosphere. He'd read the reports and had been there when she learned to take a measure of control over her movement, even without the emeralds.

They couldn't wake Patricia, and from what they'd been able to glean from the sister's breathless account, she'd shed her skin like a snake before passing out and something grew from her head.

He let go of the nonessential details for the moment. Whatever was going on with Patricia's mutations would be a problem for further down the road. First, they had to retrieve Patricia and her mother.

Stepping into Suzie's path, Walter held up a hand like a crossing guard. The forced stop stunned her into momentary silence.

"We'll need to change our timeframe. Get in the air immediately."

Suzie's eyes snapped into focus. "Of course." All she needed was a direction. She looked around the room and seeing every surface covered with something, sat down in the middle of the floor, pulled out her computer, balanced it on her knee, and began typing and clicking at rapid speed. She muttered as she worked, and Walter could tell he had become unnecessary to the moment.

He went back to his desk and pulled up the monitoring software for the lab where Dr. Liu continued to work on the mutations problem. At first he thought she was in there alone—a zigzagging whirlwind leaping from one machine to the next—but then he spotted Jessica floating above her, watching from above. He tugged his eyes away from his fiancée to check on Liu's progress.

The data Dr. Liu recorded came up in real time on his second monitor. As he'd expected, she pursued a hypothesis that her history of cancer set Jessica apart from other Liu-vians—the underlying reason that Jessica remained stable when all the other women affected by Dr. Liu's products were experiencing shifts and changes that endangered everyone around them.

Since her formula derived from a form of cancer itself, the approach made logical sense, but the data didn't support it. Jessica wasn't the only cancer survivor among the Liu-vians.

Marietta Cooper, the lightning-wielding former teacher, had won a battle with lung cancer, but that hadn't stopped her relationship with electricity from evolving into deadly force lightning bolts lighting up the park a few days ago. If Jessica had been rendered immune from further mutation because of cancer, then why hadn't that helped Ms. Cooper? It had to be something more specific. And even if it were cancer, knowing wouldn't solve anything. They weren't going to give the Liu-vians cancer to stop their power mutations. That would be like emptying a lake to put out a campfire, creating more problems than it solved.

Walter threw his glasses on his desk and rubbed his tired eyes. Would this be another wasted line of inquiry leading nowhere? It had to mean something that Jessica alone among the Liu-vians was not experiencing new mutations.

Across the room, he heard Suzie close her computer and stand up. Her pallor and demeanor had returned to something more akin to her usual appearance, though the strain of the past few days still showed around her eyes.

"We'll leave in two hours," she said.

"We?"

"Oh yeah. No way am I staying here and waiting by the phone."

Walter tried not to take the comment personally, though that was largely what he would be doing. Well, that and continuing the research. "The Director agreed?"

Suzie nodded curtly. "I didn't give him much choice."

Walter remembered the time Suzie took down an illegal fighting ring while the bad guys thought she was helplessly tied to a chair, and decided not to argue. Spending time with Jessica had taught him that cute and petite did not equate to harmless or weak. He should have known better than to second-guess Suzie's mettle.

"Come on," she said. "You'd better say your goodbyes to Jessica."

The two made their way through the labyrinthine halls of the Department facilities to the lab. Walter waited at the door as Suzie went in and relieved Jessica from guard duty.

Leaning against the cool wall, Walter wished he could melt into the plaster for a while and disappear. Somehow, an urgent all-nighter wasn't as exciting when you had a personal stake in the results—it became terrifying, and exhausting.

He pushed himself back up onto his feet when he heard the door open and had a smile and hug ready for Jessica, who plowed into him with unnecessary force.

She spoke into his chest as she squeezed him. "Can you go by the house this morning and have breakfast with the boys? Mom could really use a break."

"Of course." He automatically agreed, though he didn't really feel he could spare the time away from the work.

Jessica pulled back and studied his face, worry darkening her eyes. "Looks like you could use a break, too. Do I need to get the Director to order you to take some rest? Or can I trust you to take care of yourself? We can't have you falling apart on us, Dr. Peeples."

She was right. The law of diminishing returns came into effect past a certain point, and Walter had probably passed that point twelve hours ago. Staring at the data wouldn't get him anywhere, not until he had new data. Rest really would help.

He checked his watch. "I could get in a few hours nap before the boys wake if I go right after I see you off."

"Perfect. I'll text her that you're coming. Let yourself in and go sleep in my room. Don't go peeking at my wedding dress."

Walter aped horror, stretching his face into a grimace. "I wouldn't dare. We'll let Patricia be the only kaiju at this party—no Bridezilla, please."

Jessica punched him on the arm. "I haven't been that bad."

He tugged her back into his arms for a kiss, then whispered into her cheek, "No, not bad at all."

Someone cleared their throat a few feet away, and the couple stepped apart guiltily. Sally Ann rolled her eyes at Jessica. "I came as quickly as I could, but if this is what you needed me for, no thanks. I'm going back to Darrin."

Walter blinked. Who was Darrin? And why was Sally Ann dressed like that? He could remember seeing her in girly clothes maybe once or twice in their years of acquaintance. She looked stunning. Was that a tattoo peeking above the neckline? He forced his gaze back to Sally Ann's face and found her laughing at him silently.

Jessica gave him a shove. "Go! Take a nap and help Mom with the boys. I'll message you when there's something to report."

Walter gave his fiancée one last squeeze and went to follow her advice. A nap would do him good, as would time with the boys.

SUNDAY

THE P IS SILENT

Sally Ann found Driver on the rooftop helicopter pad, under the new air transport, closing up a control panel. He slid out from beneath the Dact and sprang to his feet, grinning from ear to ear. Sally Ann didn't need to use her psychic gift to pick up on his excitement, and looking at the ship, she couldn't blame him.

The Pterodactyl, or Dact for short, looked like something straight out of a science fiction film from the 1950s, sleek and rounded with hints of NASA-esque aerodynamic enhancements. Armed and armored, fast and quiet. Sally Ann was sure the Director had used his ability to influence perceptions and push emotions to get this project pushed through. And they'd be taking her out on her maiden voyage in a few more minutes. It seemed fitting to take the Pterodactyl to rescue the dinosaur among them.

"Everything ship-shape?" she asked, affecting a British accent.

Driver nodded and stroked the flank of the ship like someone else might touch their lover's back. Driver was more than a machine enthusiast—he had a way with all things mechanical, a freaky way, one that let him get them to perform in ways beyond their engineering specs. The eggheads called him a technopath, but Sally Ann thought Gabe's given name described it best. Agent Driver could drive anything.

With a high-tech, experimental ship like this, he had to feel like a kid at an amusement park. If the man spoke, Sally Ann had a feeling he'd be babbling his excitement nonstop.

Squeezing his shoulder, Sally Ann asked, "Everyone else on board?"

He gave her a thumbs up.

"Then let's get this party started."

Sally Ann ducked inside and found her team ready and waiting. Looking around at Jessica, now geared up as Flygirl, Suzie dressed in the simple blue jumpsuit most agents wore, and Dr. Liu in her too-big prison scrub pajama get-up, she laughed out loud. "This has to be the shortest invasion force in history. Not a one of us over five-foot-two."

Knocking on the wall behind him to get her attention, Driver stretched up to his full five-foot-seven and shook a finger at Sally Ann. She rolled her eyes. "All right, except for Driver."

"Saddle up, pilgrims." Sally Ann stowed her bag and flopped into her seat.

Everybody adjusted their buckles and waited.

Sally Ann sat tensely for several minutes, waiting and unsure what to expect, before she turned her head, looked out the window and realized they were already in the air. "Holy shit."

All the other heads swiveled toward her, and she pointed out the window at the city lights twinkling below them. "I didn't even feel it take off."

The scheduled flight was short. They would be on the ground in Indiana before the sun finished rising. Sally Ann decided she'd better take her chance at some rest now, while she could.

After making sure Suzie and Jessica were keeping watch, she kicked her seat back, dropped a forearm across her eyes, and went to sleep with the practice of someone used to taking rest when she can get it. With Driver at the helm, she had maybe two or three hours to rest. She made good use of the time.

An hour and forty-seven minutes later, Jessica yanked Sally Ann out of a steamy dream involving a luxurious tropical waterfall and a very naked reporter by shaking her foot. Groaning and holding up a hand in surrender, Sally Ann rolled up into a seated position and stretched—snapshotting the images of Darrin's bare chest in her mind and hoping she'd get the chance to compare her vision to the real thing soon. She bet he waxed.

The nap had helped. She felt less like her eyeballs had been fried in peanut oil. Quickly taking stock of her team, she saw that Suzie slept, Jessica vibrated with nervous energy, and Cindy Liu still scribbled intensely in a notebook. "Did I miss anything?" she asked.

"Not really," Jessica said. "Suzie snores. Liu wrote frantically the whole time and grunted a lot. You moaned suspiciously. Anything you want to tell me?"

Sally Ann tried to suppress the grin that sprang to her cheeks but failed.

Jessica's eyes grew wide. "Was the date that good?"

"About that. I kind of promised Darrin he could have an interview with you, to get him to hold off on reporting on the Liu-vians for now."

Jessica nodded. "I can do that. Besides, I want to make sure he's good enough for you. I'll have some questions of my own for him."

Sally Ann closed her eyes. This, she remembered, was one of the things she hated about dating—all the teasing. Still, it felt good to know Jessica had her back, both on and off the clock. She'd return the favor and bring her home unbruised.

Moving to the cockpit, she took the seat beside Driver. An impressive array of switches, gauges, and lights sprawled across the space, but Sally Ann only had eyes for the view. Miles and miles of patchwork quilt farm fields spread across the landscape in irregular rectangles of green, red, brown, and yellow. "Jeez Louise. She did grow up in the backside of the beyond, didn't she?"

Driver rewarded her crassness with a smile and a huff of breath that might have been a laugh.

"I swear I can smell the cow shit from up here. You got a landing in mind?"

He flicked a finger at a satellite view of the neighborhood where Patricia's mother lived and jabbed a thumb at an empty field, almost across the street from the house.

"Really? You can land there?"

Driver pointed at Sally Ann and shook his head, then pointed at himself and gave her a thumbs-up. Of course, he could land there, even if no one else could. With his gift with machines, he could probably have landed in a prime spot in downtown Springfield during rush hour without scraping the paint. She squeezed his shoulder. "How long?"

He held up five fingers.

Nodding, she clambered out of the cockpit and back to the passenger area to strap herself back in beside Jessica. "Five minutes," she said.

Suzie still slept, her cheek bunched up and drool dripping onto her own shoulder. Sally Ann let her be. Landing would wake her soon enough, and they'd all be going into this under-rested. Not the best recipe for success when dealing with reanimated scientists and angry reptilian women, but Sally Ann had dealt with worse conditions with less impressive colleagues.

Four minutes and fifty seconds later, they had landed, raising a cloud of dust, but not an alarm, though the denizens of the sleepy neighborhood would surely be stunned if they looked out their windows and saw what had landed outside their homes.

Sally Ann shook Suzie, who stirred and blinked dumbly for a few moments before her brain caught up to the situation.

"We're here." Suzie had her harness undone and was scrambling for the door faster than she had any right to move.

Jessica reached to grab her arm, but Sally Ann shook her head. "Let her go. They're going to need a moment."

Standing up and stretching, Sally Ann turned on the scientist sitting cross-legged in her chair and chewing on the end of a pencil. She snagged the notebook from the woman's hands, eliciting a screech of protest. Thumbing through the pages, Sally Ann listened with her psychic sense for signs of betrayal or treachery, but frustration boiled off the pages in a black cloud, thick enough to make her stomach hurt.

She tossed the notebook back. "All right, Liu. What have you got for us?"

Dr. Liu smoothed the cover of the notebook, her face gone dark and sullen. "I'm not there yet."

Sally Ann considered shaking the woman by the shoulders until the smirk slid off her face and splattered against the wall. Cindy must have spotted the intention because she raised her hands and adopted a less imperious tone. "We're looking at micrometastases here, spreading throughout the bloodstream and starting new mutations. There are too many potential factors. I'm going to need more data and time to fabricate a treatment."

As she scowled, a gleam of early morning light streaming through a window caught Cindy Liu's hair and spotlighted a strand of it, making it glow silver. Reaching over, Sally Ann yanked it from her head, making her squeak in protest. Ignoring her, Sally Ann examined the hair in the light.

Definitely silver. Not normal in fourteen-year-old people. Liu wasn't really fourteen, of course, but the rest of her body seemed to comply with adolescent expectations—acne, legs longer than make sense for the torso, a tendency to roll her eyes. The silver strand of hair might mean the doctor herself wasn't immune from the current mutation problem.

She held the hair out to the scientist who grasped it and held it up to the light. "Did you gray early? I mean, the first time?" Sally Ann watched her face carefully and saw the eyebrows knit together in worry before the woman schooled her face placid again.

Cindy Liu rolled the hair around the end of her pen and reached for her notepad, turning to a fresh page and writing out some formulas. Self-interest could be motivating, and Sally Ann was all for keeping the good doctor motivated.

Checking to make sure her baton and other weapons were in place, Sally Ann bent to retie her boots. She poked Jessica in the knee. "I'm going in. Can you babysit?"

Jessica quirked an eyebrow and seemed about to speak when she grabbed the arms of her chair instead. Around them, the Dact creaked with sudden stress, and Sally Ann sprang to her feet, readying for an attack.

Instead Suzie walked in. She cleared the entry and moved to the side, making room. When Patricia ducked into the Dact, all three women gasped at the sight of her.

She'd always loomed large in her reptilian form, but she now dwarfed all of them, as if an elephant stood next to a pack of dogs. Her scales glinted green like always, but new threads of gold ran through her flesh like stripes of ore. Strangest of all, a new growth sprouted from her head—two tall ridges protruded from her scalp and followed the curve of her head to disappear down her back.

"Let's go," she said. "I haven't got all day."

BREAKFAST AT JESSICA'S

The bedroom door creaked open and Walter heard the sound of excited whispering in the hall. He groaned and rolled over. Dim sunlight slipped between the blinds to shine through the glass of the bedside lamp, making the globe glow faintly green. Four hours hadn't been enough sleep, but it would be all he'd get. He promised Jessica he'd have breakfast with the boys and give Grandma Eva a break. Early mornings were the hardest part for his future mother-in-law.

"Hey there," he croaked. He cleared his throat and tried for a more cheerful tone. "Who wants pancakes?"

A laughing squeal followed by the sounds of two sets of feet running down the stairs told Walter he had about ten minutes to get into the kitchen, or the boys were going to start without him—a recipe for a messy kitchen at the very least.

He made it downstairs in nine, and found Max already partially covered in flour and Frankie holding the canister of sugar out of his little brother's reach. Walter took it from the boy's hands and set it on the counter, then pulled both boys into his ribs for a hug that bordered on a wrestling move. They struggled against him, but laughed while they did.

Finally, he let them go and opened the fridge, pulling out eggs, milk, and butter. "Max, go find the baking powder," he said, suppressing a yawn. "It's the one in the round can, not the box." Max scooted off to comply. The kindergartner was learning to read, but it helped to give him a hint of what to look for in the pantry.

Setting the ingredients down on the counter, he turned to Frankie. "What'll it be, champ? Bacon? Or sausages?"

"Sausages." Frankie's answer was decisive.

"Bacon!" Max called from in the depths of the walk-in pantry.

"Both it is, then," Walter said, and went back to the refrigerator.

The refrigerator was definitely better stocked now that Walter spent time in the Roark household. Eva was a wonderful grandmother and fine woman, but she didn't have much interest in the kitchen. "Why cook when Springfield has so many fine restaurants?" she'd said the first time Walter suggested they should eat at home more often. Jessica had inherited her mother's lack of interest in all things culinary. Sometimes she still tried, but the results were rarely palatable.

The good news for Walter is the boys were easily impressed with his kitchen prowess. Simple pancakes with a little cinnamon and vanilla mixed in had them ooh-ing and ah-ing as if he'd created a masterpiece. "I like your bacon," Max said. "It's not black like Mom's."

Of course, they got real kitchen masterpieces when they ate with David and Leonel, but Walter would take a little easy praise where he could get it. The boys had been pretty welcoming when he and Jessica started dating, especially considering how recently their father and mother had divorced, but, Frankie, the man of the house at age eight, considered it his job to keep the rest of the family safe. Walter could remember a slightly shorter Frankie telling him a year ago, "Mom can fly, but it doesn't mean she doesn't need my help. She relies on me."

Walter assured him he'd be someone Jessica could rely on, too. A few more days now, and they'd officially be a family, for better or for worse. Today, drawing faces on the pancakes with the butter and syrup, it definitely felt like "for better." Walter looked forward to a lot of mornings like this one, after the wedding when he would officially move in.

An hour later, the boys were happily watching Bugs Bunny, an old-fashioned pleasure he had introduced them to, and Walter hummed to himself while he washed the dishes.

His mind returned to the problem at hand as he worked. *Why not Jessica?* What set her apart from the other Liu-vians? Why didn't she suffer new mutations when so many others did?

Not her youth. That had been among the first things the research team investigated. Jessica was fifteen to thirty years younger than most of the Liu-vians, having gone into early menopause after losing her ovaries to cancer when she was thirty-two. She'd sought out Dr. Liu's Mood Lifting Tea and found that more than her mood had been lifted. But two of the other women on the watch list were also in their thirties.

Not motherhood. Her two boys were the light of her life, and now Walter's as well, but she wasn't the only mother among the affected women. Leonel was a mother, too—or should he call him a father now? When Leonel had been Linda, he'd birthed three babies. Helen, too, had a daughter. Several of the civilian Liu-vians were mothers as well. *Motherhood. Scratch. Next?*

Race didn't seem to apply. Liu-vian skin came in a variety of hues.

All the victims lived in Springfield and most of them had lived here all their lives, but they weren't from any particular neighborhoods or areas of the sprawling southern city, so geography didn't seem to be a factor, either.

He also didn't think it was the cancer. That's why Liu's research hadn't gone anywhere. Marietta Cooper was also a survivor, but it hadn't protected her from becoming a living conduit for lightning she could barely control.

Walter felt his mental wheels turning again, like a solution hovered within reach, if he could grasp it. The rest really had made a difference. It probably also helped that he'd had half a pot of coffee. The Roark household didn't drink tea anymore, not after Jessica's experience with Dr. Liu's blend. Though she had great control now, Jessica's first experiences with flight had left her struggling against the ceiling, unable to get down and afraid to move.

She still shuddered when she told the story. "Before the emeralds, I drifted helplessly. Like a balloon in the wind. I used to be afraid I'd float away into the atmosphere."

Walter dropped the skillet into the sink, splashing himself with sudsy water.

The emeralds.

The other thing different about Jessica.

Walter snatched a photograph off the refrigerator, one taken on a vacation weekend last summer. At sunset, on a lonely beach, Jessica, wearing a thin white sweater over a black bikini, smiled into the camera, wind billowing her hair around her head, back before she'd cut it short. *Beautiful.* His heart ached to look at her.

A faint green glow shone through the gauzy cloth of Jessica's pullover at the bottom of the frame. He'd always taken it for a reflection or a strange effect of the light, a lens flare or something. But he found his eye drawn there now.

Green.

The emeralds.

Jessica always kept a supply of the irradiated emeralds from Dr. Liu's destroyed labs on her person. She'd had a special compartment sewn into her bras where she stowed a piece of the gem. If her clothing didn't allow for a bra, she wore a slide of the gemstone threaded onto a long chain and dropped inside her clothing. She swore the gemstones enabled her to control her flight, transforming her from a victim of the situation to a hero no longer held hostage by gravity.

Walter suspected that was a partial truth—Jessica had needed time and practice to understand her powers and any boost the emeralds provided could be attributed to psychology. That didn't make it any less real, of course. Just less scientifically reproducible.

The UCU research team had analyzed hundreds of samples and had never been able to completely nail down the factors affecting the emeralds. Radiation, chemical interaction, magnetism. The ones retrieved from Liu's storage unit and destroyed laboratory carried strange signatures. Spectrometry and XRF analysis had shown them they were in over their heads. One of the lab techs had thrown her hands in the air after a long week of fruitless analysis declaring, "It might as well be magic for how well I understand what I'm seeing!"

Maybe the problem was that they were looking at it wrong—as chemistry rather than crystallography, physics rather than metaphysics. He needed to get a look at those rocks again.

DARRIN OPENS A CAN OF WORMS

D arrin dropped his pen on the desk only to have it roll off and go sliding across the gray tile floor. Before he could get up to retrieve it, Nicole had appeared from out of nowhere. She bent to pick it up and approached his desk, twirling the pen in her slender fingers like a tiny baton. She sat on the edge of his desk to hold the pen out to him, thrusting her breasts to within inches of his face. "Frustrated?"

Rolling his eyes, Darrin took his pen back, ignoring the breasts and dropping an elbow across his notes. His internal soundtrack thrummed up the guitar licks for "Barracuda," a tune he'd often thought could be his fellow reporter's theme song. What was she even doing here on a Sunday morning?

When he'd been the new guy at *Springfield City News*, he'd taken her overtures for flirtation or maybe even an opportunity for mentorship, but when she'd stolen his first big story idea and pitched as her own, he understood who and what he dealt with—a selfish opportunist.

Not that he blamed her. At least not entirely. It had been hard enough to make a name for himself on television news in this Southern city as a Black man. As a Black woman, she had the same hard row to hoe and an entire garden of misogyny besides. Understanding didn't mean he trusted her, though.

Maybe he was still an idealist—or worse, as naive as Nicole had accused him of being—but he wanted to think they could build each other up instead of eating their own to move forward.

When she didn't move on, he leaned back, taking the precaution of turning his paper face-down on the desk as he did so. "Not frustrated so much as stuck in a holding pattern. My source is out of pocket and I need her to move forward."

"Her?"

He nodded but didn't offer any information.

"I see," she said, crossing her legs and shifting so she looked back at him over her shoulder, perfectly smooth raven-black locks brushing the shoulders of her bright pink suit. "You want a distraction? I'll give you a slice of my story."

He squinted at her. She didn't offer to share credit for free. There would be a catch. He waited.

She sighed. "Fine. I got an in with the guy from the mall the other day—the strong man who tore the place up? But he doesn't want to talk to a woman. I figured you could do his interview, and I'll pull from it for the larger piece."

That was more like it, and he'd love the chance to find out more about the incident at the mall. "All right," he said, slipping his notes into a folder and sliding them into his locking desk drawer. "But, if I end up on the cutting room floor, we're done."

"Yeah, yeah. I'll make sure they see your pretty face." She waved a hand, stood up, and stalked ahead of him. When he stood up, she looked back and gave him a once over. Darrin tugged at his soft gray sweater and adjusted the collar of his pale blue Oxford, then spread his fingers in a "ta-da!" pose.

"That'll do," she said. "The sweater is good. Jailhouse interviews go better when you look more approachable. But you might need to stop by wardrobe. You got a little frizz."

∼

ON THE SHORT drive to the Springfield City Jail, Nicole had gone over her list of questions and filled in the background a bit. The man, Emilio Schulz, had no prior record of violent offenses. Nicole summarized him as, "Kind of dull really. The biggest trouble he'd ever been in was a car accident in his twenties." In his early forties, married with three kids, he was employed as a baker at Our Market, a co-op grocery on the older side of the city.

Not much there to suggest the kind of rage machine they'd seen in the security camera clips. "His lawyer will be in the room. They agreed to this, hoping to gain a little public sympathy for Mr. Schulz, so soft-ball them, at least at first."

"I know." Darrin tried to keep the irritation out of his voice. Nicole had been doing this a little longer than he had, but she didn't have to be so damned condescending about it. He wasn't an idiot.

They filmed Nicole's intro on the steps of the jail, Darrin waiting patiently off to the side. A few minutes of bureaucracy and he and the cameraman were admitted to a small room with a table at the center. A police guard stood at one side, and Schulz and his lawyer sat at the table. Impressed that Nicole had been able to negotiate for on-camera access without a barrier, Darrin took his place at the table and introduced himself.

"Mr. Schulz, thank you for agreeing to talk with *Springfield City News*. Could you tell us what happened that day, in your own words?"

The man looked at his lawyer like a kid asking permission. The lawyer nodded. Schulz held up his cuffed hands, shrugging an apology. "Most of it is kind of a blur. I don't remember all of it."

"Tell me what you remember."

"So, I work early, you know, at the bakery. I go in about two and I'm done at eight or nine. Then I go home and get cleaned up and go to bed until my kids get home from school. But my wife—she didn't feel so good, and she needed me to go pick up some things at the mall, so after I showered, I went."

Darrin nodded, trying to move the man forward in his story. "So, you weren't angry or upset when you went to the mall?"

"Naw, man. I mean, I wasn't exactly happy to be running errands instead of taking a nap, but whatcha gonna do, right?"

"But once you got to the mall, things changed?"

"Not right away. I picked up the sneakers our youngest needed, no problem. But, in the drugstore, looking for soap, I started to feel kind of strange. Like the music played too loud—stabbing me in my head. Since we were out of my soap, I finished my wife's bar in the shower that morning—some Chinese thing called Nu Yu, spelled like N-U-Y-U, get it? Anyway, I figured I should bring more home. It wasn't on the list, but I try to be a good husband, you know? I couldn't find Nu Yu on the shelf, so I went to ask the lady at the desk, and she kept talking on the phone, ignoring me."

Darrin kept his face placid, nodding encouragingly, but filed away the name of the soap. He couldn't quite put his finger on it, but he felt like he'd heard something about it—something not good.

The man got agitated, shifting around in his seat, but he kept talking. "I tapped my fingers on the desk, in case she didn't see me or something, and she shook her finger at me." Schulz's skin reddened under the edges of his thin, blond beard. "It made me mad—I don't know why—I'm not usually a guy who gets mad easy. You can ask anybody. But I slammed my fist on the counter, and the table it...it crumbled like I hit it with a sledgehammer or something."

He sat for a moment staring at the table between them, like it might crumble, too.

"Then it was like something in me snapped. Like the world turned red. I don't remember anything after that until I woke up in here and they told me what happened."

Darrin found he believed the man—he sounded confused and upset, more like someone something happened to than like someone who made something happen. But he pressed on—the camera footage didn't really leave any room for doubt that Schulz had been the guy who'd done all that damage at the mall. "They have you on tape throwing a security officer into a window."

Schulz nodded, his lips pushed together like he was trying not to cry. "They showed me the tape, and I can't explain it. I'm not that kind of strong, man." He looked at the guard, who nodded—they must have talked about this in advance—then stood up slowly.

"I mean, look." Schulz stretched the cuffs apart, pulling until his arms shook. He tried it again, his face darkening to a deep red from the effort. The chain stretched taut, but the links held. Then he sat back down in his chair with a huff. "These aren't even like super-strength or anything. They're normal handcuffs. If I'm the guy in that video, who could throw a person like that, why can't I break these?" He looked into Darrin's eyes, something pleading in their depths. "I don't see how it could be me. But it looks like me. I don't understand."

After Schulz had been led out and returned to his cell, and the camera was put away, Darrin gave his card to the lawyer and thanked him for the access. "Why didn't Schulz want to talk to Nicole, my colleague? She said it was because she's a woman, but I didn't get the feeling he has problems with women. Not the way he talks about his wife."

The lawyer laughed. "Is that what she told you? No, it's not her ovaries that are the problem. It's her teeth. I've seen her work, and I knew she'd chew up our unfortunate Mr. Schulz and spit him out, all in the name of ratings. I wouldn't let her do that to the poor guy."

Darrin let that slide but filed it away for future cogitation. "Did they do a tox screen on Mr. Schulz?"

"I thought of that, too. Like PCP or something? They did. Nothing in his system. Completely clean. Not even pot." The lawyer offered his hand for shaking. "For my part, I believe him. Schulz is a good man, and I intend to find out what happened to him. Thanks for giving him a platform. Crazy as it sounds, I think he might be a victim here."

Darrin thought so, too. He itched to get back to his computer for some research to help him understand the clues he'd gathered. He had a lot to think about. This story could turn out to be much bigger than Nicole realized, and boy would she be pissed when he scooped her.

WHEN LIZARDS FLY

As the Dact carried them to Ohio, to the address Dr. Liu had provided, four women stared at the fifth, who glared back at them, talons hooked into the webbing across the ceiling at the center of the cargo hold. Sally Ann, for her part, was fascinated.

Patricia in her fighting form had always been a sight—gleaming scales, yellow eyes, talons, and those monstrous feet. But this was a whole new order of things. Terrifying and magnificent—her bulk magnified to another third her usual battle size. New colors wound through her scales like coppery-golden warning signs, bringing to mind dragons and dinosaurs more than mere lizards. Most impressively, new head plates rose from her temples like the spiny ridges on an ankylosaurus. The human stance looked out of place. Sally Ann found herself checking for a spiked or clubbed tail and feeling disappointed not to find one.

After a couple of minutes of tense and awkward silence, Sally Ann tore her eyes away from the transformed Lizard Woman to examine the faces of the rest of her team.

Cindy Liu curled into her seat so that only her eyes peeked over the top of the seatback, her face avid with wonder and excitement, and scribbled fiercely in a notebook held in her lap. Of course, she would see this as an exciting development rather than a problem.

Suzie studied her lover carefully, while a range of emotions crept across her face: relief, worry, anger, dismay, determination. Sally Ann avoided examining her too closely, afraid her psychic abilities would pull her into the emotional maelstrom and drown her.

The wonder on Jessica's face would have made a great closeup in a Steven Spielberg movie: wide mouthed shock and curiosity, unable to speak and unable to look away. Stupefied.

"So, I take it we don't have to tell you about the mutation problem, huh?" Sally Ann said, moving to Patricia's side. Up close, the scales glittered hypnotically. Patricia rewarded her attempt at humor with a shrug and a grunt.

Sally Ann winked at her. "Looks like we might have to have your bridesmaid dress altered, though."

That got a laugh from Jessica, who covered her mouth immediately, face burning bright red. "I'm sorry! Can you picture Patricia in her column dress like this?"

Patricia twisted her body, turning to look at her own butt and then grinning at them—always a horrifying thing when she had her lizard face on. "What? Do these new ridges make me look fat?"

Relief washed over Sally Ann. Patricia was still in there, sarcastic and unstoppable.

"How do you feel?" Suzie asked, her voice neutral as a nurse recording symptoms before the doctor comes in. Sally Ann remained seriously impressed by her levels of self-control. If this had happened to someone she loved, she wasn't sure she could have kept it together nearly as well.

"It hurt while it was happening," Patricia shrugged, the spikes on her shoulders waggling. "The headache knocked me out. But when I woke up and found these…" she gestured at the plates sprouting from her brow like dual Mohawks made of slate. "It made sense." She sighed. "Other than not being able to change back, I'm fine now." She looked steadily at Suzie. "Truly. I'm not in any pain."

Suzie nodded once in acknowledgment, but worry still etched a crease in her forehead.

Dr. Liu sat up higher in her chair, her head slightly too large for the narrowness of her adolescent shoulders and slender reed of a neck making her look like a doll. "The new plates, are they osteodermic like your spikes, or more like the armor plating on your chest and back?"

Patricia's head snapped toward the voice, then back to Sally Ann, who held her ground despite a strong desire to back up a few steps in the presence of that terrifying visage.

The Lizard Woman growled. "What the hell is she doing here?"

Suzie spoke up before Sally Ann could answer. "We've had her working on understanding what's happening with you and the other Liu-vians, to understand these new mutations and figure out how to help you."

Patricia blinked. Twice. Once with each set of eyelids—the second ones coming in from the sides. "Wait. The others?"

Sally Ann touched Patricia's elbow. "All the Liu-vians are experiencing shifts like this."

Patricia shifted, taking a step toward Jessica that made the ship creak. "You too?"

Jessica shook her head. "Not me. But I'm the only one not affected." She pointed at Dr. Liu with her thumb. "She's working on it. Why it's everyone else and not me."

"But Leonel?"

Jessica's voice shook a little. "His strength is out of control. He's pulverizing things with the slightest touch. They've got him in isolation at the UCU."

Dr. Liu piped up, undeterred by Patricia's ire. "Helen, too. She nearly burnt down her fireproof room in her sleep." Sally Ann noticed she didn't mention her own just-discovered symptom—graying hair on the still very child-like head.

In two long strides, arms stretched above her head to use the ceiling webbing like monkey bars and keep herself balanced, Patricia was beside Dr. Liu, her face inches from the researcher's wide-eyed countenance. Dr. Liu fell out of her seat, notebook sliding across the floor, but she held Patricia's gaze.

Dr. Liu scrambled across the floor like a crab and snatched back her notebook. They all watched her digging through her cases and supplies until she emerged with a swab kit. She stood there a long moment, swab kit in hand, looking for all the world like a child encountering a lion on the path to school, afraid to approach and unable to run.

Suzie snatched the kit from her hands. "Please, Patricia. I know you don't trust her. None of us do. But she's our best hope. Will you give her a sample to study?"

In answer, Patricia knelt and opened her mouth.

Suzie expertly swabbed the cheek and capped the sample, making Sally Ann wonder again about what other hidden skills this so-called administrative assistant had. Clearly spreadsheets and organization were not her only abilities.

Sample in hand, Dr. Liu knelt on the floor and immediately began her work. After watching for a few seconds, Sally Ann gave up trying to understand what she was doing. It looked like moving things into vials and adding various elements from other vials to her. For all she knew, the woman was making a soufflé over there.

She turned back to Patricia and Suzie in time to see Suzie plant a kiss on Patricia's scaly cheek. The whole scene reminded her of *King Kong* except reptilian instead of simian. A tiny blonde and her monster.

Scratch that, she thought. The real monster wore a lab coat in this case, or at least she had until recently. She glared at Dr. Liu, half-tempted to try and sneak a peek into that brain and half-unwilling to face what she might find there. Did she even have any regrets about all the trauma she had caused?

She'd have to crack that nut another day. They had thirty minutes left until they would be on the ground in Ohio. It was time to take down Daniel Price and get back Patricia's mother.

WALTER ROCKS IN THE LAB

B ack in the UCU lab facilities, Walter unrolled the handkerchief and looked at the chunk of gemstone he'd taken from Jessica's room. Pretty enough, in the way of any shiny rock, but it wouldn't have attracted the attention of a jeweler. Too rough and uneven. Hardly the sort of rock one made into an engagement ring or anniversary present.

Picking up the slender, thumb-length shard of bright green rock, Walter held it against the light to examine the layers. It looked as if some kind of primordial slime had been frozen, bubbles and ooze gone solid at the center.

He'd examined samples before, when they'd first been found in Dr. Liu's exploded laboratory, but he was no geologist, and he hadn't really believed the emeralds important to understanding what had happened to the Liu-vians.

Past study had gleaned little of use—nothing that could explain the superpower side-effects of the formulas derived from them by Dr. Liu. The rocks had some strange properties, and samples sometimes disrupted the machines in the labs, but he'd chalked it up to magnetism or mere coincidence.

He'd spent a couple of hours reading about stone medicine. Normally, he'd have snorted at the new-agey claims of balancing qi and resonances with various elements. But he kept coming around the part about absorbing toxins and decided it couldn't hurt to try. Stranger things had proven true, especially in the Department. Many of the things Walter saw every day defied ordinary understanding. Who was he to assume stone medicine amounted to hogwash when he personally knew a woman who became a man after washing with the wrong soap?

Up until now, he'd assumed the gems were not the active ingredient that mattered. But holding the chunk of crystalline mineral in his hand, he felt something—a sort of tingling, or magnetism. Maybe his mind played tricks on him, or perhaps blind hope made him mistake exhaustion for reaction, but the gemstones felt warm and active against his skin despite the coolness of the laboratory.

One might argue they felt alive.

When he'd told Jessica's mother what he suspected earlier that morning, Eva had nodded, like the idea wasn't new to her. She'd gone with him to Jessica's room and opened the jewelry box under the bed, selected the smallest piece and handed it to him. "I worry about these, sometimes. Jessica...well, let's just say she is awfully attached to them."

Walter understood what she meant. He'd always credited Jessica's obsession about keeping pieces of the gem on her person to superstition—a placebo effect. She believed the gems gave her control over her flight, and therefore they did. None of the studies the UCU had performed had lent credence to the hypothesis that the emeralds actually acted on Jessica or affected her flight powers. Her biological signals read the same whether she wore the gems or not.

Her performance told a different story. When she flew without emeralds on her person, the two or three times the science team had been able to convince her to try it, she lost speed and direction. Her heart rate became erratic and her breathing indicated panic. No one at the UCU could find a reason to object to letting their flying hero carry the gems. "I don't believe they help her," Dr. Suggs had said. "But

I can't see how they could hurt her either. Even if the effect is probably psychological."

When Walter had said his goodbyes at the Roark house, Eva had warned him. "She isn't going to be happy you're taking them. She's possessive about the shards in this little hoard. I caught her once, sitting on the floor in her bedroom, staring into the box, this intense look on her face. She swore it didn't mean anything, but I'm not sure I believe her—in fact, I'm not sure which of us she wanted to convince."

Walter had been surprised by how many pieces had been in the case, laying there in the drawers intended to hold bracelets and earrings. He hadn't realized how many pieces Jessica had picked up and wondered if anyone at the UCU realized how large a collection she had amassed. Eva's description of Jessica sitting on the floor staring at them gave him a tug of worry in his guts. He'd have to discuss it with his bride-to-be.

But first, he had some Liu-vians to save.

Surely, Jessica would forgive him the invasion. She'd been willing to fly across the country with a madwoman for Patricia's sake. If this worked, it could save Leonel, her best friend. That had to be worth giving up a small portion of her collection.

He had a diamond blade saw brought to his workspace and practiced using it on a piece of quartz, glad he'd donned the mask and goggles as the workspace filled with dust. Quartz wasn't quite as hard as emerald, but it was near enough to give him an idea what he'd be working with. He could do this.

Ten patients suffered within the medical wing, one of them an agent of UCU, another a prisoner, the rest desperate civilians. He planned to offer each a slice of gemstone. It was no sillier than the hundreds of other things they'd been trying—and plenty of cultures believed in the medicinal uses of stones. Walter hadn't been raised in any of them, but sometimes you had to think outside your own box.

Slices made, he poked a hole in each piece and threaded a cord through, forming necklaces. He'd ask each patient to wear the gem against their flesh and see what happened. Maybe nothing would.

This could be another wild goose chase, but at least it would be a new angle to try.

If he'd been a religious man, he might have prayed. As it was, he found himself closing his eyes and pleading for success—even if he didn't know whom he petitioned.

JESSICA RECONNOITERS

o the skies. Flygirl jetted across the neighborhood as dusk
settled over the half-abandoned housing development, taking a
circuit to scout out the scene. Reconnaissance. Her favorite
assignment.

The wind already had a hint of crisp fall coolness this far north,
and Flygirl reveled in the sensation on her skin, hurtling herself into
dips and pulling out at the last minute for the sheer joy of it. It would
be even better if she could ditch the work uniform, but the dark black
armored suit she wore afforded necessary protection both from
detection and from attack, should she need it.

Wind slipped under the edges of her mask and rifled through the
fake red locks that draped onto her back, cooling her cheeks and
her mind. Free of the constraint of seatbelts and the fraught
atmosphere inside the Dact, she wished she could keep flying
forever.

Flying, once she learned to control it, had become the center of
Flygirl's world. Air pulsing around her, she could shake her worries,
her fears, her doubts, and lose herself in the moment—something she
found much harder to do in any other context. Alone with the sky
amongst the clouds, which she had once feared would be her coffin,

she knew peace and freedom the like of which she couldn't begin to articulate.

Up here, she didn't have to worry about whether Leonel would regain control of his strength and be able to fight by her side again or feel guilty about not suffering when her friends did. She could let go of her fear that Dr. Liu would make things worse by trying to make them better, that her impatience would cost them all in the end.

But she knew her companions needed her, so she spiraled through the air for only a moment before she aimed for the house at the corner of Mockingbird and Bluejay, putting on a burst of speed that nearly matched that of the peregrine falcon. She'd made reaching peregrine speeds her next goal, the way she used to work to hold a position longer or stretch her body to new lengths in her gymnastics career. Always striving to get better.

Inside the compartment sewn into her uniform, the emeralds grew warm against her flesh like something living, and she felt comforted anew by their presence.

The house looked ordinary enough, though Sally Ann had already told them it drew three times the normal power of any other house in the neighborhood and received an unusually high number of deliveries, often from scientific suppliers.

All indications Liu's intel could be relied on.

This was probably the place. That didn't mean it wasn't also a trap. Or a meth lab. Or something else entirely. Flygirl approached with caution.

The two-story mock-Tudor style reminded her of her grandparents' old house up east, a place she had visited often as a child. Something about the brown decorative timbering and triangular gables always made her feel as if she had stepped into a fairy tale.

But if this neighborhood had ever been the home of happily ever after, those days were behind it now. Shady Valley might have been an upscale subdivision forty years ago, but it was a fading rose now. Closed factories and relocated facilities had transformed the once-charming bedroom community into a whole different kind of shady.

Light shone from a couple of the rooms in the house she'd come to investigate, but as she hovered in the air above it, she let her gaze follow the street. House after house lay dark and empty in a way that said no one lived there anymore. Foreclosure signs offered low prices, but it didn't appear many people were taking the mortgage companies up on the deal. Even flippers didn't seem to want to work here.

Yards were overgrown and sidewalks cracked. Despite being surrounded by other houses, Daniel Price's hideout was effectively isolated. No nosy neighbors or inquisitive children. He could hide in plain sight without much effort.

Dropping down to hover a few feet above the roof, Jessica circled the house. She found four security cameras, simple blocky things that recorded a single angle and probably ran to an observation panel inside the house. Not wanting to call unnecessary attention by disabling the cameras, which might have brought someone to investigate, she opted for interference instead. To block the lenses, she pulled bundles of leaves from nearby trees and nested them around the cameras that observed the back of the house.

Hovering a little lower yet, she skirted the walls of the second story, angling for a view of the rooms or inhabitants, but the windows were reinforced and curtains tightly drawn. The only hint as to which rooms were occupied was the lighting. Although it was still early, light shone through three windows. One upstairs showed no movement. Probably a bedroom. Flickering light made her suspect she glimpsed the living room and someone watching TV on the bottom floor. Lastly, light peeked through the basement windows onto the garden path on the east side of the house.

All signs seemed to indicate a skeleton crew, not particularly on alert for intruders. If Price still relied on the government connections that had set him up at the abandoned campus in Indiana, clearly they weren't investing heavily in him now.

Sitting on the roof beside one of the front facing cameras, Flygirl made a survey of the front yard. A white van, sides splattered with dried mud, sat in the driveway and appeared to be the lone vehicle on the premises. She didn't see any obvious additional security measures in the yard.

Arching her back, she lifted into the air, floating over the house and landing softly on her feet near the back door. She could make out nothing through the windows, and the door itself looked ordinary but did feature a security keypad, implying they might find it harder to open than it appeared at first glance. She took a picture of it to show Sally Ann.

With a burst of energy, Flygirl bolted straight up into the air, spiraling to take in the area one last time before bulleting for the backyard of the abandoned house facing the backside of the secret lab, where the others had agreed to wait for her.

She dropped out of the sky into the center of the group, startling a gasp out of Suzie and making Dr. Liu stumble backwards. Sally Ann, on the other hand, rolled her eyes. "Drama queen. Come on, let's hear it."

Flygirl described what she had seen, and Sally Ann grew thoughtful.

"No signs of my mother?" Patricia asked.

Flygirl shook her head. "The van matches the description of the one seen leaving the parking lot the night she disappeared, and the mud spatter suggests a recent run. I couldn't get a view into any of the windows. Buttoned up tight."

Sally Ann bounced her fist against her open palm. "Looks like we'll be indulging in a little breaking and entering tonight, ladies." She turned to Patricia. "How do you feel about being used as a battering ram?"

Dr. Liu blew out an exaggerated breath that blew her hair off her acne-encrusted forehead. "There's a keypad lock on the back door."

Flygirl nodded. "She's right." She showed the picture she'd taken. "Looks pretty basic. Driver could probably get it to cooperate."

"I have the code." Cindy Liu's tone was bored, unconcerned. She seemed more interested in the cracks in the sidewalk than the discussion they were having, but Flygirl remembered how insistent she had been about coming along on this mission, how she'd used the information she had as leverage. *What was she really up to?*

Patricia leaned down to put her face next to the doctor's. "Why should we trust you?"

Cindy didn't flinch. She waved a hand. "Fine, batter the door down. I'm sure that's safer than trying to access the door with the code I stole from my father's files." She glared into Patricia's face, then smiled coldly. "No one will get shot this time, I'm sure."

Patricia seemed to increase in bulk before their eyes and Flygirl would have sworn the spikes on her shoulders grew longer. The green scales covering her cheeks seemed to darken to something nearer black, and Flygirl felt certain she was about to witness Cindy Liu's demise.

Before anyone else could intervene, Suzie, wrapped in a bulky Kevlar vest intended for an agent thrice her size, had stepped between the two former friends.

"Let her try it. If she's telling the truth, we'll get in without attracting attention. If she's lying, she'll be the first in the line of fire." She shot a glacial look at the doctor. "I'd call that a win either way, wouldn't you?"

Flygirl didn't like the idea of letting their best chance at a cure take a bullet, but she also didn't trust Cindy Liu to provide the cure in the first place. She looked to Sally Ann. As team leader, it was her call. Sometimes it was a relief not to be in charge.

Sucking in her cheeks, Sally Ann pointed at the path. "All right then, short stuff. You first."

A few minutes later, Dr. Liu stood at her father's backdoor, Patricia waiting behind her, sheltering Sally Ann and Suzie behind her bulletproof bulk. Jessica squatted on the roof, poised to jet down to the ground at the first sign of trouble.

Cindy Liu lifted the cover on a simple keypad and typed in four digits. With a glance back at the group behind her, she grabbed the door handle, yanked it down and pushed forward flinging herself through, moving with an alacrity that took them all by surprise, accustomed as they were to her languid demeanor.

She swung the door closed behind her, leaving the others locked outside on the doorstep like unwanted salesmen.

"Well, shit," Sally Ann said.

DARRIN SHOPS FOR A LEAD

D arrin had been walking around chanting "Nu Yu" all morning, feeling like the reference floated just beyond his reach. If he could get his brain to stop spinning for a moment, he might grasp it— the lost memory about where he'd heard about this soap before—but the whirlwind of his thoughts refused to be controlled.

After the jailhouse interview with the unfortunate Mr. Schulz, there had hardly been a moment to think. He had a deadline to file, an interview to record, phone calls to make, his editor to dodge, and Nicole to keep an eye on.

Then there was Sally Ann Rogers to consider—the compact, dangerous little woman had him tilted sideways, her devilish grin and raucous laugh distracting him from his work at odd moments. He wished he could have met her in some other context. But life teased like that sometimes—refusing to stay compartmentalized. You could fall in love with a source, even if it was a very bad idea.

Darrin had wandered into another daydream about Sally Ann in her yellow off-the-shoulder blouse. In his mind's eye, he'd been tugging the blouse down slowly to get a look at the rest of the tattoo that peeked out above the gathered neckline when his search finished running and the computer pinged at him, ruining the mood.

There were only two hits on the phrase "Nu Yu," and he himself had written the first article. He opened the file, a little story he'd written when he first started working for the station, an attempt to show he could do harder news than the lifestyles fluff he'd been assigned to. Watching the video, he understood why it hadn't gotten him the transfer he wanted—he came off over-eager and awkward. The whole video was off-putting. He'd come a long way since then.

"The Hidden Dangers of Over the Counter Treatments" highlighted the lack of oversight for many natural remedies and cautioned buyers to look into manufacturers carefully. He'd interviewed the manager at Our Market, a different woman than he'd seen yesterday. This woman had pooh-poohed his concerns and reassured viewers they vetted all their products carefully and were proud to give local entrepreneurs a venue to sell their wares.

The interview had been filmed inside the store. The manager stood in front of a display of bath products.

Darrin froze the frame. On the shelf behind her left shoulder sat bar soaps turned sideways so the label faced the viewer. The logo caught his eye: a woman drawn in calligraphic lines, her stride matching the length of the wrapper. Nu Yu, it said. He scanned the shelf, wishing he had a clearer still to examine.

The second article had been penned by another staffer, a few months later, the product listed as one of several that were being recalled. He jotted down the names of all the products in the list, just in case.

Viewers were asked to turn in any bars they might have at home for testing and promised a free bar of a locally made goat's milk soap instead. Even partial bars could and should be turned in. Weird. Not the usual M.O. of companies forced to recall a product. Most of these cases were about denying culpability and blaming the victims, not working to pull the product from homes as well as from store shelves.

This was the soap poor Mr. Schulz mentioned, the one he tried to replace for his wife because he'd used the last of her bar. And the soap maker? One Cindy Liu, Springfield's most interesting missing person, a person growing more interesting by the day, at least to Darrin. Her products were recalled, her house burned down, and then she had disappeared.

Pulling open his desk drawer, he pulled out the shard of green rock he'd found in the ruins of Cindy Liu's house. Beautiful, it almost seemed to glow even under fluorescent lights. Such a strange thing to be in the dirt outside an exploded science lab in the basement of a suburban house.

It looked like he'd need to stop by Our Market again and shop for some soap. Schulz worked there, so it made sense he bought the original bar there. Maybe they had more in storage that hadn't been turned in. If he could get a bar, he could have it tested, see if something in it could explain the man's meltdown.

OUR MARKET HAD a charming brick facade that gave the impression of age, though he knew the store had opened not long before he'd moved to Springfield, and he'd only been in the city a few years himself. Still, the simple design hearkened back to a simpler time of neighborhood markets that carried a range of basic needs. There had been nothing like it where he'd grown up, but it still made Darrin feel nostalgic to be there.

He'd arrived a little late for lunch and early for supper, but the place was hopping. The outdoor displays of herbs and produce were crowded with shoppers, and the small seating area buzzed with conversation and laughter. It felt like the kind of place that had been here forever. Darrin admired the thoughtful details, like wall murals with progressive quotes and a chalk wall where patrons were invited to express themselves. The smell of coffee and sweet rolls wafted on an afternoon breeze. Maybe he'd get a treat while he was here.

It took a few minutes to wind his way through the aisles to the health and beauty section. He cruised by the essential oils and supplements to stand in front of the soap section. He scanned the shelves, but failed to find Nu Yu, so he stepped closer and traced a finger across each shelf, looking.

Someone spoke behind him. "Can I help you find something?"

A short White woman, maybe 26 or 27 years old, her blondish-brown hair in dreads tied back with a blue kerchief, looked up at him quizzically. The red Our Market apron failed to completely cover a t-shirt with the word RAGE at the top.

"Mary?" he said, recognizing her as the same woman he'd tried to interview about Dr. Liu the day before.

She jumped. For a second, he thought she might run away, but she narrowed her eyes at him, making him wonder what he'd done to make her mistrust him so much.

"Mr. Berger, right? From the *City News*."

"Darrin," he said, hoping to start again on a friendlier footing.

"Okay," she said, her face remaining cold and unwelcoming. "Can I help you find something?"

"Maybe you can. I'm looking for a kind of soap I heard about. Nu Yu?"

A strange change came over Mary's face, the quickest flicker of something fierce and angry before she smoothed her expression back into the professional blandness of a shop clerk. "I don't think that's something we carry," she said. "Maybe you could try one of the other local producers. The soaps on the end are completely vegan."

Darrin couldn't have said why, exactly, but he felt Mary knew all about Nu Yu and Dr. Liu and purposefully kept mum. He pushed. "I know this store used to carry it. I've seen it here before. Do you think there might be some in the back or something?"

She shook her head. "Everything we stock is here on the shelf. You sure one of these other ones won't do?"

He changed tactics. "Do you know Emilio Schulz?"

Mary blinked at him. "Not really. He works in the bakery. Those guys start early. We don't cross paths much. Do you want me to see if he's still here?"

Darrin shook his head. "I'm pretty sure he won't be coming in today."

"What do you mean?"

"Listen. Do you have a break soon? This might take a little while to explain."

~

MARY AGREED to talk with him in thirty minutes, when she took her lunch break, so Darrin bought a coffee and a cinnamon roll and went to sit at a small table under the largest tree. He tried to organize his thoughts. He knew he must be on to something big, but he couldn't quite put the pieces together.

He pulled up the reports he had saved onto his phone and scrolled through them again. The police had been searching for Cindy Liu as a "person of interest" four years ago in a kidnapping case. She looked harmless enough in her photograph: an older Eurasian woman wearing a lab coat, the expression on her face intense and serious. Not the expected vision of a kidnapper. She didn't look strong enough to take someone by force.

The next reports covered the fire in the Riverside neighborhood, a site he'd already visited. He couldn't find any reports closing the case, either by naming the cause or accusing an arsonist. The same photograph had been used in all the reports, asking for anyone who had seen Cindy Liu to contact the police.

Around the same time, Mary's mother had been reported missing. That case had more news coverage, including a sighting of Helen Braeburn at an Urgent Care Center and a clip of a hysterical doctor who claimed she had threatened him with fire and forced him to treat a broken foot. Darrin narrowed his eyes, watching it again. The man seemed genuinely frightened. Something strange had definitely happened to him.

He wrote the doctor's name down in his notebook and turned back to the reports.

He found one final article stating that Helen's car had been located in the college impound lot. The same article mentioned the car had been towed on April 17, the date of the flamethrower incident on campus. Mary herself made an appearance in that piece, pleading with the public to share any information they might have, and asking her mother to let someone know if she was okay.

Darrin's heart sped in his chest. Helen Braeburn and Cindy Liu. It kept circling back to those two women. No one knew where Cindy Liu had gone—but Helen's daughter was right here in Springfield. He'd have to get Mary to talk to him.

He reached for his cinnamon roll and found only crumbs on his plate. He checked his phone and found he'd been sitting there for an hour. More than thirty minutes had passed while he'd pondered the story. *What happened to Mary?*

He looked around, scanning for the blue kerchief she'd been wearing over her hair. His excitement sank into his stomach and wriggled uncomfortably around the sugar and caffeine.

Damn it. She'd bolted. His lead was gone, at least for now.

Darrin stood to leave, shoving his phone into his pocket and picking up his dishes.

"She's not coming," a voice said.

Darrin turned to find a man watching him. A tall, impressively-shouldered White man, with a jutting heroic chin and bushy eyebrows, leaned against a tree with a casual air that didn't match the finely tailored suit and expensive shoes he wore.

Darrin had no idea who he might be. "Looks that way," he said, shrugging.

The man approached. As he walked, he seemed to appear and disappear, jumping ahead two or three steps in a single movement, making Darrin blink and wipe at his eyes. Maybe he was more tired than he realized. It had been a busy few days. He hadn't slept much.

"May I?" The man pulled out the second chair.

Darrin nodded and fell back into his own seat, pushing his dirty dishes off to the side. He couldn't have explained why, but he felt instinctively he should trust this man, that whatever this person wanted to tell him was of utmost importance. He folded his hands in front of him, listening intently.

The other man steepled his fingers in front of his face, and the two studied each other for a long moment.

"I need you to do me a favor," the man finally said, speaking slowly, putting pauses between each word and tapping his fingers together to emphasize "you," "me," and "favor." He leaned across the table so his face was near enough Darrin's to make him uncomfortable. His visage came in and out of focus, making Darrin's stomach lurch.

"What?" Darrin's own voice became small and shaky.

"It's a small thing, really. Insignificant." The last word stretched long, streaking through Darrin's mind like a Zamboni, smoothing out any jagged shards of worry.

Goodwill washed over Darrin. This man was a good guy. He wouldn't ask anything untoward. It was only reasonable to listen to his request. "Shoot," he said. "Let's hear it."

The man nodded. "Let this one go."

Darrin frowned. He had almost agreed without question. That didn't make sense. His job demanded he pursue leads and find the truth, and he'd almost promised to let go a juicy story go without even learning why. *What was going on here?*

He rubbed at his forehead. "I'm sorry. I'm not feeling very well." Darrin leaned away, trying to focus on the grass between his feet and fighting the nausea that threatened to bring up his cinnamon roll and coffee.

The man's voice was soothing, like water running slowly over rocks in a stream. "You should get some rest. You're working too hard."

The headache intensified, making Darrin's eyes water. Maybe this man had a point. He hadn't slept properly in days. It was affecting his ability to think clearly. He should go home and go to bed. Then he could come back with fresh eyes and work on...whatever he'd been working on.

"Maybe you're right," Darrin said. He stood, a little unsteady on his feet. "Thanks, Mister?" He realized he didn't know the man's name. At the same moment, his vision seemed to blur, the man's face morphing before his eyes into an entirely different face.

"Let me take you home," the man said, taking Darrin's arm and settling it atop his own. "You seem a little unsteady on your feet."

Nodding, Darrin let the man lead him away.

FATHER DOESN'T KNOW BEST

E verything in the past year had led to this moment, and now
Cindy would have her chance to confront her father. Even if it
meant she lost the little bit of goodwill she'd built at the UCU, it
would be worth it.

Having flung the door shut behind her, Cindy scrambled across
the kitchen and slid around the corner, hurrying down the narrow
hallway that led to the basement access. She hoped to gain a few
moments lead before Patricia and the rest of the UCU team made it
past the rudimentary security system.

She knew exactly where to go. There was only one place that made
sense to build the laboratory in this house: the basement. She'd
studied the floor plans on the sly over the past few months. Her
browser history had, of course, been observed, but since she'd also
looked at floor plans of houses in California, Paris, and Maine, among
other places, it hadn't attracted undue attention.

When asked, she'd claimed to find it soothing—imagining the
places she might go, might live, if she had her freedom. One of the
advantages of having the body of a child again was the way people
wanted to believe the best about her. Some of the guards were ridiculously easy to manipulate.

She'd used that to her advantage in her escape attempt a few months earlier. It would have worked, but her impatience tripped her up again. She'd used the chameleon formula too soon and nearly killed herself. Since then, she'd been watched too carefully to have another chance at escape.

When it came to this moment, though, she'd been very, very patient. She'd thought through hundreds of scenarios that might get her here, to Ohio, to her father's secret lab. And then the opportunity had been dropped in her lap, and strangely enough, Patricia was responsible for it, at least indirectly.

The blond girl, clearly besotted, would have done almost anything to save her beloved Lizard Woman—including taking Cindy Liu to the one place she'd been most anxious to get to since her capture by the UCU. She couldn't have designed a better opportunity for herself.

Knowing she had a matter of minutes—maybe seconds—before the others got inside, she yanked on the door handle, only to have it snap back up. Locked. She looked around for another keypad but didn't find one. Around the corner in the living room, she heard movement but kept her focus on solving the problem in front of her. She'd get caught or she wouldn't. But if she worried about what came behind her, she definitely would.

No keypad. No keyhole. Squinting, she thought about the door to her father's main lab at the campus in Indiana. She knelt and examined the handle more closely. It was ringed with a set of numbers. Of course—a combination lock. Gripping the handle again, she pushed it in and turned it to 8-10-10, August 10, 1910, his original birthdate, five bodies and lives ago. Right-left-right, like an old-fashioned high school locker. Someone should really tell him his passwords were entirely predictable.

The door popped open, and she slipped through, yanking it closed behind her. She stood for a moment, listening.

Her father's croaking voice crackled, sounding quite near. "Mekai? Is our guest secure for the night?"

Cindy held her breath. Mekai Davis? Did he still protect her father? Her mind composed a highly distracting vision of the well-muscled gunman—with his teasing smile and forthright gaze—who'd been part of her daring escape and the rescue of her father. She'd thought he was on her side, right up until she'd gotten herself captured and Mekai and her father had left her to rot in a UCU cell.

She shook herself. She'd deal with Mekai later. Right now, she needed to find out what her father was doing.

Sliding her hands over her hair to smooth it down, Cindy descended the stairs cautiously, listening. She heard sounds of drawers opening and closing, and a man humming tunelessly. As she neared the bottom stair, she picked up the faint burbling of a liquid being heated.

When she reached the last step, she leaned out around the corner. A long white table lined one wall, and her father, in the body of the long-dead scientist Daniel Price, moved among machines, peering into them and muttering to himself.

Seeing the man still in the same body he'd inhabited when she'd last seen him filled her with a glow of pride. Her serum had worked, keeping this body functional and eliminating the need for further killing. At the same time, a red-hot rage rose within her—here the man sat in another lab, free, enjoying the fruits of her labor, while she had spent months in captivity. Had he even attempted her rescue? It looked like he'd been happy to use her to affect his own escape.

"Hello, Dad," she said.

The man startled and jockeyed to maintain his hold on the vial in his hand, a vial of a very familiar-looking green elixir. Whirling, he faced her, eyes wide with shock. Before he got his borrowed face under control, Cindy read excitement, fear, guilt, and anger in his visage.

"Cindy?"

Stupid to make it a question, but she could see why her presence might come as a surprise, since he believed her safely incarcerated several states away. She didn't answer and instead took in the contents of the room. There was something familiar about the setup, and not just because laboratories everywhere have a homogeneity.

Feigning casual interest, she circled, peering at charts on the wall and running her fingers across supply bottles, keeping a healthy space between them as she explored. A bar ran along the wall, though the shelves were lined with bottles of chemicals rather than alcohol. A set of decrepit living room furniture had been stacked against another wall, making room for the table and supplies in what had obviously once been an extra living room for the people who had lived in this house.

She'd spotted the supply of emeralds in glass jars at the far end immediately and recognized them for what they were: an attempt to replicate and steal her research. But she'd let him think she hadn't yet noticed, for a little while anyway. She still didn't know why he wanted Patricia's mother, and that was an answer she wanted very much.

He'd sent no ransom note, so it wasn't leverage he'd sought.

If he hoped to hurt Patricia this way, exacting a kind of vengeance for ruining his plan to move into another body, he was barking up the wrong tree. Patricia and her mother had never been at all close—he'd have done better to kidnap the blonde.

It didn't make sense. Why risk his situation? What did he think he had to gain?

From the corner of her eye, Cindy made note of the scalpel lying within easy reach of her father's fingers and calculated the odds that he would use it against her, given the chance. She slowly turned to meet his gaze, letting her loathing crawl across her face as she did.

Price grimaced. His whole face moved when he did, though, a sign her serum continued to keep the mind-body connection and neuro-chemical systems functioning. Her stomach twisted a little in disgust. She'd made the decision to help keep the man standing, but it made her feel strange—proud of her work, and also ashamed that the work had not been worthy of her. She felt like a grave robber or a necromancer. Keeping criminals alive was not what she had envisioned for her research.

She grunted, waving a hand at his person. "How's your meat sack holding up? I see you're still wearing the same man you were when I last saw you."

"Must you always be so crass? It's unbecoming in a young lady."

222

Cindy laughed. "Are you still trying to convince yourself that 'young lady' is a phrase that applies to me? We both know I am neither young nor a lady, just as you are neither gentle nor quite a man...anymore."

"Listen here!"

There it was—the imperious tone she'd resented so severely when she'd been under his thumb, reliant on him to provide lab space, materials, and equipment—things she needed to control her own condition and to set her clock moving forward again instead of dragging her backward toward childhood.

She had gotten under his skin, knocking him off-balance, which is where she needed him. She pressed her advantage. "Why should anyone listen to *you*? A failed scientist. A failed man?"

He spluttered with rage. "My work—"

"Is a waste of resources. All this to do what? Extend your own life by a couple of decades? You might have lived this long with good diet and exercise alone." She sneered. "Hardly worth the lives of all the men you killed."

She crossed in three quick steps to the collection of gemstones and picked up a jar, holding it as if she might hurl it at his head. "And after I saved your worthless ass, you were going to steal my work, twisting it for your own ends, too?"

The scalpel was in his hand now. He held it in front of him, the hand steadier than it had been when last they met. "It's not like that. I wanted to understand and further your work. I intended to help you."

"To help me?" Cindy's voice cracked, rage purpling her face. "Bullshit."

"Language."

"Fuck my language. Don't even pretend you did any of this for me—it's all still about you, about cheating death, no matter what it costs, no matter who it hurts. What would Daniel Price think of you now?"

"Pot. Kettle. Black." He lifted the scalpel and stabbed it into the tabletop where it stuck and vibrated. "You stand there in the body of a child and dare to accuse me of selfish interest? We are the same, you and I."

"At least this body is my own. Who have you ever helped?"

His mouth compressed into a thin purplish line, a slash across the borrowed face. "I could ask you the same."

Cindy took a deep breath, swallowing the anger that burnt through her—she needed to stay in control, not justify herself to a madman. Angling for his pride, she snapped, "Don't waste my time—can you even understand my work?"

"I—understand—your." He spit as he ranted. "Impudent child. How dare you denigrate my understanding when clearly you don't even see the implications of your own discoveries. If you had, you never would have ended up where you did."

He paused, taking a more placating tone. "If we could recreate the effects on command we could overcome time itself."

"We?" She swallowed the bile climbing up her throat, pretending interest.

"Yes! With my experience and insight, and your formula, we'd be unstoppable."

She arched an eyebrow at him. "And what is this supposed insight you bring to the table? Because, from here, this unstoppable team looks a lot like exploitation and robbery."

"Heredity."

Cindy stared at him, waiting for him to go on. She knew he would. The man loved to hear himself talk.

"Patricia wasn't the only woman to use your skin cream, but the streets aren't overrun with reptilian superwomen, are they? The same with your flighty little friend and the muscle-bound man who invaded your lab. Even you yourself."

He stepped toward her, a manic light gleaming in his eye. "When I found out Patricia's mother lived so nearby, it was too tempting not to go to the source and find the anomaly that made her react when no one else has."

His voice dropped to a lower tone, confidential. "I meant to help you—to forward your work in preparation for your release."

Did he really think she hadn't considered why her product worked on some people in strange and unusual ways? She'd sold hundreds of bags of mood-lightening tea, but Jessica alone had developed the power of flight by drinking it. She'd done steady business in self-care products through farmer's markets and co-op stores for years without incident. Of course there was something different about the few women who had developed mutations.

"And you thought kidnapping an old woman and subjecting her to tests would be the best way to help me?"

A flash of anger reddened his pale cheeks for a moment. He suppressed the reaction and kept his voice quiet, but the shaking of the hand pressed against the table revealed the depth of his outrage. "Of course. If I could replicate your results, I'd have a bargaining chip, something to trade with the UCU to get you back."

Cindy scoffed at the suggestion he had any such intentions. More likely, he'd prayed she'd never get free, leaving him to appropriate her work and present it as his own. Maybe even use it to gain favor with his government contacts again, get a juicy contract and all the benefits that came with it. His self-justification stunk of desperation.

As if the obvious question had just occurred to him, he stopped and narrowed his eyes at her. "How exactly did you get away?"

Cindy slid a smile onto her face slowly. "Oh, I didn't."

Above them, a thump sounded against the floor. Angry voices whirred like bees. With surprising alacrity, Cindy's father leapt for a small, tan box on the counter. He pressed a button yelling, "Mekai!"

Cindy raised the jar of emeralds and brought it down on the back of his head. He dropped. For a moment, she stood, listening, but heard no signs of anyone coming to investigate.

Moving quickly, she checked his pulse—strong and regular. She unplugged the intercom box he'd used to call for help and bound his hands to a support post. It wasn't a great knot, but it ought to slow him down enough for someone to come and get him.

Grabbing the jar of emeralds, she headed for the stairs.

WHAT COMES AROUND

Outside the house, Patricia cursed. "I'll tear the door off!" she growled, stomping the pavement hard enough to spread new cracks in the pebbled concrete.

"No need for that now." Sally Ann stepped forward. "I got the code."

Suzie looked puzzled and a little impressed. "How?"

Sally Ann winked and waggled her fingers, shorter than explaining that her psychic gift, once limited to lifting emotional impressions from paper, had been steadily growing since the team had fought The Six. They'd have questions later, but right now, all that mattered was getting inside. She typed in the security code—using the digits she'd heard Dr. Liu chanting in her head as she'd opened the door.

It would have been more useful if her Spidey sense had warned her about Liu's intended betrayal a little further in advance, but her gift wasn't that reliable, and she'd take what favors fortune granted and make the rest for herself.

"Let's go!" She pushed the door open and dove through it, rolling to the right and landing in a fight-ready crouch, only to find herself in a perfectly ordinary and quite empty suburban kitchen, facing no immediate threat.

Behind her, Patricia growled. "Where'd she go?"

"Flygirl, you're with me. Suzie, Patricia—upstairs."

Patricia flung herself up the stairs, taking the entire set in three long strides and breaking off a chunk of the polished wooden banister in the process. Suzie followed a bit more sedately.

The downstairs consisted of a living room and a dining room, separated by a partial wall and a small room with the door closed. In the living room, the television played to an empty room, running an old cop show. Ignoring the background chatter, Sally Ann tuned in on the details. The pillow in the large armchair still carried the impression of a human backside. A mug of something sitting on the side table steamed. Whoever had been there must still be nearby.

Moving slowly, Sally Ann considered the possible hiding places as she slipped her baton into her hand, thumb on the button that would spring it out to full length. Behind her, the smallest squeak of floorboard offered warning. In an instant, Sally Ann flung herself over the abandoned chair, swinging around to face her attacker.

A broad-shouldered Black man stood at the bottom of the stairs training a gun on Sally Ann. "Who are you?"

Sally Ann swung her staff across her body, carefully avoiding glancing up at the ceiling where Flygirl now hovered, awaiting the best moment to drop into the fight. "Don't worry about me," she said. "Let's talk about you, Mekai Davis."

The man was good. The faintest twitch in his jaw betrayed his surprise at being recognized and named. Sally Ann had recognized him instantly as the man who had fought Gabe Driver in a Qmart parking lot, aiding Dr. Liu and her psychopath of a father in evading capture. She owed him a beating for that.

She shifted her staff in her hands, but Mekai never broke concentration, keeping his pale brown eyes focused and the gun aimed squarely at the lower half of her face and upper torso—the least armored and protected part of her body. "Why would a man with your training and expertise be here in Nowhere, Ohio, guarding a madman and aiding and abetting the kidnapping of a nice old lady?"

The corners of his mouth tugged downward, and he managed to

shrug with his eyebrows. "You go where they send you." His voice took on a bitter edge.

"Damn. Who did you piss off?"

Suspicion glinted in his eyes. Time to act. He would figure out Sally Ann hadn't come alone soon, and no one was getting shot on her watch—not again. Not if she had anything to say about it. She stood her staff upright at her side and tapped it against the floor.

Flygirl, taking her cue, swooped in from behind and plummeted like an eagle snagging a fish from the sea. She flew across Mekai's body in a fluid movement. Using the full momentum of her flight, she pushed his gun arm out and away from his body and twisted the hand until the weapon fell on the hardwood floor. At the same time, Sally Ann leapt forward, vaulting over the chair and pushing the button to run an electric current through her staff as she thrust it against the man's neck.

He flailed for a moment, muscular arms pulling at the staff, but Sally Ann kept it wedged in place until he finally dropped to the floor. "Help me roll him over."

Flygirl knelt beside her on the floor, and the two of them rolled the bulky man onto his side and then his stomach. Sally Ann bent his arms back and cuffed his wrists, then the two women maneuvered him into a sitting position and leaned him against the newel post at the bottom of the stairs, out of the way and easy to keep an eye on.

"So this is the guy Gabe fought?" Flygirl studied the unconscious man's face.

Sally Ann nodded, picking up the gun, removing the magazine, and clearing the chamber. She examined the room, listening for signs of anyone coming to investigate. Nothing, though she could hear Patricia and Suzie stomping around on the floor above.

Waving at the other rooms, she called to Jessica. "Find Liu." She still seethed that the scientist had slipped past her, but the slippery little woman wouldn't get away. She'd make sure of that.

MEETING MOTHER

Suzie followed Patricia up the stairs, wondering if she should have stayed back at the Dact with Driver. But once she'd gotten Patricia back in sight, she'd been unwilling to let her out again. So here she was in the hidden lair of a mad scientist, following her half-dinosaur girlfriend with an ill-fitting Kevlar vest to protect her from whatever surprises they uncovered.

"Stand still for a minute," she said. "I can't hear with you thumping around."

Patricia obeyed, and for a moment, the two of them stood at the foyer at the top of the stairs and listened. On the floor below, they could hear Sally Ann's voice, but there'd been no call for backup, so whatever was happening down there, she and Flygirl had it handled.

That hadn't been what had caught Suzie's attention. No, the sound she'd stopped to listen for had been a low, steady thumping—like a washing machine knocked out of balance, or someone pounding on a thick door.

After a moment's silence, the pounding resumed at a fast tempo. "You hear it, right?"

"This way." Patricia followed the hallway to the left, doing her best to move quietly—none too easy a task in her new armored state.

Suzie's gaze crept back up to the new protrusions from Patricia's skull, then down the glossy new golden scales striping through her customary green and brown. Entranced with the reflections on the scales, she didn't notice when Patricia stopped moving and narrowly missed impaling herself on one of the spikes protruding from her upper arm.

Refocusing, she heard it again. Slow, steady banging. The sound had shifted to a higher register as if the drummer had switched to a different kind of drumstick. "Third door," Suzie said, moving closer to examine what appeared to be an ordinary bedroom door similar to the other three lining the hallway.

The banging ceased. Taking off her shoe, Suzie banged the traditional "shave and a haircut" rhythm and was rewarded with two quick taps in response. Then the banging resumed, harder and faster. If Patricia's mother was being held here, she might be trying to signal her location. Of course, it could also be a trap or someone else entirely. Only one way to find out. Suzie slipped her shoe back on and stepped to the side, gesturing at the door.

Patricia backed up against the other wall. The narrow hallway barely accommodated her bulk, but Suzie slid around the Lizard Woman and out of the way, back into the wider foyer at the top of the stairs where she could watch for anyone coming to investigate the ruckus they were about to make.

Patricia threw her considerable bulk at the door, making the entire second story shake in response. The decorative mirror hanging on the wall at the top of the stairs slid askew and pictures dropped off the wall, but the door held.

It now featured a deep dent in the shape of Patricia's shoulder and upper arm, but it remained sealed and locked. Definitely not an ordinary bedroom door, then, despite appearances. Patricia threw herself at the door three more times, but the cramped quarters made it hard to build any momentum, and the end result left three more dents in the still-closed door.

Suzie looked around for a way to help. A small table beneath the mirror held what looked like a remote control to a television. She picked it up, considering the device, while Patricia pummeled the door, growling and cursing. The simple buttons were unlabeled and there was no brand name.

When Patricia stopped, wedging herself into the corner to try again from another angle, Suzie shouted at her to stop. "Let me try something."

She aimed the controller at the door and clicked the green arrow. A distinct click sounded. Grinning, Patricia gripped the knob and twisted, shoving the door as she did. It gave, flinging open so hard it bounced off something inside and almost slammed closed again, but Patricia had shoved a taloned foot into the doorway.

"Don't come any closer!" A woman's voice cried out, forceful despite the tremble of fear lacing the words. "I'm armed."

Patricia stepped into the darkened room, and Suzie followed, staying close enough to hide behind her girlfriend's bulletproof bulk. "What's your mom's last name?" Suzie hissed.

"Carter," Patricia hissed back.

"Mrs. Carter? Are you all right? We've come to get you out of here."

The room was dark, but Suzie made out some movement on the far side of the bed. A short, curvaceous woman of maybe seventy or seventy-five years wearing purple pajamas stood in the shadows, a bedside lamp in her hands, raised as if she intended to throw it. Sweaty strawberry blond hair stuck to her face, and Suzie spotted the shoe, shampoo bottle, alarm clock, and television remote on the floor —the items she had used to bang on the door.

Patricia seemed to have frozen in place. Suzie stepped out from behind her, holding out her hands to show they were empty. "Mrs. Carter? It's going to be okay. We're here to help you, not hurt you."

The woman's gaze bounced over Suzie and back to Patricia. The sight of Patricia would give a lesser woman a heart attack, but this one narrowed her eyes and gripped the lamp harder, raising it again.

Without taking her eyes off the looming dinosaur that had come to her rescue, Babs spoke to Suzie. "What is that thing? Who are you?"

"We're here to help, Mrs. Carter," Suzie began, but stopped when Patricia rested a taloned hand on her shoulder.

"It's me, Mom." Patricia finally spoke, her voice thick and raspy as it became when she was transformed.

Babs blanched, pulling the lamp back into swinging position again as if it were a baseball bat. "Turn on the lights," she said.

Suzie found the switch and flipped it on.

A gasp escaped Babs, and the lamp slid out of her hands and fell to the carpet, bouncing at her feet. Suzie rushed to grab the older woman's arm, worried she would be the next thing to hit the floor, and Babs seized at her with surprising strength. Suzie began to guide her toward an armchair a few feet away. "Maybe you should sit down," she said.

Still in the doorway, Patricia stood silent. This would be a great time for her to revert to her human face, but Suzie knew Patricia lacked the power to do that at the moment.

Babs allowed Suzie to help her to the chair, never looking away from her daughter. Only after she was seated did she look more fully at Suzie. "Who are you?"

"Suzie Grayson, ma'am. Part of your rescue team."

"Rescue team?"

"Yes, ma'am. Daniel Price is a wanted criminal. We've been hunting him for a while now." She exaggerated. Price was indeed a criminal, but it was unclear who wanted him or if he would even see prosecution for his crimes. The UCU had been stymied in pursuit of him after Indiana. Suzie had scheduled several clandestine meetings between the Director and shadowy figures of the government, but the details remained known to the close-mouthed Director alone.

Babs squeezed Suzie's fingers. "Suzie, right?"

Suzie nodded.

"Patty's girlfriend?"

Unsure what Patricia might have told her mother, Suzie shot a helpless look at Patricia, who blinked with both sets of eyelids and groaned aloud.

Babs's face went a little dreamy. "I thought maybe. I saw the pictures on Patty's Instagram. Annie showed me." She patted Suzie's hand. "You're a pretty little thing, aren't you?"

Suzie blushed. She'd never felt this awkward in her life. "Thank you."

Babs pushed herself to her feet and took three steps forward before she stopped. She stared at Patricia—her lips pursed in consideration, an expression Suzie recognized as one Patricia often wore when trying to make a decision. After several seconds of examination, she clucked her tongue. "Patty Jean? Can it really be you in there?"

Patricia nodded vigorously, the motion causing the yellow spikes on her shoulders to wobble, and her red hair to slide across the new plates on her head. She seemed to try to draw herself in, to appear smaller and less threatening, but the effort was useless without the ability to control her transformation. She held out her hands. "It's me, Mama. I can explain. But first, we need to get you out of here."

"Well." The woman bent, picked up the lamp, set it down on the side table, and then wiped her hands down the legs of her pajamas. She came around the bed slowly, her face opening in wonder the nearer she got to her daughter. When she stood in front of the Lizard Woman, she placed her hands on her hips and stared up at Patricia's face, a strange smile taking over her face. She surprised them all by starting to laugh.

She reached out a hand to Suzie, who took it. "Come here, sweetheart. I thought you were the biggest secret in my Patty Jean's life, but it looks like you're just the best one." She pulled Suzie into a tight hug that smelled of lavender and sweat, then pushed her back. She held Suzie's arms out and examined her, then turned back to Patricia.

"Cute," she said, hooking a thumb at Suzie, who couldn't decide if she should be offended or relieved. "Kind of young, but smart, too, I'm sure, or you wouldn't waste your time."

Hesitatingly, Babs reached out a slender, well-manicured finger and poked Patricia in the arm, eyes widening at the contact, then ran both her hands along her daughter's arms and probed at one of the spikes on her back.

"You know," she said, grinning at Suzie. "This actually explains a lot."

EMERALDS ARE A HERO'S BEST FRIEND

Walter entered Leonel's room, setting the lights a little higher. Leonel huddled in the corner, arms folded across his knees, face hidden. To look at the room, one would think there had been an earthquake. Cracks ran through the floor and up the walls and crumbled bits of wood and brick littered the floor.

Someone had gathered the pieces into a neat pile, leaving the area where Leonel rested empty of obstructions. He must have heard the door, but he hadn't raised his head to see who entered.

"Leonel?" Walter spoke quietly. "Are you awake?"

"I am," came the quiet answer. He raised his head slowly, letting his legs fall to the sides and meeting Walter's gaze with watery, bloodshot eyes.

Walter had often been jealous of the handsome hero. Once, he had even thought Leonel his rival for Jessica's heart—the two of them were so close. But now, he wouldn't trade his life with Leonel for all the gold in Fort Knox, not even if he got the super-strength and good looks, too.

The man looked terrible, exhaustion and worry hollowing his cheeks and huge dark circles blooming under his eyes. The past few days had reduced him to a shell of himself, a picture of misery that belonged in a dungeon in the Bastille, not the glossy smooth UCU facility.

Walter swallowed and made himself put on a bright face as he approached, disguising his dismay over Leonel's condition. "I have something I want to try," Walter said. "I don't know for sure it will work."

A dim light ignited in Leonel's eyes. He licked his dry lips. "I'll try anything."

He rested a hand on the floor to push himself up, but the floor tile cracked under his fingers, and Leonel snatched them back, pinning the offending hand against his chest as if it might escape and wreak havoc in the world. Slumped on the floor, he looked Walter in the face, a heartbreaking desperate hope exuding from him. His voice cracked when he asked, "What do you need me to do?"

Walter knelt on the floor beside Leonel and pulled the necklace he had constructed from his pocket, holding it up for Leonel to see. Guilt filled his stomach at the thought that he might be torturing the man with false promises, but there was no other way to find out if his idea held any weight. He had to try it on someone.

Speaking softly, Walter shared his hope that the wearing of the stones would stabilize Leonel's condition and that of the others who suffered from new mutations.

Leonel gasped. "Others? I thought it was just me." He paled beneath his golden-brown skin. "Jessica?"

"She's fine."

"Gracias a Dios."

"In fact, she's the only one that is." He told Leonel about Helen's destruction of her fireproof cell and Patricia's new developments. Jessica had sent pictures, and the two men whistled over the changes in their favorite lizard woman.

"I thought she was scary before," Leonel admitted.

Walter pressed his lips together. "She was. Now she's...bigger. And she can't change back." He went on, giving a brief summary of the happenings around the city among the Liu-vians on their watch list.

"The Lightning Woman in the park was the first, we think. And now I'm wondering about the man at the mall."

"But not our Jessica."

"No. Not her." Walter rested the emerald in the palm of his hand and explained his hypothesis that the gemstones and not the cancer made Jessica different from the other Liu-vians.

"I see. You want to try this out on me first, before you offer it to the others. In case it doesn't work. I will be your guinea pig?"

"At worst, I expect it will do nothing at all. At best...."

"I will do it." There was no hesitation in Leonel's voice.

Leonel submitted meekly, careful not to touch Walter as he placed the necklace around Leonel's neck and arranged it so the cut of gemstone rested flat against his chest. Though the lights in the room were still dim, the jewel glinted against Leonel's skin, shining as if lit from within.

"It is warm," he said.

Walter nodded. He'd felt the same thing, holding the rock in his hand. "Do you feel any different?"

Leonel shook his head. "No. But I didn't feel any different when I destroyed my kitchen either." He looked around at the destroyed hospital room. "Or this furniture. Until I touch something, I don't feel any different."

The two men sat in silence for a long moment.

Finally, Leonel asked, "How will we know if it works?"

"We'll have to test it." Walter picked up a chair leg from the pile of ruined furniture by the window and laid it in front of Leonel. "Pick it up. Try not to break it."

Leonel eyed the chunk of thick wood warily, before reaching out to rest a finger on it. Both men held their breath as they watched. Walter half-expected it to crumble to dust before their eyes.

It remained intact.

Letting out a shaky breath, Leonel extended his hand and wrapped his fingers around the leg loosely, forming a cup with his palm, the way he might have picked up a kitten. A glimmer of hope flickered in his light brown eyes. He tightened his grip slowly, and the wood cracked.

Walter fetched another chair leg and held it out to Leonel. Frowning, Leonel took it, and transferred the object to his other hand, reverting to a looser hold. Slowly, he tightened his fingers, experimenting to find the balance between destruction and strength.

Watching, Walter held his breath. From what Jessica had told him, the reaction had been instantaneous—the first time she flew with the gems on her person, she gained control over her mercurial relationship with gravity. But this wasn't medicine. He had no idea how long an exposure might be needed, or what size fragment of the gemstone might prove enough for efficacy. It would all be trial and error, and the best he could strive for would be to minimize the error.

As he continued to manipulate the chair leg, relief flooded Leonel's face. Walter ignored the tears that began to stream from the hero's eyes. Leonel wept easily under normal circumstances, and the past few days had been trying beyond compare.

Walter wanted to cheer and run a victory lap around the room, but he knew that a step forward did not yet make a full victory, so he forced himself to be more circumspect. "I'm going to send someone to run some tests and help you find your balance."

Leonel stood, stretching his arms toward the ceiling, pulling his posture erect for the first time in days. He bounced the chair leg in his palm, like a weapon. "Thank you," he said, holding an arm toward Walter, but stopping before taking Walter's hand, caution overtaking his enthusiasm.

Sweeping a hand through the heavy waves of his hair, Leonel grimaced. "When we are sure I will not break it, I would also like a shower, please."

Walter smiled. "I'm sure that can be arranged."

FEROCITY RUNS IN THE FAMILY

S ally Ann knelt to look into Mekai Davis's face. She couldn't figure him out. His record showed a stellar service history full of commendations and awards, yet he had been stationed in podunk Ohio guarding a walking corpse. It reeked of retribution, the way her own assignment to desk work had, back before the Director recruited her. She had refused to protect a rich and influential criminal, and since they couldn't fire her, they tried to make her quit. She'd genuinely like to hear this man's story someday.

She updated Gabe, asking him to come to the house. "Bring the wagon," she texted. Davis was a big fella, a good two hundred and fifty or two hundred and seventy pounds, by her estimate, and all muscle. If they had to haul Davis and Price back with them, the extra hands would be useful and so would the wheels. Plus, she wanted to give Gabe a chance to get back some of his own. She hadn't forgotten his busted face after that fight.

Flygirl landed beside her. "Nothing on this floor. Want me to try upstairs?"

Sally Ann listened. She could make out Patricia and Suzie's voices and another woman's voice—older, probably the mother. No explosions of outrage. She shook her head. "I don't think she's up there."

Mekai Davis remained still—so still Sally Ann doubted he was actually still unconscious.

Gesturing to Flygirl to keep her distance, the team leader squatted beside the man and poked him with her staff. His head lolled more forcefully than the gentle push warranted, and she laughed.

"Faker."

Mekai opened his eyes and glared at her. "You electrocuted me."

Sally Ann stood, shortened her staff, and clipped it in place at the small of her back. "Nah. I shocked you. You seem plenty alive to me. If I'd electrocuted you, we wouldn't be having this lovely little chat."

He narrowed his eyes at her. "What do you want?"

"Come on, now. Are we pretending you don't know who we are and why we're here?"

Mekai turned to point up the stairs with his chin. "Are you here for her?"

Sally Ann didn't answer.

"Good," he said. "I didn't sign on for kidnapping old ladies." He knocked his head against the bannister. "I didn't sign on for any of this. I should be in Washington, DC, guarding someone important to our country—not in Nowhere, Ohio babysitting a madman."

"Madman?"

All three of them jumped, and Flygirl didn't quite make it back to the ground.

Cindy Liu stood in the hall, a jar of emeralds in one hand and a hard drive in the other. "That's a little harsh, don't you think, Mekai?"

Flygirl crossed the room in a flash, leaping over the staircase and landing behind Cindy, blocking any retreat.

Sally Ann grunted her approval and stepped toward the pair of them, casually sliding her baton back into her hand. "I don't know. Seems pretty accurate to me. Where is your crazy, kidnapping, body-snatching old man, anyway? Did you kill him again?"

Cindy pointed behind her with the hard-drive at a door still standing open. "Downstairs. Still alive, or at least as alive as he was when I got here." She nodded at the man on the floor. "I see you've met Daddy's pet."

Mekai's face darkened dangerously, but he remained silent.

"We were having a pleasant little chat. Mekai put on a good show of remorse while he discovered the cuffs he's wearing aren't standard issue and that he won't be able to escape them as easily as he imagined." She tilted her head at her prisoner. "Ain't that right?"

The man's carefully expressionless face admitted the truth of her accusation.

No one else had come to investigate, suggesting Davis and Price were the only two people on the premises. The mighty had fallen, indeed. Sally Ann's phone chimed. A status update from Suzie. The old lady was okay.

Sally Ann waved her closed baton as if directing an airplane to land. "Come on over, Liu. There's room for you next to our Mr. Davis. Can't leave a woman your age standing around needlessly. It's hard on the knees. Besides, you guys are old friends, aren't you?"

Cindy grimaced, but after a quick glance at Flygirl's avid face, she obediently sat down beside the agent, though she kept hold of the hard drive and the emeralds. Davis glowered.

Moving into position to stand guard over them both, Sally Ann called out to Flygirl. "Why don't you check on the rest of our team, Flygirl?" She glanced up at the ceiling. "It's gone a little too quiet up there."

FLYGIRL DIDN'T WASTE any time arguing. Leaping into the air, she flew directly to the top of the stairs and jackknifed her body to make the corner. Downstairs, someone whistled, a slow exhalation of surprise. She thought it might have been Mekai.

A bedroom door bent almost concave made it obvious where the Lizard Woman and Suzie had gone. Flygirl floated up to the ceiling and flew just below it—her backside brushing against the Artex ceiling as she moved cautiously toward the room, listening for signs of what she would find and hearing only murmurs of muffled voices.

When she popped her head in, peeking in from the top of the door frame, a woman screamed. The Lizard Woman whirled while Suzie put an arm around the older woman. Flygirl grabbed the door frame and swung her body down, landing at the Lizard Woman's side. "Everything okay?"

The older woman, who had to be Patricia's missing mother despite the lack of physical resemblance, rested a hand on her heart and stared into Flygirl's masked face for a moment before turning a stern expression on the Lizard Woman. "Patty Jean, you might have warned me. What's next? An invisible ninja?"

Flygirl suppressed a laugh. A cute, little old lady in purple pajamas yelling at the Lizard Woman as if she were a wayward child might be the best thing she'd seen in a while. And calling her Patty Jean! Flygirl still hardly dared to use Patricia's full first name, let alone a nickname. Part of her still wanted to say "Yes, ma'am" or "Yes, Ms. O'Neill" every time Patricia spoke.

Smiling, she held out a hand. "I'm Flygirl. You must be Patricia's mother, Mrs . . .?"

"Carter, but you can call me Babs. Everyone does."

Not every seventy-five-year-old woman who'd been kidnapped, held against her will, and then confronted with a Lizard Woman and a flying woman could keep her equanimity, but Babs Carter stood solidly on her own feet, giving Flygirl's hand a firm shake. A quick assessment assured Flygirl that Babs was unharmed, at least physically. In fact, she looked damned good for a woman her age, purple pajamas or not—good genes. "All right, Babs, let's get you downstairs."

Babs gripped at Suzie's arm, a gesture Flygirl suspected was for show more than from actual need for comfort. "Are you sure? What about the guard? What about Daniel?"

"All taken care of," Flygirl reassured her.

"I'll go first," Patricia said. "Just in case."

Babs walked over to the bed and grabbed the pillow, tucking it under one arm.

"What?" she said, when the others stared at her. "It's a very good pillow. My neck hasn't felt this good in years. Besides, I can use it to smother Daniel when I get my hands on him." Babs grinned, all determination and challenge, and Flygirl finally saw the similarity to the Lizard Woman of Springfield. Maybe Patricia resembled her mother more than it had first appeared.

Patricia paused and peered down the stairs. Behind her, Babs still clung to Suzie's arm, but her head swiveled nonstop, taking in the details of the time capsule from the 1980s decor. She pointed out the crooked mirror, still hanging askew from Patricia's assault on the bedroom door. "I think I had that mirror when Patty Jean was a teenager. Where are we?"

Patricia flexed, making her body as broad as she could. "Stay behind me, Mom. I'm bulletproof."

Babs paled, whether at the consideration of flying bullets or the idea that her daughter could deflect the bullets with her flesh, Flygirl couldn't have said. But the woman jutted out her chin and gave a quick, decisive nod, the flash of ferocity in her visage reminding Flygirl of the Lizard Woman in human form again.

Letting go her hold on gravity, Flygirl floated back up to the ceiling, a position she'd learned often kept her out of harm's way while affording her an element of surprise, but she couldn't see past the bend in the stairs. Impatience rose in her, even though she acknowledged the sense in sending Patricia in front as a shield for the rest of them. She didn't like that Sally Ann was down there alone.

They rounded the landing, and Flygirl breathed a sigh of relief. The two captives had been moved to the sofa and Driver stood behind them, weapon at the ready. Sally Ann turned, relief flashing across her face before her usual cocky smirk hid her concern. "It's about time. What took you so long?"

Sally Ann's phone rang, startling all of them. She pulled it out and frowned at the screen before clicking to answer. "Rogers here."

Flygirl watched Sally Ann for a clue about what to expect, but the woman's face revealed nothing. After listening in silence for what seemed a very long time, she said, "I see," and hung up. All the mirth had gone out of her eyes, and Flygirl knew she didn't like the orders she'd been given.

"Seems like Tweedle Dee here still has some friends in high places. We're to leave them here and report back to base, ASAP."

"What?" Babs' face purpled with outrage and Patricia moved to keep her from hurling herself at Sally Ann. "You mean Daniel's not even going to jail for this?" Her voice rose in pitch, and her arms, still wrapped around the pillow, shook with rage. "He kidnapped me."

The corners of Sally Ann's mouth raised, far enough to reveal the dimple in her left cheek. "Oh, don't you worry. He'll get his. Not from us, but retribution is coming."

Mekai's eyes widened. Sally Ann laid a black business card bearing a phone number and no other words on the coffee table. She tapped it with a fingertip, looking Mekai in the eyes. "Call this number when you're ready to make a change." Then she nodded at Driver, who raised his gun and lowered it hard on the back of Mekai's head. The man slumped into the corner of the sofa, and Dr. Liu, still seated beside him, jumped up.

"What did you do that for?" she cried out.

"He had it coming." Sally Ann winked at Gabe Driver. "And we need a little time to get in the air before he makes a move." She dropped a small key on the coffee table beside the card, then waved to the group. "Let's go."

SALLY ANN'S FAITH

Sally Ann brooded as the Dact made its way across the sky back to Indiana. She should have been elated—the mission had been a success, and no one on her team had acquired so much as a skinned knee—but her joy and relief remained muted beneath an undefined dissatisfaction and worry. It didn't feel like a win. Not completely.

Leaving Daniel Price free rankled, even if the Director's talk of jurisdiction and assurances that Price would be brought to justice helped a little. Whatever partnership he had brokered with the people behind Price would lead in the right direction, she told herself. She almost believed it, too—all except for the tiny skeptical monster poking at her guts with its taloned fingers.

Damn, she missed the days when her faith in the man had been less complicated—when she'd believed what she saw matched reality. Ignorance really had been bliss. Knowing the man could manipulate her emotions and cloud her judgment brought every interaction into a harsh spotlight of second-guesses and suspicion. Constant skepticism and doubt exhausted her, leaving her weary in a way that time in the gym or in battle never did.

At least she had her team. She lifted her head to take in the others.

Babs chattered incessantly to Patricia and Suzie, and Sally Ann admired the old lady's ability to let go of trauma so quickly. Babs had a full, contagious laugh reminiscent of old movie stars and cocktail parties. Sally Ann had a feeling that for years to come, Babs would use this story to rule the bridge club, or bingo parlor, or wherever old ladies in the middle of Indiana gathered to gossip.

Even now, still dressed in borrowed pajamas and recently rescued from a kidnapping, she projected glamour and confidence as she peppered Suzie and Patricia with a barrage of questions.

In another mood, Sally Ann would have enjoyed Patricia's obvious discomfort over all the inquiries about her Lizard Woman alter ego and the probes into her love life with Suzie, but she was too deeply troubled to take the delight she might have.

Jessica, too, seemed melancholy. She stared off into the distance, eyes glassy in the shadows of her mask, suggesting her mind wandered somewhere else entirely—somewhere dark and unsettling. Knowing Flygirl, she had Fuerte on her mind.

Sally Ann did, too, remembering the strong man cowering in his hospital room, afraid to move lest he break something else. Watching Jessica, Sally Ann noticed the twist of her comrade's mouth, an expression she was starting to recognize as guilt. Only Jessica would feel guilty for staying healthy when others fell ill. Ridiculous, of course, but very Jessica—she'd sacrifice nearly anything to protect others.

Sally Ann sighed quietly. Recovering Patricia's mother solved half the problem. They still had to recover Patricia, the human version trapped in her scalier self, and find a way to help the rest of the Liuvians.

That broached the question of Cindy Liu, who had the opportunity to escape and didn't take it. Instead, she'd confronted her father, confiscated scientific information, and then returned to her captors. After her trick at the door, she'd expected to have to chase the teenaged senior citizen across suburbia, but the scientist had surprised them all by meekly returning. For a moment, the woman had felt like part of the team, a confusing idea that didn't fit with her previous conception of who Cindy Liu was and where her limits might lie.

Sally Ann's psychic abilities didn't give her the ability to predict the future, but she considered herself a good study of character and had a decent track record at predicting what others would do. Cooperation with her captors was not on her bingo card for a game of What-Would-Dr. Liu-Do.

But here the woman sat, hands calmly folded in her lap, face serene, staring out the window even though there was nothing to see but the occasional wisp of cloud or the shadows of trees. She seemed almost at peace. Or was that something else in her face, something more like smug satisfaction?

Letting her physical gaze grow fuzzy, Sally Ann reached out with the unnamed part of herself that gathered information from paper and sometimes people, a move she immediately regretted. It was like opening the door to a room and finding a rave going on inside. Emotions and thoughts plowed into her from all sides in a confusing, noisy mess. She slammed the mental door closed and rubbed her temples, feeling as though something had scraped at the inside of her skull, leaving scratches in the bone.

When her vision cleared, she found Dr. Liu watching her, an avid curiosity burning in her coal-black eyes. Sally Ann shuddered. It was like being observed by a tiger, lying still in its cage, tail twitching against the bars, waiting for the moment you let down your guard and it could eat you. Sally Ann stared back unblinking, and eventually Liu looked away, but Sally Ann didn't feel as if she'd won, more that the tiger had decided this wasn't yet the moment to show its strength.

Her musings came to an end when the Dact landed in the same field in Indiana where they'd picked up Patricia. A glance out the windows showed a small crowd gathered in front of the Carter abode —Patricia's sister and stepfather at the center, and a gathering of others that might have been friends, family, or nosy neighbors.

Annie must have gathered everyone together to wait with her and her father. That was always the danger with civilians—they didn't know when to keep their mouths shut. The PR guys would have to get creative with this one.

In a quick consultation, they agreed Patricia, Suzie, and Babs would go in, and Patricia and Suzie would be back on the Dact in fifteen minutes or Sally Ann would tase them herself.

The cargo ramp lowered and the Lizard Woman of Springfield, flanked by a tiny blonde and a curvaceous older woman, stepped out into the night.

THE LIZARD WOMAN IS OUTED

S uzie led the way, Babs still grasping her arm. The woman's grasp was fierce. When Patricia stepped into the light, a gasp went up from the gathered crowd. Some children who had been chasing each other around seconds before pulled together into a tight knot of bodies, the older ones automatically taking the hands of the younger ones. The adults' faces went slack with wonder, and they reached for each other. The night had gone so quiet, Suzie could make out the frog song from the pond in the backyard.

After a pause, Annie pushed her way through the group and let loose a whoop of joy. "Patricia! You did it! You brought her back!"

The girl ran down the short hill made by the driveway, hurrying toward the three women disembarking from the helicopter. She stumbled on the loose gravel and landed on her butt, but sprang back and flung herself at Patricia's middle, wrapping her arms around her scaly sister's midsection. Relief shone in her eyes as she swung around to grab her mother by the arms and tug her back toward the house.

"Mama's home!" she called out, pride and delight making her face glow under the yard lights. As she dragged Babs into the knot of gathered people, the silence lifted, becoming a tangle of voices talking all at once. Suzie watched in amazement, trying to imagine her stoic

Patricia growing up in such an atmosphere—the two-story house that listed a bit to the westward, yard littered with toys and odd lawn ornaments.

The contrast to Patricia's sleek and tasteful condo in Springfield couldn't be larger. How strange to imagine the intimidating red-headed woman who collected designer handbags and reveled in expensive theatre tickets growing up here, where the air smelled sweet and dusty, and you could see more stars than city lights. She'd always imagined Patricia had grown up much like herself—in an affluent household concerned about manners and appearances as much as right and wrong. Urban, sophisticated.

Behind her, Patricia stopped moving, too; the second time in a single night Suzie had seen her freeze—a hesitation completely unlike her. The Lizard Woman glanced back over her shoulder at the Dact like she was thinking about getting right back on it. Even though Suzie looked forward to a long soak and a good long sleep herself, she couldn't let Patricia slink off into the night without taking leave of her family.

Suzie looped her arm through Patricia's far larger and scalier arm and grinned up at her girlfriend. "Come on, sweetcheeks," she said. "Time to introduce me to your family."

Patricia's eyes widened, the fearful look comical in the scale-covered reptilian face. Suzie laughed. "After what they've seen tonight, I don't think they'll be shocked to find out you have a girlfriend. What are you afraid of?"

By the time the two of them covered the few yards to the top of the driveway, George had wrapped Babs in his arms, and two little kids clung to both her thighs. Her grown children gathered around here in a huddle, everyone talking at the same time and waving their arms in excited gestures.

Suzie let go of Patricia's arm and gave her a little shove.

Patricia growled but took another step forward. "Mom?"

At the raspy rumble of her voice, the group went silent again. Babs disentangled herself from her the arms of her husband and her grand-children and walked over to Patricia, a little wiggle making the wide legs of the pajama pants billow around her like the skirts of a gown. "Bend on down here, Sweetheart," she said.

Patricia obeyed, dropping to one knee, and her mother wrapped her in a hug, avoiding the shoulder spikes, and planting a kiss on her bumpy cheek. Somebody gasped in surprise. Someone else laughed, a nervous titter like a night bug. Everyone else sank into a shocked silence, staring with moon-eyes at their mother or grandmother embracing a monster.

Then Babs surprised Suzie, pulling her into her hip and giving her an uncomfortably tight squeeze and a wet smacking kiss on the cheek that tickled Suzie's ear. Suzie shot a look at Patricia, hoping for rescue, but found Patricia hiding her face with her taloned hands, shaking with laughter.

Turning to the group now staring at them, Babs cleared her throat. "This is Patty Jean's girlfriend, Suzie. She might look like a stiff wind would knock her over, but she's a formidable woman—just the kind to keep our Patty Jean in line. Let's welcome her to our family."

A half-hearted cheer made its way through the gathering, along with some muttering and whispering.

Stepping in front of the pair, Babs made an X of her arms and flung her hands to the sides, a defiant light flaring in her eyes. Suzie saw in that moment where Patricia had learned to shut down dissent and take control of a room.

Babs spoke softly, but with intensity, her face growing fierce. "I know how some of you all are, but if any of you have a problem with this, you'll have to take it up with me."

Several of the adults shuffled nervously. No one spoke.

Clapping her hands as if she'd been asked to give a toast at a party, she smiled prettily. "I am home safe, thanks to my daughters and their friends. I know you all have questions, but you're not getting any answers tonight. I'm tired and need a bath and a fourteen-hour nap."

Everyone laughed.

She grabbed Patricia's hand, and Patricia lumbered back to her feet, towering above the rest of her family.

Her mother patted her arm. "Patty Jean has got to get back to

Springfield tonight. She's got some superhero business to handle. But she and her Suzie have promised to be here for Thanksgiving, so you'll have plenty of time to figure out how not to stare."

Suzie shook her head. They'd made no such promise, but she had a feeling she knew where'd they'd find themselves this November. Babs made it hard to say no. Like mother, like daughter.

DARRIN'S LOST DAY

Gasping, Darrin woke. His heart raced with a wild panic, and his shirt stuck to him with sweat. His head felt like a bruised orange, squishy and rotten from the inside.

He sat up slowly, his stomach roiling at the change in orientation. He had to sit still for some minutes, hands over his eyes before he felt he could open them and look around without vomiting. When he did, he saw the sagging, overstuffed bookshelf and realized he was on the sofa in his own apartment. Why had he been sleeping on the couch? He couldn't remember coming home.

When he tried to recall what had transpired, a jagged flash of light cut across his memory, making his head throb anew and his stomach lurch. He breathed through it, determined to understand what had happened to him. The last thing he remembered was going to Our Market, but couldn't remember why he'd gone.

A few blurry images remained—his own hand on a coffee cup, the light through the leaves on a tree, Mary Braeburn's narrowed eyes, and a man he didn't recognize, lips sliding into a wide smile that seemed to grow larger than his face.

That last bit didn't make any sense. Had he been drugged?

Stumbling to the bathroom, Darrin turned on the shower and let the room fill with steam while he contemplated himself in the mirror. One of his eyes twitched a little in its socket, and he splashed cold water on his face, trying to jolt awareness into his senses. It didn't work. Everything felt fuzzy and strange, like he watched the world through a gauzy curtain he couldn't pull back.

Peeling off his shirt and jeans, he dropped the clothing into the hamper then pulled back the shower curtain. Still wobbly on his feet, he steadied himself against the wall to step over the side of the tub and into the stream of hot water. Turning around, he let the water beat against his back as he rested his head against the cool tile.

He tried again to retrace his steps. He'd gone to work that morning —was it still Sunday? He called out to the smart device he used to listen to music while he showered, "Alexa, what's the date?"

Yep. Still Sunday.

He straightened, pushing against the wall with his palms and stretching his back while he excavated his memory through the haze burying it. Restless after the unsatisfying ending to his date with Sally Ann the night before, he'd gone to work early. Nicole had come by his desk, wanting a favor. The favor turned out to be a jailhouse interview with Emilio Schulz, the strong man from the mall. He'd turned in his package, and then he'd gone to Our Market, which is where the trail seemed to run cold. He could remember arriving at the co-op store, but it was like the day stopped there and leapt forward to now.

He called out again. "Alexa, what time is it?"

Ten p.m.?

It had been past the lunch hour when he'd arrived at Our Market. That meant he'd lost nearly eight hours, a shocking gap in his memory.

He'd been tired. He could see falling asleep on the sofa, but that didn't explain why he couldn't remember what happened at Our Market or how he'd gotten home.

As the water ran over his skin, he tested for pain and injury, trying to guess what ailed his body and whether that might affect his mind. He felt more hungover than sick, but he'd never been blackout drunk in his life, not even when he'd been an exceptionally stupid twenty-something in love with nightlife. When he overindulged, he usually felt like Roderick Usher, light sensitive and able to hear his next-door neighbor breathing through the walls, not like a man getting over an eight-day flu.

Whatever this was, it was new. Darrin had never been susceptible to headaches, generally speaking, but he felt as if something had clawed its way out of his body through his skull. His teeth and jaw hurt too, like he'd held them clenched the whole missing eight hours. His eyes still felt twitchy.

Turning off the water, he stood listening to the drips fall against the bathtub for a long minute before he reached for his towel. He should check his phone and his notebook. If he'd emptied his pockets before he laid down, they were probably out on the coffee table.

A few minutes later, he emerged from the bedroom dressed in pajama bottoms and a t-shirt softened to near-transparency from years of washes and wears. His phone, as expected, lay on the coffee table sitting on the wireless charging pad. *Good. At least it wouldn't be dead.* Picking it up, he thumbed over to his calendar, then his email, but didn't find anything to suggest what had happened during his lost hours.

He checked the saved files, feeling he had downloaded something there related to his story. Weird that he didn't feel certain what he'd been working on. That worried him even more than lost time—and his imagination raced straight to the scariest possibilities like brain cancer and having a stroke before he reined it in. Focus, he told himself. One thing at a time.

Odd. The most recent saved file dated from last week. He saved things to his phone nearly every day. The idea that he'd gone six days without downloading information for a story to his files felt so unlikely the hairs on the back of his neck rose.

The trash was empty. His agitation rose. Darrin didn't clear out the old files that often—usually only when he started to run into memory problems on his phone. The software deleted files from the trash after a certain number of days, but the only way the trash would be completely empty would be if someone had emptied it manually. That someone hadn't been him.

His notebook! He still liked to work on paper for some things and always carried a pocket-sized notebook with him. There were dozens of them in drawers around the apartment. The one he'd been carrying today should have been there with his phone, but it wasn't there. Getting down on all fours, he peered under the table and the sofa, finding a lonely sock and a missing remote control. Digging through the couch cushions uncovered a couple of pens and a magazine that had gotten wedged in the cushions, but no notebook.

Had it still been in his pockets?

Springing to his feet made his head complain, but he ignored it and lurched toward the bathroom, his heart again fast in his chest. He dumped the hamper over and dug through the dirty clothes, finding the pants he'd been wearing. The pockets were empty, except for a receipt from Our Market for coffee and a cinnamon roll, time-stamped for 1:30 p.m. that afternoon. He tossed the laundry around, patting it all down for lumps, but the notebook didn't turn up among the shorts, exercise clothes, socks, underwear, and work clothes from the past few days. He didn't find it under the cabinets or fallen into the garbage can. It was gone.

Darrin stumbled back to the hall and slid down the wall, holding his head in his hands. His emotions swung between anger and horror. It didn't help that his head still hurt, even after the shower and a dose of Tylenol. He picked up his phone, wanting to call someone, but not knowing who to reach out to. Not the police, certainly—what would he even say? My notebook is missing, and I can't remember how I got home? At best, they'd laugh. At worst, someone would come to do a wellness check—and those didn't always go well for people of his complexion.

The closest thing he had to a suspect was a funhouse mirror image of a man he couldn't recall ever having seen before. His imagination could have conjured him from whole cloth, built a composite out of late-night talk show hosts and old movie actors. He had no idea if the man had even been there at all.

Scrolling down his contacts, he got to Sally Ann Rogers. She hadn't said where she was going when she took off the night before, blazing through the night on her motorcycle, but she'd been in a hurry. Even through the headache, his body responded to the thought of her—those shoulders in that yellow blouse, the curve of her lips when she laughed. The kiss she'd surprised him with when they'd parted. More than the physical, though, he'd felt he could talk to her.

What had she said? "My hours are strange, but I suspect yours are too." When she'd said she'd wanted to see more of him, he knew that this wasn't what she had in mind. She'd probably hoped for more "wine and song" than "whine and what's wrong." But he didn't know who else to call. He pressed the button.

THE DIRECTOR GOES TOO FAR

Sally Ann knocked but didn't wait for the Director to acknowledge her presence or invite her to enter. She burst through the door, eyes blazing with anger. "What did you do to him?"

The Director looked up from his coffee cup, surprise and irritation vying for control of his face—a face that looked blurry to her because his power vied with her own for control over her perceptions. Mary Braeburn jumped up from the chair next to him, the redness in her cheeks suggesting that her own conversation with their boss had run a little warm.

"I assume we're talking about our Mr. Berger?"

His voice was irritatingly calm, and Sally Ann felt the tug of the man's siren call, urging her to calm down. It stoked her anger all the hotter until it blazed brighter than a searchlight cutting through the mental fog, keeping her focused.

"Damn right, we're talking about Mr. Berger. I did what you wanted. We already had a deal. He agreed to sit on the story in exchange for an interview with Jessica and the promise of a future interview with all our powered agents. There was no reason to do this."

Mary cleared her throat. "I'm the one who called Steven in."

Sally Ann wheeled on her, ready to let fly with her venom, but she saw that Mary already wore apology in her slumped shoulders and downcast eyes.

"Darrin showed up at Our Market today, asking about Nu Yu. I panicked." She glared at the Director, who still calmly sipped his coffee as if he'd weren't the focus of all the rage in the room. "I thought Steven would give me a red herring to use to keep Darrin busy, or suggest a believable lie. Instead he said he'd 'take care of it.' If I'd known this was his idea of taking care of things, I'd never have called."

The Director set down the cup on the side table. His mouth had thinned to a barely perceptible line, and his face flickered again, flashing between his real appearance and something akin to a Baldwin brother—meaty and artfully unshaven, sporting an impressive chin.

"Stop it!" Mary and Sally Ann yelled together.

Letting the facade fall, The Director—now recognizably "Steven" without the added psychic glamour and manipulation—returned their twin, blazing gazes without blinking. "Until we have a treatment, we have to keep this under wraps. Even if Mr. Berger sat on the story, his continued investigation would have raised curiosity, and then we'd have other curious parties to fend off."

He shrugged, trying for nonchalance. "It's possible I pushed him too hard."

Sally Ann's fingers itched for her baton, but she clenched her teeth instead. "You think? Darrin lost eight hours today. He woke confused, with no memory of how he ended up back in his apartment, worried he'd had a stroke or something."

The Director had the good grace to blanch. "That was—I mean—I didn't intend..."

Arms crossed over her chest, Sally Ann let him flounder. He flushed red and grimaced and cajoled in turns. From the corner of her eye, Sally Ann saw Mary raise a hand to her lips, perhaps to hide her amusement at his discomfiture.

The man started eight or nine excuses before he threw his hands in the air and growled his exasperation. "All right."

Sally Ann cocked her head to one side, waiting.

Steven's face seemed pinched, but he finally said the words. "Okay. I'm sorry. I admit it. I went too far." A pulse throbbed in his temple, and his face had gone even paler than its usual pasty hue.

He raised his watery light blue eyes to Sally Ann's. "Is he all right?"

Sally Ann narrowed her eyes, but she nodded. "He will be." *He better be, for your sake.* The strength of her emotion terrified her. Did she already care so much?

The Director spread his hands and lifted his head to the ceiling. It seemed a kind of prayer. Interesting in a man who had only ever expressed contempt for religious faith.

The three of them went silent for a long moment. He couldn't take back what he had already done, and Sally Ann gave him the benefit of believing the apology sincere and trusting it would be accompanied by an effort to do better. If it wasn't, she'd be there to call him on it—and so would Mary, apparently.

Finally, Sally Ann spoke again. "We can talk more about Darrin later. Right now, tell me about Daniel Price and why he's not in cuffs in one of our cells right now."

"It's complicated."

Mary coughed—a thin disguise for her accusation of "Bullshit."

At the same time, Sally Ann barked a harsh laugh.

The Director raised a questioning eyebrow. "Is this funny?"

Sally Ann shook her head. "Complicated is what men always say when they don't want to tell the truth."

"Ah, I see," he said, shooting an apologetic look at Mary that made Sally Ann wonder again what exactly was between her boss and Mary Braeburn.

He snapped his gaze back to Sally Ann. "Sometimes, however, it is also true."

Crossing to the Director's desk, Sally Ann grabbed the large chair and rolled it over, placing it to form a triangle with the two armchairs. She dropped into the soft seat, happy to get off her feet. "Let's see what you can do to simplify it. You've got maybe fifteen minutes before everyone else arrives."

"It's really a matter of jurisdiction." Both women listened as Steven detailed the conversations he'd been in with Betrand Dietrich. A shady figure with deep pockets and heavy influence on a national level, Betrand was the man who'd funded a crackpot named Anton Lorre and his longevity research in Project Osiris more than half a century before and who'd protected him ever since, through five bodies, names, and identities. A man who sought a successor and thought Steven might be the man for the job.

Steven couldn't suppress his enthusiasm—his face lit like a child who had been promised all the sweets he could eat. "This could be a chance to go national, to help the country instead of just our little city. Imagine what we could accomplish with that kind of funding."

Sally Ann could imagine, but the excitement tasted coppery-bitter rather than minty-fresh, mixing with doubt and worry to leave her mouth dry and her heart rate elevated. Watching the Director rhapsodize, a ripple of something cold traversed her spine. The gleam in his eye reminded her of something—something that gave her pause. It reminded her of Dr. Liu.

THE COLOR OF OBSESSION

W alter waited, pacing the perimeter of the landing pad on the roof of the bank building. Sally Ann had bounced from the Dact and taken off running like a woman on fire, but the rest of the team remained on board, including Jessica. Normally a patient man, Walter twitched with agitation. What was taking so long?

He knew no one had been injured. The Director had shared that much, along with the information that the mission had been a success, that Patricia's mother had been safely delivered back to her home, and that Patricia herself would be on the Dact when it landed. So, why didn't the rest of them disembark already?

At last, two agents burst through the access door and onto the roof. They went aboard and came back out a minute later, escorting Dr. Liu between them. One kept his hand on his weapon. The other carried a jar and what looked like a hard drive. Dr. Liu kept a hungry eye on the jar, and when they crossed near Walter, he saw the greenish glow and understood.

Additional samples arriving. *Good.* They'd need more. The UCU would be forming a whole new research team, focused on understanding the emeralds and their effects on the Liu-vians.

When Patricia stepped onto the landing pad, Walter took an involuntary step backward and almost tripped over a perimeter light. He'd grown accustomed to her Lizard Woman alter ego, but this was something of another scale. Gargantuan, gilded, and astounding, her every step reverberated in the bricks beneath their feet, and tall armored plates protruded from her head. When she got to the door, she had to twist and go in sideways, head ducked. Behind her, the petite Suzie looked as small as a child, but joy emitted from her like a beacon.

Staring at Patricia, he almost missed it when Jessica finally walked across the concrete helipad. "Jess!" he called.

She flew to him, covering the meters between them in a bounce and landing neatly with her feet between his, a favorite trick. He pulled her into a hug, holding her there until he could feel her heart as if it beat within his own chest. She floated up to put her face at level with his and kissed him soundly.

She sighed when they parted. "I needed that."

"Me too."

She tugged her mask off and fluffed the short blond hair beneath. "You know what else I need? A shower."

He let her lead him down the stairs and through the halls until they reached the right turn to the locker rooms. He caught her arm, pulling her to the left instead. "Come with me," he said. "There's something I need to show you first."

Sped by a desire to relieve her worry, Walter pulled Jessica along at an uncomfortable pace until she finally let go her hold on the ground and floated alongside him. Though she shot him quizzical looks, she didn't say anything more until they turned in to the medical wing. Then she stopped, pulling her fingers from his. She swung around to look him in the eyes, her body floating out behind her. "Is it Leonel?" she asked, her voice nearly a sob.

"Yes, but it's not what you think."

Walter scanned his card. The door to Leonel's room slid open, and the two of them slipped inside. The room had been put back into order, though the cracks in the floor tiles and drywall remained. A bunch of white daisies in a blue glass vase decorated the side table beside the bed, and his husband David sat in a chair, holding hands with Leonel, who slept peacefully, damp hair stretched out across the pillow.

Jessica gasped. "He's all right?"

Walter nudged her forward. "See for yourself. He's been asking about you."

Jessica knelt beside David, patting the man's arm. "How's our patient?"

"So much better," David said, pulling his fingers free from Leonel's. "Sleeping now, thanks to our Dr. Peeples."

Jessica widened her eyes at Walter, but he shrugged and pointed at the bed where Leonel stirred. Yawning and pushing himself to a sitting position, Leonel rubbed his still bleary eyes. Once he'd cleared the sleep from his eyes, his face broadened into a grin. "Jessica, I'm so glad to see you," he said.

"I'm the one who's glad to see you," she said, face awash with wonder. "What happened?"

"Walter didn't tell you?"

"Not yet," Walter said. "I brought her straight here—to let her see for herself that you're okay."

Shifting in the bed, Leonel reached into his hospital gown and pulled out a strand of dark, waxed cord, a small green disk glittering at the end of the pendant. Without removing the necklace, he rested the gem in the palm of his hand, holding it out so Jessica could see. "It's the emeralds. Walter figured it out. You didn't change when the rest of us did because you always wear them."

Jessica's face darkened, and Walter stepped back. He'd expected relief and excitement, but the look on her face bespoke barely contained rage. Her eyes flashed, and then the moment passed, and she was hugging Leonel and telling him how relieved she was that something had worked. Walter wondered if he had imagined the spike of anger.

Leonel tucked the pendant back into his hospital gown and laid a hand over the spot where it rested against his chest. He flopped back onto the pillow a little roughly, and Walter held his breath, half-expecting the bed to crumble from the impact. It didn't, and Leonel blinked at them sleepily from the pillow.

Walter wondered how long it would be before he could take Leonel's control over his strength for granted again. As he watched, David slipped his fingers into Leonel's, his face showing only love when Leonel's squeezed the hand gently. So much trust. At least they still had that, despite the conflicts and disagreements that had threatened their marriage in the past few years. He would hope he and Jessica would find a similar faith in one another as they built their life together.

"He should rest," David said, brushing Leonel's hair back from his forehead. "We can talk more tomorrow."

Jessica took the hint with good grace, and Walter bowed his good-bye, making David promise to call him directly if there were any changes. And then they were back in the hall.

"I don't understand," Jessica said as they walked together. "Dr. Liu seemed so certain the cancer made the difference—that I didn't suffer like the others because I was already a survivor. How did you know she was wrong?"

"You're not the only one."

She blinked. "What?"

"There's another survivor among the Liu-vians. The lightning woman, from the park the other day. You remember?"

She nodded.

"She's a survivor, too. Lung cancer. But that didn't stop her from scorching Patricia and blackening the lawn at the park. Once I realized that, I knew there had to be something else different about you."

Jessica's fingers sought the small lump in the neckline of her costume, where Walter knew a shard of emerald lay ensconced in a mesh pocket pressed against the flesh of her upper chest, near her heart.

She froze in mid-stride. "So, if I didn't carry these..."

Walter gripped her hand, frightened by the thought of what might have happened to her—how a ramp-up of her powers might have manifested. Would she have lost her hold on gravity entirely? Floated into the stratosphere unable to return to earth? "I'd have kept you tethered. We'd have found a way to help. I wouldn't have let anything happen to you."

Something snapped to attention in Jessica, and her gaze went from soft and dreamy to intensely focused on him. "How did you do it? I didn't know the UCU still had samples from Dr. Liu's lab."

He shook his head. "We didn't. But your mother gave me a bit from your collection."

There it was again, the flash in Jessica's eyes. Her body went stiff next to him.

"She did?"

Feeling suddenly wary, he nodded. "Of course. We knew you'd want to help the others—Patricia and Leonel."

"Yes, of course." The words were positive, but her voice had gone flat and cold.

Walter tried to look into her face, but she evaded his gaze, looking instead at something down the hall. "Jess? Are you all right?"

She shook herself and offered him a tense little smile. "Yes, just tired. It's been a long couple of days. I still need that shower."

He had a feeling she held something back, but they started walking again. "Well, then let's get you to the locker room."

When they arrived at the doorway, he leaned in to give her a kiss. "Welcome home, Flygirl. See you when you're clean."

She stopped him before he'd taken three steps. "Did you use all of it?"

He squinted, confused.

"The emerald. The piece you took. Is it gone? Or can I get it back?" Her fingers clenched at her sides, grabbing at the air.

"No," he said, keeping his voice even and calm. "I still have some. We cut off slivers to use with the Liu-vians. We'll need to run more tests to identify its special qualities and figure out how large a piece is necessary to stabilize the victims, and if it burns out over time or anything like that. I should keep some on hand, in case there are more victims we don't yet know about."

She nodded again, her face closed and distant, as if her mind were miles away. "I see." She turned and went into the locker room, waving over her shoulder.

Walter stood alone in the hall for a long moment after she'd gone inside, a creeping dread rising in his guts. Eva's words from that morning echoed in his mind. *Possessive*, she'd said. *Intense*. Walter added another adjective as he made his way back to the debriefing. *Obsessed*.

PILLOW TALK

Freshly showered, Patricia lay in bed, flat on her back, red hair dampening the pillow. "God, it's great to be able to lay on my back again."

Curled next to her, Suzie smiled. True. If they had not been able to reverse Patricia's transformation, she could not have rested on her back without spearing the mattress and pillows with her long yellow spikes. An image of Patricia stuck there like a scaly hedgehog pinned to a pillow had her suppressing giggles. "I hadn't thought of that."

Patricia grimaced. "I owe my mom some new furniture, by the way."

Suzie could imagine. Patricia's Lizard Woman persona played better in the outdoors, even before the new mutations had expanded her girth and created new protuberances, spikes, and plates. The bull in the china shop had nothing on the Lizard Woman in a living room, especially in a home as cluttered with knick-knacks as Patricia's mother's.

The few minutes Suzie had spent in the Carter house had been enough to leave her claustrophobic. It was good to be back in Patricia's condo with its sleek furnishings and lots of open space, even if the furniture was all Patricia-sized instead of Suzie-sized.

Reaching up, Suzie stroked the smooth, flat disk of emerald Patricia now wore around her neck strung on a bit of black necklace cord. Walter didn't have a new career as a jeweler, but Suzie still thought it one exquisite piece of bling. It had gotten Patricia back into her skin and back into bed beside Suzie, where she belonged. That made it more precious than diamonds to her.

Rolling onto her belly, she stretched her body across Patricia's and flipped on the lamp. Still draped over Patricia, she pincered the slice of stone between her fingers and stretched it out on its cord, holding it to the light. Three shades of green swirled together, making a mottled sickly mixture, resembling acrylic or plastic more than a gemstone of dubious monetary value. This slender miracle didn't sparkle.

"It really doesn't look like anything special, does it?" Suzie lay it back against Patricia's skin and rested a palm over it.

Patricia laid her hand over Suzie's. "It does match my scales."

Sliding down Patricia's body, planting small kisses in a trail, Suzie paused at the belly. "Maybe we should have it made into a navel piercing."

Patricia rotated her hips, looking down at her toned torso. "Not bad. I think I could rock it." She tugged Suzie back up, so they lay face to face, and ran a finger down Suzie's slender, pinkish arm. Her voice went low and soft. "We could get one for you, too. I've never bought you jewelry."

Suzie sat up and stared into Patricia's face. Had that been a sort of declaration of love? Patricia wasn't exactly mushy-gushy. But for Suzie, Patricia's bold and independent nature had always been a selling point. Too much talk about feelings got on her nerves, and she'd always liked that Patricia didn't seem to need to analyze their relationship too deeply.

But she did love the big lug, fiercely, even if they never said it out loud.

She must have stared too long because Patricia finally sat up, too, stretching her long arms out to grip the headboard above her and rolling her neck which made a series of loud pops. "For a little while, I

269

thought I might never feel my own skin again. I never expected to be glad to see this crepey neck and all these freckles. Hell, I'm even glad to see the lines on the backs of my hands."

Suzie lunged and planted more kisses on Patricia's flesh. Before long, they were tangled in one another's limbs again, panting with exertion and both in need of another shower. Suzie's stomach growled loudly, so she pulled herself loose, slipped into the bathroom, and turned on the shower. While the water warmed, she pulled her hair up into a knot atop her head. She hummed to herself as she stepped into the stream of warm water.

As she lathered up her body, she called out, "What'll it be, sweetcheeks? Should I make eggs? Or should we get takeout?" Suzie really only knew how to make eggs, and Patricia didn't have much interest in cooking either, so the two of them had an extensive collection of takeout menus in a drawer in the kitchen. "I could go for Chinese."

Patricia didn't respond, so Suzie finished her shower and stepped out. Wrapping herself in a giant towel that covered her from chest to knees, she peeked out around the bathroom door. "Patricia? Did you want the shower?"

Opening the door a bit further, she saw the bedroom was empty. Maybe Patricia had already put in an order. Suzie pulled on a sweater and a pair of panties, then padded out to the living room. She found Patricia standing in front of the big picture window, wrapped in her bathrobe and staring at the city view. The building lights shone in the darkness like a promise.

Suzie slid her arms around Patricia's waist and rested her head against the armored plate on her back. "Everything okay?"

Patricia remained silent, so Suzie let go and circled to stand in front of her girlfriend. "Babe? You're making me nervous."

"Sorry. Just thinking."

"No need for too much of that now," Suzie said, moving toward the kitchen to grab a menu.

"I'm a selfish old woman."

Suzie stopped. Twice in one evening Patricia had called herself old, a sure sign she was brooding over something. "I don't know about that."

"I'm sixty years old, Suzie. What's a woman like you doing with an old broad like me anyway?"

Suzie frowned. "Having the time of my life."

"Don't."

"Don't what?" Irritation cracked her good mood and oozed into her voice.

"Don't pretend it doesn't matter."

Suzie threw herself into the sofa and pulled a pillow against her belly. "Why would you assume I'm pretending? Have I ever failed to tell you when something mattered to me?"

"Well, maybe it ought to matter to you. You have your future to consider."

Suzie snorted. "What are you? My guidance counselor?"

"Stop being ridiculous."

"You first." Suzie really wished she'd ordered food before she'd hopped in the shower. Being hungry didn't make this easier.

Patricia sighed. "All I'm trying to say is you don't have to do this."

"If by 'this' you mean you and me, of course I don't have to do this. I wouldn't be here in that case." She patted the sofa. "Sit down, Amazon. It's hurting my neck to look at you."

Patricia complied, perching on the front edge of the cushion as if she expected to have to flee at any moment.

"I'm here because I want to be. The life I have with you is amazing, and I wouldn't trade it for anything else. We have adventure and laughter, and I am more myself with you than I have ever been with anyone else. Why would I give all that up?"

Patricia flushed nearly as red as her hair. "What if something like this happens again?"

"Then we'll deal with it, together."

"I don't want you to have to take care of me."

Suzie shook her head. "That's too bad. I'm going to take care of you. And I expect you to take care of me. That's how it works, you know, when people love each other."

Shock widened Patricia's eyes.

"That's right," Suzie said, leaning closer so Patricia couldn't evade her gaze. "I said it. I love you, you pain in the ass." Her stomach growled again. "Now show me you love me too. Order me some Chinese food. I'm starving and it's all your fault!"

Patricia grinned. "Yes, ma'am."

A FEW WEEKS LATER

CHAPTER 50

Fuerte paced back and forth in the green room until Patricia finally growled at him to sit down. He did, but sitting down didn't help. He bounced his knees and drummed his fingertips against his thighs so rapidly that Flygirl eventually grabbed them and held them in her own.

"*Cálmate*," she said, blue eyes smiling behind the blue and silver mask of her show costume, false red locks curling against her shoulder blades.

Fuerte smiled. "Do you even know what that means?"

"Not exactly," she admitted. "But I've heard David say it often enough. I figured it meant something like, 'relax, you big bonehead.'"

Patricia snorted.

"Close enough," Fuerte said.

"What are you so nervous about anyway?" Patricia asked. "People love you. I'm the one who ought to be crawling the walls. They're scared of me out there."

"Can you blame them?"

Patricia rested a hand on her scaly bosom and affected a drawl worthy of Scarlett O'Hara. "Why, whatever do you mean, sir? I assure you I am a ray of sunshine. Ask Suzie."

"She might be a little biased."

A knock sounded at the door, and a short White man clutching a clipboard and sporting a large headset poked his head in. "It's time."

The three of them followed the young man to a soundstage with a bright orange sofa and a lime green armchair arranged into a conversation circle around a rug with the television station logo emblazoned across it. Red theatre seats rimmed the stage, but they were empty, except for one woman from legal at the UCU, probably there to make sure Darrin stuck to the agreed upon limits. Bright lights shone down on the seating and a large, old-fashioned looking camera waited. Fuerte whispered, awe-struck, "It's like being on Johnny Carson."

"Who?" Flygirl asked, blinking.

Fuerte and Patricia both groaned.

"I forget how young you are," Patricia said.

Flygirl laughed. "I'm kidding. I know who Johnny Carson was. Jeez."

Darrin entered from the opposite side of the set, and Flygirl elbowed her companions, cuing them to put on their game faces. The handsome young reporter shook each of their hands in turn and thanked them for agreeing to the interview. He came across warm and professional, and even when Patricia used her second set of eyelids to blink sideways at him, he kept his cool.

Fuerte had just learned this reporter and Sally Ann were dating and watched the man with interest. Darrin Berger might be the one doing the interview, but Fuerte would be judging whether the man was good enough for their team lead. His manners were impeccable, and he was undeniably handsome, but only time would tell if he proved a trustworthy and kind person.

"I thought we'd chat for a little bit first, then film the demonstration bits your legal department agreed to." Darrin waved at the other side of the soundstage where a collection of props were gathered.

Flygirl spoke for them. "That'll be fine. My friends here are a little nervous about being on TV, I think."

Darrin spoke to the group, his voice soft and measured. "I'm not here to try to embarrass you or make you look bad, I assure you. But the public is dying to know more about you three. I'm grateful to have the chance to do this interview."

He held an arm out to the sofa and chairs. "Isn't the set lovely? *Springfield Today* agreed to let us film in their space." They spent a few minutes deciding who would sit where, eventually putting Flygirl in the chair nearest their host and Fuerte and Patricia on the sofa, two hulking figures that dwarfed the furniture. Patricia shifted into the corner, spikes sheathed and her legs crossed so one taloned foot hung in the space in front of them. Fuerte remembered to sit with both feet on the floor, thighs spread, even though his instinct was still to curl up with one foot beneath himself.

The camera crew adjusted the lighting and affixed a lapel mic on each hero's clothing. Through it all, Fuerte fidgeted. Over the years, he'd grown a little more accustomed to the public eye, but this would be the first extended interview any of them had done. He was grateful Patricia and Flygirl were there to keep him from making a fool of himself.

After a quick introduction, Darrin jumped in. Fuerte fumbled through his answers, but Flygirl handled it like a pro. If they ever did this again, he'd have to get some tips from her. When they talked about their costumes, Flygirl demonstrated some gymnastic moves and talked about aerodynamics. She even worked in a joke about keeping bugs out of her teeth when she soared over the city.

"And what about you, Fuerte? Can you tell us about the special features of your costume?

Fuerte raised his hands to the half-sunshine mask that covered his upper face. "My favorite part is the mask," he said. "The spikes imitate the Aztec Sun Stone to represent my culture, it protects my privacy, and it's beautiful." He ran a hand down his leg to point at the tall, calf-hugging boots. "As for the rest? Well, I think I look a little like a pirate, but I have good freedom of movement, and my new shirt is less embarrassing."

Darrin smiled. Behind him on a screen, a picture of Fuerte wearing the original shiny shirt he thought of as "the gigolo shirt" displayed. His new shirt was still red, but more matte than shiny and more fitted than flaring and offered Kevlar protection as well. Everyone laughed at the image, and Patricia poked Fuerte's shoulder. "I don't know, I think you rocked it."

"Speaking of new looks," Darrin segued. "Patricia, you seem to have gone through a bit of a makeover as well. Can you tell us about that?"

Patricia stood, and the camera pulled back to keep her in frame. She concentrated and expanded until fully extended, the new head plates, arm spikes, and layers of scales shuttling into place. Darrin gasped and Patricia hammed for the camera, doing a few body-building poses before she pulled her transformation in to the level she preferred for walking around—spikes hidden and bulk toned down to something nearer her human-sized form, but still completely green, and features transfigured far enough to disguise her human face.

"Wow," Darrin said.

Patricia nodded. "You might say I've grown."

"Indeed, we might."

Patricia talked for a moment about the special materials the UCU had developed so that her clothing would survive transformations and how protective gear wasn't as necessary for her. Fuerte imagined the final cut would show footage of bullets bouncing off the Lizard Woman's scales to illustrate the point.

"Unlike your colleagues' costumes, yours is pretty simple, and you also go by a pretty common name, Patricia."

"Well, I'm plenty startling enough on my own. I don't think I need a special uniform for people to know who I am when I arrive on the scene."

"No, I guess not," Darrin admitted.

"And the public named me Lizard Woman, which is descriptive, I suppose, but a little awkward to shout on the battlefield, so I stick with the name my mother gave me."

Fuerte could see Darrin was dying to ask more about Patricia's family, but the woman from legal who watched from the audience stood and took a few steps forward, reminding them all that personal life details that might compromise secret identities were not allowed, so he didn't inquire.

Instead, he shifted the conversation to recent cases, including the Lightning Woman in the park and the strong man battle that had been dubbed "The Brawl at the Mall." Flygirl fielded those questions deftly, making the canned statements from the UCU sound sincere. The more Fuerte watched her do this kind of work the more he thought Jessica could have had a career as an actress if her life had gone another way.

She finished with a warning about dangerous products that might still be on the market and a new request that anyone with bars of "Nu Yu" still in their homes discontinue their use and turn in the samples at their local police station where they can be disposed of safely. "The soap doesn't affect everyone, but, as you saw with poor Mr. Schulz, the effects can be quite dramatic and dangerous."

"Luckily, the effects on Mr. Schulz proved temporary," Darrin said.

After a few more anecdotes about the less glamorous aspects of crime fighting and recognition of the UCU's partnership with the fire, police, and rescue services of Springfield, Darrin asked them each for any final words they'd like to share with the audience.

This one, Fuerte was ready for. "True heroism isn't flashy and doesn't require unusual powers. It comes from the heart, and consists of doing the right thing. That makes all of us heroes."

ACKNOWLEDGMENTS

I don't write in a vacuum, and because I write I often don't vacuum, so I owe full gratitude to my family who make sure we don't live in squalor when I'm playing with my imaginary friends. I couldn't enjoy my writing life without your support. The dust bunnies would gain sentience and eat me.

My thanks, too, to all the people along my path who've helped me live my dream.

Mrs. Alsdorf, who back in first grade whispered to me, "You know you could write your own poems, if you want to," and helped me realize that "writer" really was a job.

Alicia who wrote that terrible tennis love story with me when we were in high school.

JD, who taught me how grammar was about clarity and connection as well as correctness.

The string of librarians who shoved the right books in my hands just when I needed them.

My critique partners who keep me honest.

The first reader who wasn't someone I knew in "real life" and left me a positive review.

The writers in my community who answer all my questions with such patience and kindness.

You all rock! Can we keep doing this, please?

ABOUT THE AUTHOR

Samantha Bryant wishes she were taller, faster, and stronger, so she writes characters who are. Her body of work is half horror and half hero, which also describes her day job as a middle school teacher. If you can't find her, she's probably out in the woods getting lost on purpose. Don't worry, she always comes back. Until then you can find her at http://samanthabryant.com

ALSO BY SAMANTHA BRYANT

FRIENDS OF FALSTAFF

Thank You to All our Falstaff Books Patrons, who get extra digital content each month! To be featured here and see what other great rewards we offer, go to www.patreon.com/falstaffbooks.

PATRONS

Dino Hicks
John Hooks
John Kilgallon
Larissa Lichty
Travis & Casey Schilling
Staci-Leigh Santore
Sheryl R. Hayes
Scott Norris
Samuel Montgomery-Blinn
Junkle